D0307973

In Search Of Emily

Susan M. Nelson

RocketDog
Books

Copyright © 2009 Susan M. Nelson

All rights reserved. No part of this book may be reproduced in any form without the written permission of the author and the publisher, except for brief quotes by a reviewer.

This novel is a work of fiction. The depiction of characters & events are fictitious. Any similarity or resemblance to events or persons, living or dead, is coincidental.

Cataloging in Publication data
Nelson, Susan M.
    In search of Emily / Susan M. Nelson.
    p. cm.
    ISBN 978-0-9841250-0-5
    Romantic suspense novels. gsafd
    PS3564.E4762 I5 2008
    Fic

Book design by RocketDog Books
Published by RocketDog Books
Cover design painting by Lindsay Ann Metcalf
Author photo (with Lily) by Bill Musser

Printed in the United States of America

To my sister Sherry, who
wishes she were Emily.

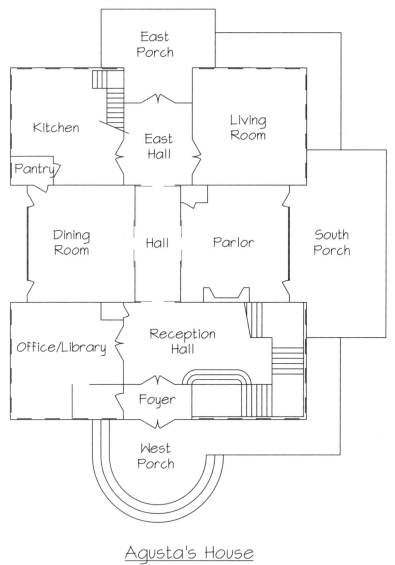

Agusta's House
Main Floor

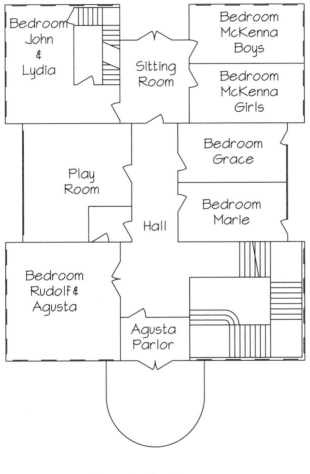

Agusta's House
Second Floor

I

It was raining when I packed up the car. It was raining when I stopped for lunch at Curt's Cannonball diner at Cannon Falls, Minnesota three hours later. It had been difficult driving in the grey. None of the familiar landmarks had been visible: no golden ochre cornfields, no rusty sienna weeds in the ditches, and no deep dark reds in the woods, no dairy farms in Iowa, with the black and white ladies calm and serene. In Minnesota, no open prairies with every natural color possible, no cattle grazing on still green grass and no Amish farmers in their clip-clop horse-drawn buggies. It was just me and the tedious wet.

I only saw Curt's because of the red light stretched across the highway. Curt's was a comfortable roadside diner, gas station and trucker's motel just off Highway 52. The counter was shaped like the long side of an eight cut in half and there were tables around the edges. Even in this weather, it was busy with every kind of Midwesterner possible, farmers, families, old-timers, and, of course, truckers of all shapes and sizes. A sign said they served the best breakfast in the state, and I believed it. Most of the diners were having breakfast even though it was early in the afternoon. Strong coffee, freshly baked pie and fried food was the fare. The soup was terrific and warmed me up, and I got coffee to go. The tall, reed thin attendant in the baseball cap filled the car with gas and flirted a little. Cute.

It was a typical autumn Midwest rain. The water came down in thick, gray sheets turning the world into a monochromatic landscape. It was hard to tell where the road stopped and the ditch began. Or the sky and the ground, for that matter. "Sten grå kallt," or something like that, according to Grandpa Algot Lind. It took me years to finally realize it meant "stone grey cold," rather than a Swedish curse, which was the way he uttered it. The kind of weather that colored all thoughts. My God, I won't get there before dark! It was going to be a trick to find the place in daylight, impossible after dark.

But, I was on my way to a favorite memory from childhood and I couldn't wait for the weather to cooperate. I decided I had to get there today, no matter what unforeseen circumstances tried to prevent it. A place I had not seen since age ten, twenty-two years ago. A very magical place to a child and God knows I needed some magic in my life these days. It had only taken me a few minutes to decide to respond to the legal letter I received. Now I wondered if perhaps my abrupt actions had been too hasty. But then, that was how I did things. Never think it out or I would never do it. The more I think the less action I take.

So here I am. Driving in a downpour in a very old, small car. A faded two-door hunter green Saab 95 with a grey leather interior, affectionately known as the sow bug. She was on her very last rusty legs. Her shape was that of a hard shelled beetle and I thought of it as my 1930's era gangster's car, only cute and free of danger. The world held no other vehicles like her. It was extremely fun to drive, low to the ground and somewhat, but pleasantly so, noisy.

I had left my home and my marriage with very little deliberation. I simply wanted out. I had wanted to leave for a very long time, but it was easier to stay and, as usual, take no action. Hard as it had been to admit I had made a mistake in my choice of husbands, which was exactly what I had done. The lawyer's letter gave me the excuse I needed to act. I took my dogs, my oil paints, canvas and my parrot. I didn't want it to look like I wouldn't be returning, although that was probably true. Maybe I thought my husband would sic his friends in the Highway Patrol after me and fetch me home. But then, perhaps not.

I reached over to the passenger seat to rub Lily's ears for the reassurance we both needed. She looked at me with worry and apprehension. Lily, a 100-pound Great Pyrenees dog, as white as almost new snow with grey ears, she thought she was tiny, but I suppose that came from growing up with twenty pound dachshunds. They were lap dogs, so she was a lap dog also. Rain frightened her because it might thunder any minute.

"It's not that kind of storm, baby," I tried to calm her. Eyes straying to the windshield, she ignored me. Sullivan, or Sully, a red, longhaired dachshund, and my current wiener dog, lay uncharacteristically quiet in my lap. He was on his back with all four feet resting on the steering

3

wheel, which couldn't possibly be a safe way to drive, but I did nothing to stop him. Pearl, the small grey and white parrot, slept soundly and safely in his cage and under his blanket. Thank the Gods for small favors! That screeching would do in my frayed nerves, in this small space, with barely enough room for my tiny family.

With hours to go and tired of the two CDs I had with me, Nora Jones and Beethoven's Seventh, which had been in the car for months already, my thoughts strayed to the letter once again. I don't get much mail, and did not often check the box, so this expensive paper caught my eye immediately. From the law firm of Anderson/Erickson, on Payne Avenue in Saint Paul. I had grown up in Saint Paul, Minnesota, but hadn't lived there for a lifetime and knew no one there. All my relatives were long gone to the west coast or the cemetery.

Payne Avenue was known to me though. A Scandinavian neighborhood often visited by my paternal grandparents and then by my Dad and myself. Swedish bakeries and butcher shops lined the sidewalks. Strolling down the avenue always filled my fanciful imagination of women in long skirts and men in those white shirts with the enormous flowing sleeves. I loved looking in the windows of the old world gift shops. There were blue and yellow flags everywhere and Swedish was still spoken at the bank and post office. Names like Jacobson, Svensson, Anderson, Nelson, Erickson, and Lindquist abounded. Jacobsons Bakery was a favorite. You could smell it floating in the air up and down the block: cardamom, almond, and fresh rye. The trips there were practically the only memory I held onto of life with my father.

Actually, that was not true. I was being unfair, but still, at an adult age, I resented his unbending staid ways. He was unwilling to compromise or even to listen to any reasoning other than his own. Life with my father colored my views concerning my relationships and attitudes toward men to this date. From a very young age I learned that Dad was always right. Even if I had evidence to the contrary, he was right. I learned I was better off not to argue or disagree, no matter what the topic. If I tried to tell him my idea, I was ridiculed and scoffed at, even in front of my few friends.

When I was in school, I gave my thoughts less credence than those of my male classmates. Somehow, my mother and I were much less important than my father or, for that matter, any man. My first date, at age fifteen, was a disaster! Ronnie Burns kissed me constantly while we were supposedly watching a drive in movie. Later, I wasn't able to recall what the movie was; his sloppy wet mouth was all I could remember. It was so unpleasant; I wouldn't accept another date for years. And yet, I didn't know how to deal with the situation. I didn't know how to say no to a man. This leaving my husband was probably my first action on my own, without any input from a member of the male race. It felt good. Really good. 4th of July celebration good. I knew I had turned a corner in my life of a second-rate member of the human race. I was free. I was happy. I was doing what I wanted to do.

Howard, my Dad, was an incredibly handsome man. Tall, shiny black hair and a smile that could melt the polar ice caps. I have a photograph of him standing with his father and three brothers, all of them dressed in short-sleeved white dress shirts and black trousers. They are all smoking and holding drinks. Smiling at the camera, they look like a small Swedish mafia, self assured, happy with themselves and their lot in life. Knowing, that in their world anyway, they were kings. Absolutely on top of the world. They were a force to be reckoned with.

I wanted Dad to love me. I wanted his respect and approval. So I was always trying to earn it. By the time I was twenty five, shortly before his death, the realization finally hit me. What I wanted simply was not possible. Not unless I could magically sprout a penis. My life changed for the better in that moment. I just stopped trying to fix things with Dad. But I still wasn't standing on my own feet; I switched from a domineering father to a worse husband. Ah, my father, my husband, there was an incredibly long and complicated, but dull story. I shook my head and concentrated on the road, and the letter.

"Dear Ms. Lind" I had not been Ms. Lind since before marriage and that salutation alone startled me.

"We have the unfortunate duty to inform you of the death of your maternal grandmother, Augusta Jane Svensson. She died six years ago this past August. We are sorry this news is so late in coming. Your grandmother left an odd will, and it took us some time to locate her next of kin. In her will, Augusta Svensson specified no one but her granddaughter was to live on her property in Minnesota. If you could not be found, we were to use the money in her estate to maintain it until such funds were depleted. You, Ms. Lind, are her only remaining kin and are to inherit her entire estate. If you choose not to live on the estate, you are to forfeit the inheritance entirely."

6

The letter went on to explain in detail what that inherited property consisted of, but all I could think of was the cottage by the lake. My mother's cottage by the lake. In truth, I often remembered that house and the summers spent there, but assumed it had long ago been sold, destroyed, or turned into a lakeside resort. I should have known better. My grandmother could barely tolerate my mother, her own daughter, and me coming to visit her. But we did, every summer for ten years. Long, perfectly glorious summers. When Mom died, the lake side summers died also. In fact, for a very long time I felt that the Emily part of me, also, had simply slipped away; slid right through my fingers and disappeared completely. I was just a girl, any girl, but Emily was no longer living in me.

My father was not welcome at my grandmother's house and nothing more was ever mentioned of the place or of Grandmother. When I would question Dad or ask to go to the lake, I was met with a silent, stony stare. Eventually, I just stopped asking. Dad was as lost to me as Mom. Even at age ten, I knew what subject to avoid. Anything at all to do with my mother or her family was taboo.

The lawyer's letter gave a phone number and I dialed it.

2

I was just north of the Twin Cities now and the rain was letting up some. I was not used to driving in such traffic, living in a nearly microscopically small Iowa town with no traffic lights and only a handful of stop signs.

"So far, so good," I said to Lily. She was nervously turning around and around in her seat and whining at the window. "Want to stop for a bit?"

We were driving through Anoka on Highway 10, and I spied a small park with a covered picnic area. Lily, my oh so brave dog, wouldn't pee while her head was getting wet. She and Sully wandered around on their flexi-leads, Sully pulling his out the full fifteen feet, Lily leaning on my legs. Finally, we accomplished our mission and climbed back into the warm dry car. Sully had only managed to bathe in one puddle.

The weather had made the day darker than it should have been, and I was worried about the rest of the drive. As it was, I nearly missed the turn-off onto Hwy 169, completely. God knows where we would have ended up. Small towns with pretty names flowed by: Zimmerman,

Princeton, Milaca and finally, Mille Lacs Lake. I remember always wanting to go by way of Elk River just because I liked the name so much, but Mom said it was too far out of the way. I had to pull over to the roadside lookout I was so excited.

"Look, Lily!" I exclaimed, "When I was a girl I thought this was the ocean." Lily looked but it was still too grey for her. I gazed out over the choppy, ice drab water until it blended into the equally grey sky. One color, no line to separate the greys as the lake was too wide to see the far shore. Even on a clear day.

Oh my God, memories of Neapolitan ice cream, soft, Indian beaded moccasins and fishing with Dad and his father overwhelmed me. While my father had never been at the cabin, he often came this far north just for the fishing and time spent with his father. I was occasionally allowed to come along.

"I fished right here," I told her, pointing. Grandpa Lind was a real fisherman. He entered contests and usually won them, and I and my cousins would be at his side. His photograph was in the St. Paul Pioneer Press almost every winter, holding one large fish or another. I could bait a hook, catch a sunfish, scrape scales, and bone it before I was four. Grandpa had a sign that said "Old fisherman never die, they just smell that way!" For me, warm smells of sweet pipe tobacco spoke of Grandpa, not dead fish. He had also been a carpenter and outfitted the fancy railroad cars when he worked for the railroad in Saint Paul. He and I would walk from his house to the tracks just to watch the trains come and go. Often there were gypsies camped in the spot we liked, so we would bring a chicken or two with us. Grandpa said if we were generous, they wouldn't steal any. It seemed to be true. Grandma Bengta was the only woman in the area who never complained of losing eggs or chickens. Grandpa Lind was a terrific grandfather and I spent a great deal of time with him. Grandma Bengta was the sweetest person I have met to date, a very proper Swedish lady who wouldn't let her husband kiss her in front of us.

Their tall stucco house on Saint Clair Avenue was once a dairy farm. Now it one of the busiest streets in St. Paul, with houses and businesses lined up like Roman soldiers. I loved that house. It wasn't large by today's standards, but it felt big to me, and so mysterious. Full of dark corners, polished wood, and deep closets. A small three season porch faced St. Clair Avenue, where we would sit and watch the ever busy squirrels. The city bus stop was at the corner just one house down, and I loved watching the people get on or off and speculate about their lives. The living room ran the length of the front of the house. The carpeting was dark and soft. I remember a forest green sofa that I would sink down in and fall asleep with my head in Grandma's lap.

A formal dining room and kitchen sat behind this room. Grandpa's desk was in the corner piled with his papers and unread newspapers. There had been a photograph of me standing at Grandpa's desk, with his soft wool cap on my head and his pipe in my hand. I loved that photo. I wonder whatever happened to it. The heavy mahogany table could seat the entire family and my cousins and I would play for hours under it, safe from adult eyes. Through a swinging door was the small kitchen, whose space was nearly all stove. A tiny table seated four and that's where I would eat my breakfast of Swedish coffee and toast that Grandma cut into quarters. The room was neat as a pin, everything always exactly where it belonged. At the back of the house were an unheated pantry and the back door going out into a minute-sized yard.

Between the kitchen and living room was a dark hallway no longer than four feet, with the refrigerator on one side and the basement door on the other. Halfway down these steps was a door that led outside, which I always thought was so clever. The cellar was the size of the house and was lined with narrow shelves absolutely filled with neatly tied bundles or boxes labeled in Swedish text by a female hand. An old fashioned wringer washing machine was really the only reason to be down there.

The staircase that led to the second floor was grand. Dark wood and heavy posts. Halfway up was a landing where my cousins and I could listen to adults when we were supposed to be resting. At the top were three bedrooms, a closet, and a bathroom. The octagon-shaped hallway had shiny hardwood floors with wide planks. The bathroom floor was covered in tiny black and white ceramic tiles and a beautiful claw-foot tub that was so deep I needed to be lifted out of it. The largest room, where Grandpa Algot slept in later years, once held Dad's three brothers. A closet sized room tucked off to the side of this was Dad's space. Later, it was transformed into a sewing room with an old treadle machine where Grandma sewed doll clothes for me and my cousins and patchwork quilts for us all to snuggle under when we visited. Shelves from floor to ceiling were stacked with dozens of closed boxes.

Some were tied with string and others wrapped in brown paper. Many of these were labeled in Swedish and, we were sure, full of interesting things like linens from Sweden, old letters and cards, clothes we had given to Grandma on birthdays, which were still wrapped in tissue paper when she died as they were "much to nice for this old Grandma to wear." I would give anything to have those cards and letters now.

Another room had belonged to my aunts and then later, to an unmarried uncle who stayed with his parents until they died. I was never allowed inside of it.

Grandma's room was the third. It had a high bed and white coverlet with matching lace curtains. When I spent the night, I would lie in that bed and listen to the sad, quiet sounds of the mourning doves in the grape arbor. The room smelled of lilacs always. Sweet and soft. After Grandma's death, my aunts found hairnets stuffed with her brown, fine hair. She always wore these nets on her hair and I never thought it odd, but I'm sure she was losing her hair and covered up that fact with these hair filled nets. Ah, we woman are so vain. Grandma always wore rayon or silk dark dresses and dark stockings. The dresses favored tiny flowers or solid colors, black and grays. Funny, that would be the type of dress I would choose for myself

. A narrow sidewalk went to the one-car garage and a trash barrel where most of the household trash was burned, a practice no longer allowed. Tall, old-fashioned hollyhocks stood next to the garage. Some years they grew taller than my grandmother. Still, after all these years, I can never see that flower without remembering her. Up against the back door was the largest purple lilac bush in the Midwest. Or, so it seemed to my eyes. Grandpa had built a grape arbor there, with a bench underneath. On hot days, it was always so cool under the ripening fruit.

All of my family on my dad's side was from in or around the Twin Cities of Saint Paul and Minneapolis. I knew and loved them all. It is strange to think of them now, after so many years. It is a long and complicated story, but to simplify things, growing up I always felt that I was very special to all my dad's relatives. Well-loved and a favorite. When my mother died, I began to doubt this idea. People were kind, but not what I expected, distant perhaps.

When Dad died, I was hit with a lightning bolt of realization. I watched as my aunt distributed Bengta's jewelry and personal items to my cousins, but not to me. Everyone was available to me, but not particularly loving and I immediately felt such a fool! It was so obvious to me then that the close family ties were simply in my mind. They were nothing I could count on. I was nobody's special or favorite anything. It seemed that while Dad was living, I was part of a family, tolerated and included. But when he died, I lost all of them as well. Even the best-friend cousin, who was my own age and had grown up with me, disappeared from my life. When she married into the Catholic Church, I was so sure I would be a bridesmaid that I planned for it. However, she never asked me. To this day I feel her rejection, still fresh and sore. I realized I was truly alone in this world. I also realized that Mom couldn't have loved me as much as she said, since she left me too. These thoughts completely devastated me for many years and can still bring tears to my eyes. Everyone needs to feel they are somehow special to someone else. Everyone. I cannot believe that I was so blind.

Mom's family was always a mystery, especially Grandmother Augusta. Her, I knew not at all and loved even less. In some ways, I felt foolish for letting her back into my life dead or not, after all these years. But, I was very curious about Mother's side of the family. I think I was hoping to find a little of her on this trip. After all, she had grown up in Grandmother's house and lived there until she married Dad. The marriage, from what little I knew, was not a welcome one for Grandmother Augusta, and Dad was not allowed to visit. Or, maybe he simply chose not to put himself in that uncomfortable position. So each summer we went without him. I never understood, and it did not occur to a ten year old to ask. Why did my mother even go back there? So many questions! Was there anyone left to answer them? Why did it take me so long to look for these answers? I think perhaps that it was easier to let everything go, just like I had with my marriage.

The rain started up again in earnest as I moved the car back onto the highway. There no longer was much traffic to confuse me. The summer people were back in their real lives and the locals knew enough to stay out of this weather. Another hour and a half or so and I turned off onto a secondary highway and stopped to consult the map sent by the law firm. This part of the trip was a blur in my memories because I was too busy waiting for the first glimpse of the lake or the mailbox shaped like Uncle Sam, to pay attention to the roller-coaster road.

With my heart pounding, I soon made the turn onto the straight narrow gravel road that led to the lake. Up and down several roller-coaster hills with a bit of lake showing at the top of each. As I came over the crest of a long hill I saw it! The lake as it always appeared in my first glance. Then, I turned again. This time on a winding gravel path, rather than an actual road, that led to the house. Past raspberry and blackberry vines scratching at the car, we crawled up the lane. This path was so overgrown it was hard to distinguish it from the surrounding growth, especially in this dim light. It was almost like trying to drive in a forest except there were no fallen tree branches. I thought it would be too dark to see the lake, but then, there it was again. And just when the house came into view, a shaft of sunlight broke through the dark sky and lit up the place like a spotlight. Sunlight sparkled on rain drops, wet window panes, very long grass, and it took my breath away.

The house was enormous. Two floors and a full attic and nearly the size of city block. The rooms had to be huge. It looked like something out of an Alfred Hitchcock movie, part deep red brick and narrow white siding with a dark red tiled roof. Part of my view of the mansion was obscured by overgrown tree branches shading the house so thoroughly those parts were lost in the shadows. Oh my dear lord, what have I gotten myself into?

As the dogs and I exited the car, I did what I had always done upon arriving: I turned to the lake and walked to the end of the dock. It was in great need of repair, but held our weight. I was finally here, Bay Lake, Minnesota, the most wonderful place on the planet. Nearly dark now, the sun setting on the water, I was immensely glad to be here, in spite of any misgivings I might have convinced myself existed. It was so silent. A quiet experienced nowhere else. I had forgotten the gentle sound made by the breeze flowing over the water just before dark. The only additional sound was the gentle lapping of the water against the dock and an occasional splash of a fish. I often imagined my mother, standing here just as I was, in a light cotton summer dress, flowing against her bare legs in the soft lake wind. She could spend hours just staring out onto the lake. Daydreaming, I guessed. As the breeze lifted my hair, exactly as it had moved hers, I knew the magic was still here. I stood there until the sun was gone and the dogs grew restless. They weren't particularly good at motionless daydreaming.

Back at the car, I reached for the oversized key and moved toward the house. On the front porch, feeling like I was standing in the center of a small roofed Athenian temple, I hesitated. I never had been in there, I realized. Mom and I always stayed in the much smaller guest cottage by the water. No one ever said, but I think I reminded Grandmother of my Dad, and she couldn't bear to look at me. Putting the key back in my pocket, I made a decision.

"Come on, guys, we'll sleep in the cottage." The cottage was between the house and the lake with the lane, if it could even be called that, in between. It had a friendlier look than the cold forbidding house and I felt better as we approached the door. This house I knew like no other.

There was no electricity or water turned on there yet, and I didn't want to attempt to locate the fuse box in the dark. But I also couldn't go in the main house. Not yet. With the last remaining light, we entered. I do not think anyone had been there since Mom and me. With shocked eyes, I saw my forgotten books and crayons on the table under several inches of dust. One of my Mother's pearl earrings sat next to the sink and an old, dried out lipstick lay on the floor. There was no more daylight and the windows were covered in a wire mesh and opaque plastic for winter, making the room even darker and full of shadow. But it was a comfortable and still familiar space, so I swept the dust from the center of the room, using the small amount of dusk showing through the still open screen door, took out my sleeping bag from the car, and fed the pets. I was too exhausted and overwhelmed to eat anything myself, so I crawled into the bag and snuggled with Sully and went immediately to sleep. Home. I felt that I was finally home.

3

I awoke from dreams of breathing in moist, humid, almost wet rainforest air to find Lily stretched out on top of me with her nose against mine. Sully was growling threateningly from inside the bag, nervous about being stepped on, and I remembered where we were. My new life was starting today.

Coffee. I needed coffee first! The dogs knew better than to ask for anything until there was a steaming mug in my hands. Not today, though. In all my excitement the only supplies I packed were for the pets. Lily, watching me with a wary expression, and Sully oblivious as they ate their kibble. I uncovered Pearl's cage and was greeted with a chirpy "Good morning, how are you?" And then a more somber "What 'cha doing?" as he looked around the unfamiliar territory: "What are you doing to me?" He wanted to know.

The weather had done a complete turn-around. The sun was bright and there was no wind. It was a warm day for September in Minnesota. One of those cherished Indian summer days that I wished would last forever. Leashing the dogs, we went out for a walk. What a beautiful world it was! Even more so than memory. Birch and poplar trees grew in clumps, with their intriguing and ragged parchment bark. Pine, oak, and willow were scattered around the yard. So many trees and so thick, I wondered if you could even see the lake from Grandmother's house. The grass grew thin and sparse here in the sandy ground; denser near the bigger house where once a real lawn grew and was tended. Against the water grew these odd little hollow plants. I don't know what they are really called, but Mom and I called them pull-aparts because the stems grew in sections and we could pull them apart and stick them back together again. Next to the lake stood the two trees we would stretch the canvas hammock between. I decided at that moment, we would make the cottage our home rather than Grandmother's forbidding monster of a house.

From the end of the dock I could see there were no boats on the water. No signs of other people. In the distance I heard the sound of a lawnmower or chainsaw, but it was a mile or so away, across the bay. The cabin was in a tiny bay of its own, completely out of sight of others. Except for a loon or two, it was silent. It was a steady quiet, a comfortable and dependable quiet where no unexpected noises would interrupt thoughts. Absolutely no people sounds unless I made them. A barely noticeable breeze stirred the long, thin grass as a red-tailed hawk soared above looking for a meal. It eyed Sully briefly, decided he was too big, and flew off. There was a memory of a rowboat either tied to the dock or lying on the shore, but none to be seen. Red. It had been painted a barn red.

Of course, it had been at least six years since any people had lived here.

Stomach empty and desperate for coffee, the dogs and I climbed into the car to head out into this strange but familiar world to find supplies. Wondering if Petersons General Store was still in existence, I drove in the most likely direction. At the end of my lane, I turned left and drove past cabins closed up for the season and those that were still occupied. Some folks lived there year round, and you could tell who they were by the kind of cottage they lived in. Some had a thin stream of smoke coming from chimneys. There were huge vegetable gardens and fruit trees at these places and piles of sawn and chopped wood. Good idea, I thought. It would be cold soon and I had no idea what sort of heat was available at either house. I'm sure Grandmother had heat, but I didn't remember if there was heat in the cabin. The only source of heat I remembered from childhood summers was a fireplace.

Another three miles up the rough gravel road and I found it. Petersons General Store. I remembered five cent pony rides in the parking lot on hot sweaty afternoons and double scoops of ice cream for a dime. The hand-painted sign was so faded it was hard to read, but I was thrilled it was still here after so many years. A long, low rectangular shape, the building consisted of a poolroom bar on one side opening into the store on the other. White clapboard siding and no windows, it didn't look promising. But I remembered a treasure trove of everything interesting to a child, bubble gum to bait, comic books to sweatshirts with Bay Lake printed on them. Anything the summer people could want. The stooped, crooked man behind the counter looked too old and frail to be there, but wasn't familiar to me. Instant coffee, bread, milk, peanut butter, canned soup, canned pears, cheese, cereal, bottled water, and Milkbones. There were no fresh veggies or fruit, so a trip to a town was in order. Wherever that might be! I piled my purchases at the register and smiled brightly.

"That's it," I said.

"Well," Mr. General Store rumbled, "You know we can get whatever you want. Let me know by Tuesday and it'll be here on Friday."

"Great."

"So, what do you want then?"

"I'll have to think it over."

He rang up my food and studied the box of Milkbones a bit. "Got a dog, do ya?"

"Two of them. They are out in the car," I offered with another smile.

"Haven't seen you before....." So I proceeded with a shorter version of my story.

"And now I'm here for awhile. Maybe all winter."

"Lind, you say. Ain't nobody here by that name." He sounded suspicious.

"My Grandmother was Augusta Svensson." That brought a closer look.

"Didn't know she had family anymore."

"Apparently no one did, since it took the lawyers so long to find me." He bagged my groceries slowly, watching me with a close and curious expression.

"You must be Marie's girl." He finally smiled back. "Look like her, you do. The same curly brown hair, those rosy cheeks, eyes so dark blue they almost look black." No one had ever compared me to my mother. All I had were my memories of her; I had never seen a photograph. No wedding pictures, no birthday party celebrations. Nothing. There were later photographs of Dad and me, or his folks, but not of Mom.

"Really?' I was pleased and I was sure he could see that. "Did you know her?"

"Watched her grow up. She was a friend to my children. Moved away when she was eighteen or so."

We walked to the door and he handed me my sack. "Ain't no Linds around here." He repeated with a grin.

"There is now."

"Welcome home." What a wonderful sound those words were! I did feel at home, for the first time in more than twenty years.

4

When I pulled in behind the cottage, I got my first really good look at it. It appeared to be in much better physical condition than I expected, and although it was still painted an unusual shade of pink, the roof was nearly new and the chimney had been repaired. Who? I wondered, still cared for this place?

The cottage greatly resembled the family bungalows built in old Saint Paul neighborhoods in the 1930s and 40s. There were two entries: one on the south into the kitchen, and the other, rarely used, at the front. Approximately thirty-five feet by thirty-five feet and less than a hundred feet from the shoreline.

There wasn't a proper beach here, the water simply lapped up into a pile of smooth rocks. The lake was very shallow at this shoreline, though, only a couple of inches so you could easily put a lounge chair in the water for sunbathing. The sand at the edge of the water was a light speckled tan but out farther where the water was deep, when I would stretch my toes down to the bottom they would instantly be buried in this mysterious silky mud. I could barely feel all sorts of things hidden down there. I never learned how to swim under water, so the mystery remains.

The kitchen and living space was one large room separated by short walls between to give the appearance of separate spaces. The sink, next to the door with a corner cupboard between, had a cold water faucet that brought in lake water, which meant drinking water needed to be carried in. A huge, round oak table with mismatched chairs took up most of the kitchen space. There was also a small ancient refrigerator against one of the short walls, but no stove. On the other short wall sat a side table with shelves below and an ancient toaster on top. This appliance was genius. The shape was slender, two pieces of metal joined at the top and slightly angled out at the bottom. Each side had two pulls that folded the sides down so the bread could be placed on the heating elements. When it was closed, it turned on and toasted.

The cupboards were still cluttered with dishes in various patterns and colors. Half-pint and pint jars became our drinking glasses because both Mom and I were so clumsy we tended to break the more fragile glasses or lose them outside. Dinnerware and knives were stuffed into the drawers. There were dozens more than necessary as most of Grandmother's old and unwanted silver ended up in the cabin. Pots, pans, and skillets, too, were all stored haphazardly. Nothing matched anything else and I liked it that way.

Behind the kitchen, in the back of the cabin, was a smaller bedroom and a ladder leading to an unfinished attic where the floor extended only down the middle of the room about twelve feet across. If you stepped off the floor you would fall through to downstairs.

Both the kitchen and living room had a line of crank windows the length of the walls. Great views of the lake and trees were visible from there once the mesh screens were removed. These windows faced west and I remembered the sunsets as glorious. Most of the living room's north wall held a hand-built brick and pine paneled fireplace. All floors were polished pine covered in places by beige tattered woven mats. Pine also covered the walls and ceilings: long planks on the walls and squares on the ceiling. Two more bedrooms opened off the living room on the west. The doors were built of thin pine wainscoting on the front and plywood on the back, making them heavy, if not unusual. The wall between these two bedroom doors held a huge mirror that reflected the line of windows and the lake. It looked like a painting. Below this was a daybed with dozens of pillows. It was a cozy warm space that I loved. Mom was everywhere. I swear I could smell her perfume. And maybe even see her standing at the sink or lying on the daybed.

"Well" I said aloud, "Let's clean this place up a bit."

"Okay, okay." This from Pearl.

I found the fuse box hidden in a corner of the smallest bedroom and flipped the switch. All the lights came on, including the refrigerator. Surprise! I started with that appliance and worked steadily until the place was at least cleaner and dust free. There were rags, newspapers, and cleaning brushes under the sink. I struggled with all the mattresses to get them outside and into the fresh air, along with what few blankets were salvageable. None of the sheets, pillows, towels, or other fabric had any useable life left in them. They were moth eaten and had been nested in by field mice. The mattresses and upholstered furniture had been covered by heavy plastic sheeting and the blankets had been safely tucked away in a trunk but were extremely old and worn. A list of necessities was started.

The antique carpet sweeper worked better than the new vacuum I used at home. I had to grin when I realized that what I had just thought of as *home* was no longer any concern of mine. I removed the tattered coverings and plastic from the furniture and washed the windows with cold lake water and old paper. That let in more light than I expected and I was taken by surprise at how wonderful it all still looked. I could almost see my mother smiling at me with approval from the sofa.

Time to walk the dogs and scout around outside a bit. I decided to try Lily without her leash since she hadn't been more than three feet away from me since we left Iowa. Sully, on the other hand, was totally without sense and could not be trusted. I wondered for a moment why it was that I loved him so intently. He did not come when called, had no manners to speak of, absolutely never listened to me and thought everything I owned was for him. Although his absolute favorite toy was an empty dog food bag, he had managed to destroy many of my shoes and other various belongings during his first year. A rocket of a dog my husband called "Spudnuts" for reasons only a man could know. But he was a cuddle dog and a lover and sought me out several times a day for a quick snuggle. He had this spastic little movement he did when he thought he was being ignored: he followed me and whenever I stopped, he

26

would flip over on his back, directly in front of me. With the most pathetic groan and whimper he would kick all four legs in jerky motion. He was like an overturned chubby beetle trying to right itself. He thought he was the center of the universe and this was his reminder that I was supposed to think so too. Sully continuously had to show me something or other, like a rock he wasn't able to pick up or a bird that had mysteriously flown away before I could come to his barking. Ah, it is so difficult to be a dachshund.

When he slept, a part of him, or sometimes all of him was as near to me as possible. Not only would he get under the blankets, but he would crawl up under my nightgown. My personal hot water bottle. Other dachshunds I had raised had the good sense to hide in shame when they'd committed a naughty sin. Not Sully! He would meet me at the door, tail wagging, sit up on his butt and bat his nose with a front paw, knowing just how impossibly cute he was. I'm ashamed to say that it worked, too. Every time.

Another dachshund from years back, Lola, had been trained to relieve herself on newspaper. She would get just her front feet on the edge of the paper and poop. Because of her body length, the poop would be on the floor. Lola would observe this situation in some distress and then bat the poop onto the paper with her paw. Problem solved. Dog love is so unconditional. I would do anything to keep them happy.

I met Lily after she was just born. I knew immediately that I had to have one of the three puppies and I visited them every day. I think Lily knew who I was before her eyes were open. I'd sit on the floor of the straw-filled barn and she would slowly squirm her way to my lap on her soft belly. So, when she was finally old enough to come home with me, we were already inseparable. She constantly walked next to my legs, as close as possible without either of us tripping over the other. If I dropped a hand to her, she would suck on my fingers as we walked along. It seemed to be sort of a security thing for her as she's always been slightly leery of the world. Even now, if I leave a room she comes, if only briefly, to see where I am.

The boathouse to the right of the dock had nearly collapsed in on itself. The large white garage door was in pieces and all I could see inside was a hand powered lawnmower that you would need Paul Bunyan himself to push through the long grass by the main house. I was saddened by the loss of this building. No matter where I was out on the lake, I could see where home was by the beacon of the white door in the sun light. It was even visible in the night because it was so large and so white. Still no sign of a boat.

The only other building was an outhouse positioned somewhat behind the cottage on the way to the house. Hidden amidst a stand of willow and lilac bushes, if I hadn't known it was there I would have missed it the night before. Last night's experience with spider webs helped me to decide what to clean up next. All it needed was to be swept out but a couple coats of paint wouldn't hurt either. More supplies to go on the list. Toilet paper was, in my opinion, worth a trip to the store. Just beyond the outhouse stood a rickety fish cleaning shed. I was afraid if I touched it, the poor thing would collapse completely. So I left it for now.

It was too late for a start on the main house. Or was that just another reason not to go there? For heaven's sake! Did I think Augusta's ghost was in residence? Or that she had booby trapped the place knowing I would come back?

No. I just needed real food. So back to Petersons. No matter what time of day or night one went to the General Store, it was open. I went to the bar first to see about hot food. I lingered at the pool table for a moment. A memory maybe? I was standing on a wooden box and someone was telling me how to make the shot. Who was it? Then, nothing.

"You lookin' for Myron?" A voice behind me asked.

"I don't know. Can he cook?" I turned to the sturdy man in the red lumberjack shirt who laughed. He had thick, dark brown wavy hair graying at the edges, and grey friendly eyes, somewhere around age fifty I'd guess.

"Don't think so," he said. "But Selma, his wife sure can."

A sweet looking tiny and wrinkled snowy white-haired woman came smiling into the room from the store. She was chubby and dressed in an old fashioned print dress. She wiped her hands on a faded apron.

"Hi there, honey. You must be Emily! I'm so glad to meet Marie's daughter again!" Smelling of freshly baked bread, she wrapped me in a hearty hug.

At hearing those names, a fleeting shadow seemed to pass over the man's expression, but was gone in an instant, leaving me to doubt it had been there at all.

"I am Selma and this oaf is my eldest, Robert."

Robert grinned at us and said, "This girl is hungry, Ma."

"We can surely fix that. Be right back." She hustled back through the door.

"Dad told us you were here." Robert was seated at the bar now. "What do you think of the old house?"

"I'm ashamed to admit I haven't been inside. Ever. My Mom and I always lived in the cottage."

"Yeah." He was quiet for a time. "Always thought that was a shame. Augusta was a tough one. Didn't seem to care much for anyone. But, the place is all yours now."

"Yes. I think I want to live in the cottage, though. The house is a bit much."

"You'll need some help getting it ready for winter. If you plan on stayin'."

"I have no plans other than staying. I love it here. Where else could I go? I'd like to make this my permanent home. I don't know how much help I'll need, but I sure do have questions." That last burst of speech came out of nowhere and embarrassed me somewhat. After all, how much could this man know? Quite a lot, as I would find out later.

Selma came back with a huge basket filled to the top with parcels of all sizes and smells.

"Wow. I thought maybe a hamburger."

Robert really chuckled at that. "Hey," he smiled "You said you were hungry! To Mom, that is an excuse to fatten you up."

I laughed too, and left the store with promises to return for a "real meal" soon.

5

The next morning was bright and alive with life. I had slept really well with a full stomach for the first time in days. The bed was comfortable enough with the sleeping bag and two dogs for warmth, but I was aware I would need to do something for heat soon. I lay there content for a few minutes watching the sun make gently swaying shadows and soft patterns on the walls. Outside there were sharper, brighter patterns through the leaves and branches. The ground looked speckled. I knew the sunlight patterned the rest of the world in similar ways but I only noticed it here.

With a mug of cold instant coffee in my hands, I took the dogs out. Lily was beginning to relax and trust the weather again. Both dogs were very interested in the lake. Sully ran up and down the length of the dock looking for a spot to jump in. When he finally did, it took him completely by surprise. He couldn't get out fast enough and it was clear I was to blame for this misfortune! After shaking most of the water off we breakfasted on Selma's leftover chicken and bread while sitting on the edge of the dock gazing over the lake. Sully turned into a vulture, hanging his head and neck as far as he could over the end of the dock. I could see his brain figuring out how he could snatch those fish right up out of the water. If he could just reach…

Lily napped up against my body. I knew she was comfortable by the way she did this, flat on her back with all four legs straight up in the air and snoring lightly. She stretched and rolled right off the dock and into the lake! I thought she'd be terrified and I jumped up to help her, but she seemed to love it. She actually did it several more times with the briefest of hesitation. It looked so great, I tried it. With much laughter, we allowed ourselves to dry off. After feeling like I'd been living in a state of near hibernation for so many years, my damp skin, as it absorbed the autumn sun, felt like it was waking up. I packed up Selma's unfinished lunch and patted my full stomach happily. Selma was indeed a terrific cook, a talent I had yet to cultivate.

A sound caught my attention, and I looked back over the water. A birch-bark canoe carrying a single man paddled past. Something about him seemed way too familiar. He lifted a hand in silent greeting as he floated past. I blinked, and he was gone. A memory? Had he really been there? If so, the dogs had failed to register his presence.

"Okay," I told myself. "Time to see the house."

Leaving the dogs behind, I started over. A moist breeze smelling of fresh lake water and green floated in over the lake. I cannot explain that smell but it was so familiar to me; I stopped to just breathe it in. The air here was completely different than anywhere else I had been. Somehow cleaner and clearer. Even my skin smelled different. It was a smell I associated with sunlight. Colors were more vivid, sounds sharper, air clearer; why would anyone leave? I walked back out on the dock and lay on the rough wood. I needed to spend a few minutes absorbing the sun on my skin and the smells that so made me think of my mother and our private summers together before those tender memories flitted away.

An osprey flew directly over my head and I watched as it dipped its beak into the lake. It was an incredibly graceful sight and I vaguely remembered a game I had played during some of my long and isolated childhood hours. Maybe I could still do it? I concentrated all my thoughts on that osprey and watched it so intently that eventually I saw the lake through his eyes. I could feel the wind in my feathers, lifting me in its breeze and the cool water under my feet as I soared over the lake, trees, and empty cabins. I was happy that the lake was quiet and still, that the people were gone for awhile. Refreshed by my flight, I landed in a pine and spent time preening my feathers carefully. Slowly the osprey faded away and Emily was back. I sat up and located the bird again. He was sitting at the top of a pine just behind me. Where had I learned this game? Why had it stopped?

As I stood to move to the main house it occurred to me there was no hurry here. I could do what I needed to do and that was to relax and take all this in. I was beginning a new life here in this old and well loved place, and I could take as much time as I needed. There was no husband or father to try desperately to please. Only me, and I was easy. I sat back down.

Tiny fish were milling about doing what fish do, I suppose. Swim, eat, and swim some more. The water was so many colors of blue, grey, and green that it was like an animated painting. Looking around, I saw no one so I stripped and jumped in. I had learned about skinny dipping from my Mom. She loved to swim, and we pretended this naked swimming was our secret little sin. The water was deliciously chilly.

I swam out a ways to test the soft muddy bottom, turned back, and dried myself using the sun as a towel. Stretched out at the end of my rickety dock, I felt peace. When I had drowsed and dried, I slipped back into my dirty clothes and went to find the hammock. In it's usual place, stuffed under the attic ladder, it was covered in dust and cobwebs so I hauled it out to the lake, stripped again and rinsed it thoroughly. Shaking out as much water as I could, I spread it out where I had been lying. I could hardly wait to hang it and daydream like I did at age ten. Back then, I had planned out my entire life while lolling in that hammock. Of course, nothing turned out like that plan. Does it ever?

There were still blooming flowers at the edge of the yard, so I picked them all and took the bouquet inside. Mostly mums, marigolds, Black-eyed Susans, and a few daisies, they added a lively, cheerful friendliness to the cabin. There didn't appear to be a vase, so I used a quart canning jar which suited very well. I set them in the center of the table. I made myself a peanut butter sandwich for lunch and ate while watching the tranquil lake lap against the shore. Someone had piled many rocks against the restraining wall at the edge of the water. They were smooth and varied in color from slate grey or black to a greenish blue, tan, speckled, and chocolate brown. Smaller colored pebbles like these had been embedded into the cement walkway between the cottage and the water and they gave it a natural path look, pebbly and rough.

Scrounging in the cupboards, I found an old pair of Mom's shorts that she had used as a dust cloth once or twice, shook them out, and donned them to go back outside. This time, I took the dogs and we played in the water, splashing and fish-chasing to our hearts content. After air drying yet again, I put the dogs inside and headed to the house.

The house key had to be the original, fancy iron filigree and quite heavy. It slid easily into the lock. The door opened into a foyer with a wide oak door to the left and an arched entry straight ahead. The foyer could be lit by a chandelier overhead and there were long, narrow, leaded glass windows on either side of the front door. I went straight through the arched doorway into a kind of reception area where the ceiling was domed like a small cathedral. There was a twelve inch ledge about a foot and a half below the ceiling and a painted scene above that wrapped around the room. The remaining walls were painted a soft orange/gold and the oak floor was bare. Built-in fern stands were part of the woodwork at the corners. A second but identical arch, led the way into the rest of the house. My, what a first impression!

To the right was a straightforward Mission-style staircase with oak steps about ten feet wide. They went up to a landing, turned, up to another landing, and so forth. I imagined from the top, you could look straight down.

The door on the left opened to a library and office. These walls were lined with bookshelves full of books, both in Swedish and English, and maybe some in French or Russian. I wasn't sure as I was terrible at languages. It was a decidedly masculine room with heavy, Mission-style furniture. A large desk and library tables were pushed up against walls. The desk chair sat between two windows that also had built-in cushioned window seats. In the corner was a tiny room, a water closet, I believe it was called. A small sink and toilet with the water tank high on the wall above with a brass pull-chain to flush.

Between this room and the front door was a small waiting area. All of this was carpeted with Oriental rugs, faded and worn but still lovely. Back in the reception hallway, I walked into the house a little farther and discovered more extra-wide doors, on both sides of the hallway. These doors could be slid back into the walls to turn these rooms into one large one. The hallway walls were lined with framed portraits with names and dates on brass plaques beneath them. Ancestors, I presumed.

On the right, was a parlor with velvet, forest green drapes keeping all light at bay. Opening them changed everything, and the electric lights were not needed. The charm of the room was unexpected. It was warm and welcoming and full of old-world style. More Oriental rugs covered the floor.

Suddenly I remembered a scene, or remembered the story of something. Mom and another girl sitting on these carpets playing with very small dolls and their furniture, clothes and even dishes. The patterns in the rugs were the hallways, gardens, and roads. Did I play this game or did Mom? It had to have been Mom as I had never been in this room. At least I didn't think I had.

What I could see of the furniture under the white sheeting, was oak and heavy. After six years, I could still smell the lemon oil. A fireplace large enough to live in took up an entire wall. Framed paintings in a similar style to the one in the reception room adorned the walls that were papered in a faded forest green, maroon and grey stripe. Four feet from the floor, a line of crank windows like those in the cottage looked into what must have once been a formal garden. Flanking the string of windows were two doors of matching construction, opening onto the stone and granite porch.

A worn Bible written in Swedish lay on a pedestal table alongside a well used rocker. Grandmother's chair, I was certain. It had its straight back facing away from the windows. What had been wrong with this woman! There was a small drawer that was hard to see because of the carved scrollwork. In this was another Bible. Odd though, it wasn't exactly a Bible, but I could read nothing in it. It appeared to be Russian maybe?

Across this hallway from the parlor was a formal dining room. The walls were lined with ornately carved side boards and glassed in china cupboards. Delicate china, glassware, and linens were still kept here. On the outside wall was another long row of crank windows with two glass doors opening onto another granite porch. A long polished table seating twelve, with matching chairs was in the center. The ceiling in the center of the room was maybe twelve feet high, considerably lower around the edges, the same as the parlor. In the parlor, it lent itself to more intimate settings, in the dining room, it accented the table. Another huge chandelier hung over the table.

Behind a small barely noticeable door in the far corner, was a butler's pantry that exited into the kitchen. A large airy country kitchen with pale yellow walls and red and white checkered floors spoke of more informal family gatherings. Lots of windows, lots of light. Under an oil cloth stood an enamel wood cookstove complete with warming ovens and a water reservoir. It was a gold/beige color and had been in the cottage all the years that I remembered, which is where I wanted it now. However, it most likely weighed as much as my car.

A stairway leading both upstairs and down was built into the inside corner of the room. Under the stairs that led up was a door leading back to the hallway. The hall was slightly wider here. An additional set of double sliding doors opened into a remarkable, neat, and formal living room with lots of tall, narrow windows and furniture that looked hardly worn. This room wasn't used much, I guessed. Full of furniture nobody sat in.

The last room on this level was another bathroom, again with sink and toilet only. A little fancier, for female guests.

I did not like basements, so there was no contest as to which way to go next. But first, there was something nagging at me about the foyer, so I went back. The wall across from the library waiting area was very strange. It was hand carved and almost looked like a map, or a code, or something quite odd, very modern and totally unlike the rest of the house. There were knobs and bumps and crevasses on the highly polished wood. I would have to look more closely at this in better light. It struck me as strange that my mother had never described this oddity to me while talking about the house she grew up in. This was surely something she would have mentioned.

I went up the main stairs to the second floor where I expected the stairs to continue to the attic, but they did not. The landings were wide and roomy and at the top was an inside balcony that looked out over the stair well and down to the first floor. Immediately to my left was a fussy sitting room with exceedingly large overstuffed and matching chairs. They appeared to perhaps have belonged to giants especially since they were placed beside tiny pedestal tables. Fringed lamps, both on the floor and on several tables, lit the space. Oak wainscoting covered the walls four feet up, and the remainder was wallpaper in small roses of various colors. It was a feminine room despite the size of the furniture, even though it was attached to the master bedroom. A balcony opened to the front of the house and fit the entire top of the Greek entry below. It was surrounded with wrought iron filigree fencing. The view was magnificent! Standing there I felt like I might have been in some mountainous country, tucked away in a castle overlooking a dense forest. There should have been jousting knights and fine prancing horses below. The bits of the lake that were visible from here might have been a moat.

Okay, into the master bedroom! Square with lots of built-ins: wardrobes, chests of drawers, benches, and tables, all built into the woodwork and all of the same heavy

Mission-style. Fern stands at the corners, like downstairs. An overly tall four poster bed sat in the middle, so that you could walk around it. The bed itself was ornately hand-carved and high off the floor. It was older than anything else I had seen. Maybe it arrived with the family from Sweden? I remembered stories of Great-grandfather's skill as a carpenter, but they were vague.

The most surprising features in this room were the walls. Every available space was covered with photographs or paintings of the same girl. First as a child and then as a young woman. At closer inspection, I realized the pictures couldn't be the same person because they were of such different times and dress. I did recognize my mother, and some of them looked like me, but they were taken in this house, so they were not me. Two of the photographs had two girls in the frame maybe ten years apart in age. In one, the two were in bathing suits and holding hands, laughing and getting ready to jump in the lake. The younger, Mom I assumed, was about seven and looked like pictures taken of me at that age. There was a painting over the bed, high up on the wall. I think it might have been Grandmother, and a very young girl in pigtails holding a newborn. Another woman, short and dark haired, who looked nothing like Grandmother, stood slightly away from the others and did not face the camera. It was easy to pick out the women, Grandmother and the girl, who must have been my mother. But the baby? Who was that? Mom was far too young here for the baby to have been me. It was so confusing!

One armoire still held Grandmother's clothes; dresses, skirts, blouses shawls and embroidered slips and night gowns. Beautiful and expensive things. Many drawers had been emptied of possessions and anything else that might possibly have told me more of my Grandmother's life. But, it appeared that she had been in the process of removing herself before she died.

Back into the hallway, the next door opened to a large bathroom. Claw-foot tub, toilet, and pedestal sink. The floors were covered in braided rugs of many colors, reminding me of an old Bible story about Joseph and his coat. In one of the rugs was a scrap I knew! It was a dress I had worn for my birthday. I did remember Mom saving old clothes and bringing them here to Augusta, so she must have braided the rugs. Did she even think about my mother and me while she ripped apart our clothes?

Next was a play room or school room. It was painted light green and had flowery curtains at the large windows. The outer wall of this room didn't extend out as far as the master bedroom, so it was somewhat narrower. From the windows, you could almost see into the window of the master bedroom. It was the same at the other corner. Shelves were built in all around the room with a table and chairs in the center. There were still toys and books on some of the shelves. There were also some toys that would belong to a boy, trucks, and a baseball bat. I leafed through a couple of books and found they were text books: arithmetic, science, and geography, with childishly scrawled names on inside covers: Grace, Marie, Alice, and Ruth. My mother's book had red hearts of all sizes drawn in a circle around her name. It looked like she had been about to add another name as there was a plus sign drawn beneath her own. A first love?

Across the hall were two smaller, identical bedrooms. One held only an unmade single bed and empty chest. The paint was so faded I couldn't tell the color. No rugs and no curtains, it was completely bare and somehow sad. The other, was obviously the room of a much loved child. The walls were the blue of sky and the floor was carpeted in forest green. Mothers favorite colors. I felt like I was in the woods on a cool spring day. But there were no secrets to be revealed about Mother or Grandmother here. Nothing, but the furniture, no books, no forgotten dolls, no letters. Nothing. I don't know what I expected to find, just something more than I had. I wasn't able to sense Mom in here.

Back in the hall again, what I thought was a solid wall at this end was actually a door that slid back into the wall of the playroom to reveal a wider hall with several more doors. I took a quick look, but would thoroughly explore later. It was empty anyway. Straight ahead of me were tall windows that looked out into the backyard full of gardens still blooming, the flowers poking heads up through the long grass. To my right were two small bedrooms much like those in the other hall, except they had built in bunk beds rather than just singles. Across this hall next to the playroom, was a larger bedroom and small bath. This room would be over the kitchen, I realized when I saw the narrow stairway that descended. Odd, I thought. How do you get to the attic? I must have missed a ladder or stairs somewhere. Realizing the day was advancing rapidly, I decided to leave the attic for another time. Besides, I had no idea how to get up there.

Descending this back staircase, I entered the kitchen again. Afternoon shadows made it all look a little unnerving and I made straight for the entrance. As I passed the door to the basement, I shivered slightly. I doubted seriously that I would ever venture there! Not without more than two dogs to protect me from whatever demons might be lurking in that dank darkness.

6

After days of resting and relaxing, absorbing the lake life into the very fiber of what was me, and feeling marvelous, the like I'd never known, I discovered I had an abundance of energy. It was time for a walk, a stroll around my home, I reminded my delighted mind. We, the dogs and me, were in great trouble of becoming dock potatoes with all this lazy time. Sully was already plumper.

I remained somewhat bothered by the fact that I had located nothing in the way of journals, legal documents, or letters. I had learned nothing of Grandmother except that she had excellent taste. Either the knowledge will come eventually...or not. Did it really matter all that much? Not in my present state of mind.

I found a pair of tennis shoes, and the leashes, stretched my muscles, and left the comfort of the cabin with the dogs. We took a very long walk which included a stroll in the lake. Lily even ventured to get her feet wet again with a little less coaching from me. She seemed to have completely forgotten her joy at rolling off the dock. Sully was having too much fun without her, and that was not acceptable. Sully couldn't figure out how to catch the minnows without sticking his head under the water and was frustrated enough to try stepping on them. What a sight he made! Whining and moaning in disgust, he finally gave up and sat in the water waiting for me to lift him back onto the dock. I put the wet dogs in the cottage and set out once again for Petersons store.

This time I was greeted by Mr. Peterson. "Hello there little Miss Emily." His voice boomed out of his frail, grey body.

"I'm not little anymore, sir" I laughed.

"Well, that's what we called you for ten years, when you were, so I guess it will stick. What do you need today?"

"Just some canned food that will taste good cold. There isn't a stove in the cottage anymore." Mr. Peterson looked off into space for a moment and I thought he had forgotten me.

"I remember now! Twelve years ago or so before she passed on, Augusta decided she couldn't cook on her electric anymore. Brand new stove, too. She had my boys move it out and the wood cookstove in." He shook his grey head. "Selma thought she was crazy. Augusta didn't cook. Lydia, your grandmother's friend, did."

"I'd like to get it moved into the cottage as soon as I can arrange for it."

"Which one?" he asked, with a twinkle barely visible.

"The wood stove. I don't know if it is just for sentimental reasons or if I am a glutton for punishment. Besides, the warmth will be great."

"There are a lot of downed trees just behind your place. Year's worth. Augusta had her wood delivered from the saw mill. Her handyman, me, refused to do it anymore."

"Weren't there a couple of people who lived in the house with her? Employees or something?" I inquired. "I thought she had hired help."

"By this time it was just Augusta and Lydia, who was a bit younger than your grandmother. She cooked and did light housework. Sometimes her daughters helped out, but usually it was just the two of them in that big house. Once a month, a team of professional cleaners from Brainerd came in to do a thorough job of it."

Just then a man I hadn't met ambled in. "Hey Pop," he said. He gave Mr. Peterson a swat on his shoulder and looked at Emily with curiosity.

"Emily, I'd like you to meet my son." This man was a shorter, stockier version of Robert, and maybe slightly younger. No grey in his hair.

"Ray, this is Emily Lind. She is Augusta's granddaughter. Marie's girl."

"Sure. Little Miss Emily!" He laughed and held out his hand. "Expect you don't remember me, but I used to babysit you."

He did seem familiar. Especially the laugh. It was very musical, very contagious.

"My wife told me you had moved into the cottage. She thought you might need some help." My goodness but this was a helpful clan.

"She does, actually. Wants the old wood cookstove moved back into the cottage. Soon. She's down to eating cold food from a can." Mr. Peterson didn't waste time getting to the point.

"We can do it right now. I'll just collect Robert and we'll be over. He's cleaning the fish we caught this afternoon." Turning to his dad, he added, "Sunfish for supper tonight."

To me he said, "Are you sure you don't want the electric stove?"

"I'm sure. Maybe in the spring. Right now I want the heat."

"Okay then. We will meet you there."

I purchased canned food, soup, vegetables, beans, and peaches. A feast of easy food. When I got to my car, there were a couple of bundles of campfire wood in the backseat. I guess it will be a warm supper after all.

Back at the cottage, I got the food put away and the dogs leashed. We were on our way to the house when the brothers pulled in. Two additional men sat in the bed of the truck. They had some kind of homemade platform on wheels that looked like it could move anything. With much laughter and several grunts, and groans, and what looked like a sprained muscle or two, the stove was dismantled. It was a lucky thing that the enamel appliance came apart in several pieces: the round iron burner lids, the water reservoir, warming ovens, two of the three oven doors and the drawer that held the wood or coal, and the base. They needed a crowbar to separate the pieces since they had been sitting in place at Grandmother's for such a long time. Once all the parts were back together in my kitchen, and that part went much easier, we found only a small scratch in the enamel. The indentations were still deep in the floor from when the stove had sat there in the past. Like me, it was home again. The stove might have been smiling, but it was only the design of the pulls and temperature gage, shadowy and vague.

The brothers' personalities were very different from each other. Ray was always smiling and laughing, making jokes and telling funny stories about life at the lake. Robert was solemn, even when he laughed. I'd catch his eyes on me every time I looked at him. I thought maybe he had something he wanted to ask, but he never did.

I thanked them for the wood and the help and they went on their way. Ray ran back to the cabin with a package of newspaper. "Here's supper," he said.

Sunfish.

7

I did not want to open my eyes the next several mornings. The lids felt puffy and glued together with sleep and my body was sore and tired from exercise it was not used to. And it was warm and cozy in my sleeping bag. Neither of my companions was eager to rise and they snuggled in tighter when I moved. I had to pee, though, and I'm sure they did too. When I wasn't able to hold it any longer, we all raced for the door. A considerably cooler day faced us. There would be no splashing in the lake on this day. Clouds and a stiff wind came off the water. This might be a good day for that shopping trip. I found an old Minnesota map in the glove box of my car and checked it out.

There wasn't a town of any size closer than thirty miles and I was becoming so comfortable here I did not even want to go that far. What was it Myron had said at our first meeting? It was something about ordering anything. That sounded like a plan. So, coffee mug in hand, I made my daily trip to the general store.

"Good morning, Miss," Mr. Peterson was again at the counter. "What do you need today?" I pulled my extensive list from my pocket and began to read: "Warm clothes, boots, mittens, dog food, parrot food, real coffee, vegetables, fruit, a saw, batteries, flashlights, toilet paper, towels, sheets, pillows, dish soap, people soap, shampoo, and turpentine." Mr. Peterson had a wide, silly grin on his face when I finished.

"You sure that's all?"

"Well, there's water, juice, and Band-Aids on the list, too." I looked on the backside of the paper. "Plastic to winterize the windows, tape, and a rowboat."

Myron Peterson was still laughing. "We'll need some help," he told me. He went into the back of the store and when he opened a door, delicious smells wafted out. Their home must be back there, I realized.

Soon he returned with a smiling Selma, who took my list.

"Let's start with the clothes. What do you already have?" she inquired helpfully.

"Two T-shirts, one pair of jeans, tennis shoes, one pair of underwear, which I am *so* tired of washing every night and putting on damp!"

"Oh my." She was slightly taken aback either by my candor or lack of packing skills.

"I left in a hurry," I offered by way of an explanation. She put an arm around my shoulders and led me into her home. "We can fix you right up. As long as you aren't too fussy. You just wait right here, honey." Selma bustled off and I looked around. The living room was small and crammed with overstuffed but comfortable furniture. It looked like it had raised a family. Lots of photos of children through various ages lined every flat surface. Proud parents, proud grandparents, I thought. A real family. I had all but forgotten...

Selma soon returned with her arms so full I wondered how she could see her footing.

"Let's see what fits, shall we?" We spent the next several hours laughing and joking, me trying on clothes and Selma baking scones. When we were finished, I was better outfitted than if I had spent the day at L.L. Bean. There was even an Air Force parka lined with fur.

"These are all from one child or another," Selma said. "I knew they would come in handy one day. The parka is my eldest grandchild's. He lives in Hawaii now, so he won't need it, but you surely will. Winters are not a picnic in this part of the state."

Myron joined us for coffee and scones when the clothes were all packaged up.

"I ordered most of the other stuff on your list," he said. "Except for the things we already have, of course. But I need more information." We covered the specifics until we both were satisfied.

"Before we get all this stuff, you should look around Augusta's." This from Selma. "She had the most beautiful linens. I'm quite sure everything is still in the house."

"I have been in most of the house, but I haven't seen anything I could use yet. I still need to check the closets and cupboards, though."

"Lydia packed a lot of trunks to store in the attic years ago. If I remember correctly, there were several linens, towels, bedding, and the like. She didn't want to leave it all for Augusta who was already ill."

"What did she die of?" I realized again how little I knew of her. Selma and Myron made eye contact over their coffee cups and hesitated before speaking.

"How much do you know about your mother and grandmother?" Myron spoke. I laughed without any humor.

"Almost nothing."

"Do you know about Grace?"

Before I could reply, the door burst open and a windblown Robert burst in. "I've got the turpentine, Pop, but what do you need it for? You've got gallons of......"
He broke off when he saw me.

"Oh. Hello, Emily." He had a drawing pencil tucked behind his ear and paint brushes in his hand. Something in the back of my mind just clicked and I stood up in my astonishment, knocking over my chair.

"You." I uttered. "You are R.G. Peterson!"

"Yes ma'am! I fear I must admit my guilt." The entire room was chuckling at me.

I was completely embarrassed and too shocked to speak for a second. I stuttered, took a breath and said, "I know your paintings..." I finally got out. "Mom took me to many of your shows when I was young. We spent hours and hours looking at your paintings. She even took me to Chicago to see them. I cannot believe this. I love your work! So did Mom." R.G. Peterson was an extremely well-known and expensive wildlife painter. His works were available in quality prints that had always been outside of Mom's budget. Besides, Dad was not fond of art. Especially art you had to pay for.

Robert blushed and his parents looked quietly and with some sadness I thought, at each other. He held out the jar of turpentine. "This must be for you. Do you paint?"

"No. You paint. I play."

It wasn't until I was back at home that I realized I hadn't learned about Grandmother or Mom. And who the hell was Grace?

8

When I woke, I heard Lily rooting around somewhere. I could hear her snuffling in corners. Good, I thought, she's feeling more at home. When I stretched, Sully poked his head out from under my arm questioning this movement and wondering why his nap had been interrupted.

"Up and at 'em, big boy! We've got exploring to do." The fire in the cookstove was still warm from the evening before, and the water in the kettle was hot enough for instant coffee. I drink Swedish coffee, anyway: a third strong coffee with two thirds milk. Um, perfect!

After dressing more warmly and breakfasting the pets, I took my coffee and we strolled to the end of the dock. The tang of autumn was in the air but the day was warm again. I took my shoes off and dangled my feet in the lake, feeling like a ten year old girl once more. Thinking about Robert and yesterday, I knew I was no closer to answers. Coffee finished and still barefoot I headed to the big house deciding on the way that I would never go back to Iowa and my unhealthy marriage. I remembered seeing a telephone in the library and wondered if it still worked. Probably, as everything else seemed to.

Entering I figured I would call Marcus, my husband, and get it over with. He probably hadn't even realized I was gone, yet. I was composing a message when he answered on the first ring.

"Emily!" he shouted in my ear. "Where the hell are you!" It was a demand, not an inquiry. I was immediately transported back to the ranch style house we shared. A cold, barren abode that never had been a home to me. We were married, yes, but we were never friends. He was master of his domain and I was there to support his every whim. I was not allowed to work outside the home, because Marc might need something. For example; "Where are my clean socks?" Answer, in the drawer where they always are. "I can't find the peanut butter." In the refrigerator on the top shelf where it always is. "I don't want soup for supper, make me bacon and eggs." This after spending all afternoon making the beef vegetable soup he had asked for earlier. "I have to go out tonight. Don't wait up; it will be a late meeting." Uh huh.

"I have nothing to eat and no clean clothes." Marcus was, as usual, complaining bitterly.

"Cook something, or go out. Use the washer and dryer." I was falling back into helpful wife mode. Enough of this.

"Marc," I said. "I won't be coming back."

"You got that right, Emily! I filed for divorce today." Marc was a law clerk in a self important small town office. "The grounds are desertion. You up and left me!" He spat that out.

"You left me years ago," I responded in a weary voice, so tired of this. So tired of dealing with Marcus, the 37-year-old spoiled child, who looked like a Greek god, but who was rude and vicious with his words. Thick, styled blond hair, blue eyes that were a little devious, broad shoulders and a killer smile.

"May I remind you, you left me! I did not desert you!" He was still yelling, each word hitting my ear like a bullet.

"What about Kerry, Linda, Bridget, Connie, and Luanne?" This was answered with a full minute of dead air space.

"Well, I certainly hope you won't be asking for anything from me!" he sputtered.

"Marc, there is nothing you will ever be or own that I could want. Now, you go fuck yourself! Everyone else does." With that I disconnected the call. I was surprised at myself.

Such language! I giggled. Okay, that was easy. I was unhappy it took me so long to stand up for myself, and to break that tie. Was Marcus always such a jerk? I didn't think so, but what had happened? I did not like to think about it anymore, but I had an idea.

I had spent my childhood trying to please a father who had wanted a son. Neither I nor Mom had ever been forgiven for this slight. Nothing was ever right, or good enough. Every mistake we made was done to spite him. To make his life harder. As time went on, the distance between us grew wider until there were days then weeks, where I wouldn't see him at all. I would often be awakened during the night by arguing and slamming doors.

Dad's raised voice was the only one I would hear. I think Mom was quiet during these storms. I learned from these incidents over time, that the opinion of the female meant very little, if the male wanted something else. I also learned to keep my real feelings and ideas to myself. I learned to respond with what I knew the other person wanted to hear. It made me weak, but I figured that was normal. So, I was quiet, shy, and on my own. When Mom withdrew from me also, my anchor in the world disappeared.

The year I turned ten, after we came back from the lake so I could return to school, Mom simply sat and stared out the window. I would make her tea and sandwiches but she wouldn't eat. She patted my hand and told me she would always love me, but we no longer talked about things.

One day I came home from school to find the house full of people crying and talking quietly. Dad told me Mom was gone. Dead. I knew she had died of a broken heart, but I didn't understand what caused it. There was no memorial service. I never got to say goodbye.

After that, Dad was around more, but I always felt it was out of duty to a child he couldn't care much about rather than parental concern. Whatever it was, it wasn't love. His parents took up most of the slack and I felt that they loved me. I don't think they understood my father either. Grandma Bengta said some men should never be husbands or fathers. They are too self-centered or hard-hearted. I'm sure he didn't think he was a bad father. After all, he never hit me, but I wasn't important either. I grew to believe that because of that unimportance, he couldn't be bothered with discipline or interaction.

One story about Dad that Grandma Bengta used to explain how I wasn't the only one he couldn't show love to, was this: "When Howard was eight or nine years old, he put his younger brother Thomas into his red wagon and wheeled him to the street with a sign pinned to Thomas's shirt that said, 'five dollars or free'. I asked him why, and he said Thomas took up too much time and had stolen his toys."

That is the kind of man Marc was. Exactly. In our marriage, anyway. I spent too many hard years trying to please him, when it just was not possible. I took up too much of his time and stole his toys. If I rented a movie, he would send me back to the store for a different one. If I dressed one way he would tell me to change clothes. He would interrupt me when I was speaking and then never ask what I was going to say. I don't think he realized I had even been speaking to him. He would criticize me in public, when he bothered to take me out at all. He would complain the house was messy so I would spend hours cleaning it only to have him mess it up again within minutes of coming home. Then he would look around and complain again. When we were first married, I would look forward to his coming home from work. But within five minutes of his arrival, I wanted him gone. Always negative, always angry about something that was my fault, always hurtful. And it wasn't without his realizing how he sounded, it was done on purpose. Once he brought me flowers and I was too shocked to speak. The next day they were gone. When I asked what had happened to the bouquet, Marcus said he had given it away because I wasn't grateful enough. Let's see, I think it was Connie that time.

Shortly before I finally left, he had stopped by the house to change clothes before going out again. I could hear that the car was still running. Before Marcus could leave once more, the front door burst open and this young, terribly skinny woman breezed into the foyer.

"Marcie! I'm hungry! What's taking you so long, honey?"

"Excuse me?" I barred her way from dashing into the rest of the house even though I really didn't care that she was there.

"What have you done to my boyfriend?" She demanded, taking a dainty sip from a silver flask that I vaguely remembered having received as a wedding gift. "Connie, luv, I asked you to wait in the car." Marc, by then, had come into the room dressed to the nines. He was unable to meet my eyes when he took the woman's arm in leaving. I hope he heard my shriek of laughter follow them out.

I think what bothered me most though, was his absolute lack of interest in anything I did or that was important to me. He never once asked me how I had spent my day. He never looked at my paintings. My opinions were never solicited. I wasn't loved or caressed or hugged. If I touched him, he shrugged off my hand with irritation. We never made love. Or, I guess I would have to say that we never had sex, as love had nothing to do with the act.

59

He always yelled at the dogs. I would have to cover Pearl's cage when Marc was at home, because of "that damn racket!"

He never included me in his activities or asked what I wanted to do. I had only accompanied him to one of his office parties. Now, of course, I knew it was because of his many girlfriends, but at the time, I was hurt and lonely. I blamed Marcus; I blamed Howard, but never myself. Until I really dwelt on my past, that is.

Soon I was reliving all of my mistakes, all my faults, and never once thinking about the good things. Funny how long it can take to realize what is really going on! What a relief to be on my own for the first time in my life. I felt wildly free to explore my own thoughts and to express my own ideas without worry or consequence. I called Marc's lawyers and asked that the divorce papers be sent immediately. I mentioned that I wanted nothing more than what I had already taken with me. They were pleased.

9

I felt the need to be outside in the wonderfully cleansing sunshine. Not in Augusta's house. The answers I was seeking would have to wait. I collected the dogs and we trekked into the woods. Most of the leaves were now on the ground, still damp from the earlier rain. The air was incredible. Moss was soft and thick as a quilt in places and it smelled like outside is supposed to smell: moist ground, disintegrating leaves, air fresh with earthy fragrance, wet dirt, and a vague scent of decaying vegetation. It reminded me of the smell of spring, not autumn. No human odors at all. I hadn't thought about the rudeness of city smells until they were no longer present. I rested on a log and let the dogs explore on their own a bit, with Sully still leashed. Sunlight filtered down through the dense willows swaying in the slight breeze. So perfect. So quiet. So necessary after my most recent thoughts.

I was daydreaming and idly glancing around me when I noticed several neatly stacked hills of roughly sawn wood, precisely laid out on ground that had been measured out and sectioned. Each piece, marked with numbers and letters written in white ink in a very tiny script, was a reminder of something else, somewhere else, which was illusive at the moment. The pieces were numbered in sequence; the letters appeared to be a sort of code readable only to the person who etched them. What could this be? I picked one up and recognized that it was the perfect size for the cookstove. I could use this.

"Hey! Put that down! What do you think you are doing?" A very angry man came from around a stand of trees. I took a firmer grip on the wood still in my hand, thinking I might need to use it on this guy.

"A better question is: who are you and what are you doing here?" This was one too many jerks today and I was angry, not afraid.

"You don't own these woods!" he snarled.

"Oh, I think maybe I do. That would make you the trespasser and the one who needs to answer questions, not me."

"I have a permit signed by the owner, and it isn't you."

"Maybe you should show it to me." I waved the stick around a little, feeling like David against Goliath. He dug in a pocket of the jacket lying on one of the piles that I hadn't noticed, and pulled out a rumpled dirty paper. The dogs came dashing into the clearing with hackles up and growling loudly. Sully had tangled his flexi-lead around one of the piles and was straining against it. I made no attempt to restrain them as they swarmed around the intruder dismantling the stack with the leash. I didn't know they could be protectors. But then, they had never had the opportunity before now.

"Hey!" he shouted again. "Get these dogs away from me!" He raised an arm as if to swing at Lily and I stepped forward and cracked the stick over his raised forearm.

"DO NOT EVEN THINK ABOUT IT!" I could be fierce where my babies were concerned.

"Put that wood down before you crack it!" He was red in the face and yelling.

"Not until you back off, buddy!" He stepped back and I called Lily to heel. I had to grab Sully's collar and shorten the leash on him, because he would not back down. We stood ten paces apart and glared at each other, breathing hard. The dogs were losing interest so I thought I should hurry this on a little. I grabbed the paper he held out. It was indeed a permit of sorts. While not a legal document, it was signed by Augusta herself.

"She's dead."

"I know that! But she still gave permission and it takes some time for this project. I just never got to it before now and I didn't think it would matter. Besides, you..."

I interrupted him sharply because I was not remotely interested in his project by this time. I just wanted him to go away.

"I think you should leave until I can figure this out," I said.

"Who are you?" he asked again.

"Augusta's granddaughter. And you surely do not know how to make friends. Now go away."

"You gently put that wood down and I'll go. But," he threatened, "I will be back to finish this project!" I dropped the stick. He picked it up and carefully laid it on the pile, picked up his jacket and stomped off. So much for a relaxing walk in the woods. *Just another jerk.*

Back at the house, I phoned the firm of Anderson/Erickson. Maybe they could tell me something.

"Mr. Anderson, this is Emily Lind."

"Hello! Ms. Lind, we have been trying to find you yet again." There was a smile in his voice. "We have the deeds and bank accounts to deliver to you, along with various personal papers. Where should they be sent?"

I didn't think there was mail service at the cottage so I said "I am at Augusta's house. Please send them there. Mr. Anderson, I am impatient for some answers here. Why are the phone still hooked up and the heat and electricity still working? There is even running water. But, most of all, what can you tell me about my grandmother and my mother?" I did realize that I was jumping all over the place with these questions, but it had been a frustrating day.

"Most likely there are answers in these documents, but they are sealed and are for you to open. Augusta was a woman of very few words. There is also a small silver key. Have you come across something that is locked?"

"No, but I still have a lot of exploring to do in the house. It's huge! I need to find some help."

"Well, there is enough money to do nearly anything you want to do, so go ahead and hire someone if you like. The utilities are hooked up because we called the appropriate offices when we knew you would arrive. We will FedEx all the information we have. You will have it tomorrow morning. Good luck and please call if you need to, Ms. Lind. We are prepared to assist you in any way we are able."

Okay, so not all men were jerks.

I glanced around. Something that will be locked. That sounded promising. Wasn't there a comment about trunks in the attic? You could certainly lock a trunk.

10

The following morning I resolved to return to Grandmother's house and discover something, anything that would lead me to information. Up to the second floor. I was feeling a little like Nancy Drew from the dozens of Carolyn Keene novels my mother had purchased for me over the years. They were completely unrealistic, but I loved them. I would pick out an apple, the largest in the bin, and the newest Nancy Drew, and climb to a comfortable spot in the maple tree just outside the house. I could read up there for hours and never be discovered. Nancy Drew and her pals got me through many lonely times. She was also a good role model for a young girl. I learned that she could think for herself and figure out any mystery. It's too bad it took me so long to put into practice what she taught me. Anyway, as much as I wanted to go straight to the attic, Nancy would be methodical and check out the remainder of this floor first.

At the landing at the rear of the second floor was a second, small parlor only slightly less roomy than the one in front. The furniture was faded, but looked comfortable enough. A table with four straight-backed chairs sat in the corner by a window. I remembered Mom telling me of growing up with another family living and working here also. McKenna. Or was it Nelson? That was the name. I think both families had come from Sweden together. That would have been Augusta's parents, the Lundquists I thought, who came from Sweden with the Nelsons. The family had worked for the Lundquists in Sweden too. Isn't it odd to find out you know more than you thought you did?

Maybe there was some information about the McKenna or Nelson clans in these rooms. So I started with the first one and found nothing but beds and an empty chest of drawers. Disappointed again, I went into the closet. There was a single carton on the floor, taped closed. Written in a small, neat hand was the name Jackson. Would there be no end to these mysteries, I marveled?

I pushed the heavy box out into the brighter parlor and ripped off the tape. Inside were several notebooks, many photographs, some jewelry, a small stack of what appeared to be love letters to someone named Lydia from John, and a much worn oversized Bible. Embossed in gold leaf was the name McKenna and the inside covers had a kind of written family tree, two, actually, Nelson and McKenna, a more modern who begat who. Beginning in Ireland and Sweden and ending here with the birth of a child, Jackson, who, I figured out, was only a couple of months older than me. Interesting. Was he maybe a cousin? No, not possible as Mom had no siblings. Did she? I knew so little about her and I had loved her so deeply.

Oh my gosh! Maybe Grandmother's Bible had this same sort of family list. Dropping the book back into the box, I dashed down the stairs. Turning the corner into the kitchen, I ran straight into Robert.

"Slow down, Emily! There is no fire here." He steadied me before I fell.

"Oh, no!" I blurted before I could help myself. With him was the belligerent man from the woods. This couldn't be good.

"We have a problem..." hostile man began.

"I see you still have few manners." This guy brought out the bitch in me.

Robert grimaced. "Hold on and let me referee this please."

"Go ahead." I sat at the table but did not invite them to join me. Robert did anyway.

"Emily Lind is Augusta's granddaughter and Marie's daughter. I saw recognition and now belief in the man's eyes. It told me the angry man could believe Robert if not me. "This is Jackson McKenna, Emily. He is Lydia's grandson."

That was a jolt. "The same Lydia who lived here with Grandmother? Why didn't you introduce yourself?"

"I was worried about my project you were so carelessly throwing around." He was making me furious and I wasn't in the mood to listen. I stood up and went for the stairs.

"Show yourselves out, gentlemen," I said over my shoulder.

"Emily!" Robert demanded. "Come back here and..."

"If you tell me to act like a lady, I'll scream," I threatened. "Jackson, shut up!" I yelled as he opened his mouth.

Robert burst into laughter. "Do you hear yourselves? Am I dealing with a couple of spoiled toddlers who don't know how to share?" I think we both blushed. I sat back down and gestured to a chair to show that I, at least, was an adult. Jackson stood.

"Okay Jax, tell her about the project. Nicely," he added after getting a glance at Jackson's stormy face.

Jackson took a deep breath and began. "About ten years ago I was cutting wood for Augusta and Lydia and I got disoriented in the woods..." I raised an eyebrow.

"It was almost dark! Anyway, I stumbled onto this house that was beginning to fall into the ground. The part I tripped over was so unusual that I spent the night there so I could really check it out in better light." I raised the other eyebrow.

"I wasn't sure where I was and I didn't want to lose it!"

"Continue, Jackson." Robert encouraged him.

"There was a type of house building in the mid 1850s called cordwood construction. It was used by the Scandinavians in Wisconsin, Upper Michigan, and also in Canada. Some people think the Swedes brought it here, some think it is a Canadian thing, and some say it's Siberian or Greek. No one really is sure. I didn't think there were any examples here except for a few barns, and they are only partly cordwood." Okay, this was interesting. And familiar.

69

"I know about this. It's also called stove wood or stack wood," I volunteered. Jackson's jaw dropped.

"That's right." He was astonished. "How do you know...?"

"I'm from Iowa; there's a museum there, Vesterheim, and they have a 1850s stove wood house. Continue if you please," I said in my most lady-like voice. Robert grinned and chuckled.

"I work for several museums, including Vesterheim and the Swedish Institute in Minneapolis. I find things they are looking for and get the museums together with the artifacts. Like unusual buildings. I dismantle them carefully," he glared at me. "Number each of the logs in sequence, move it all, and reassemble. There are thousands of pieces of wood, each about fourteen inches long. Sometimes they are shorter or longer, but this one is exactly the length for a wood cookstove. They are stacked width-wise in mortar, so the buildings are very well insulated. The lime in the mortar keeps the wood from rotting. It's ingenious, really, and it can take years to study, and that's why I was upset with you." His eyes slid over to where the cookstove had been and seemed relieved it was no longer there. I didn't have the heart to tell him where it was, or that I was using it.

"So do it then. Just do not hit my dogs."

"I would never...I won't," he seemed surprised to find himself sitting at the table. In his enthusiasm, he had finally taken a seat. He reached up and absentmindedly brushed an errant lock of black curly hair out of his eyes. His skin was a sort of dark ivory and his eyes, a piercing blue. He was strong looking, but not over six feet tall, and he moved his body with a certain grace and confidence. He was very appealing to look at.

"Before you leave, there is a box upstairs with your name on it," I remembered.

He stood, looking at me with curiosity.

"On the second floor next to the stairs," I told him. When he left to get the box, Robert patted my shoulder and said

"Good girl. We'll get out of your way now." He tilted his head slightly to the side. "Sometimes you are so much like her. Your mother, I mean. She had a short fuse, too."

For supper that night, the dogs and I feasted on canned soup and peanut butter with jelly sandwiches. I was running low on kibble and couldn't remember when Myron said it would be in. I needed to talk with him and Selma again. They knew more than they had let on. So did the others.

"Is it good good good?" Pearl wanted to know. He was sitting on my shoulder and trying bits of sandwich. "Oh dear," he said moving his tongue around his beak trying to rid himself of the peanut butter. Pearl was acting like he hated the peanut butter, but he always begged for more and was alert to the twisting of the jar lid. He'd fly in out of nowhere the minute I picked up the jar.

"Oh dear me," he uttered once more.

"You sure got that right," I agreed. "What a day!" Jackson McKenna was weird, definitely, but also intriguing. Maybe we both needed another chance. There was something interesting there. Besides, Robert liked him and I liked Robert.

I took the dogs out after the sun set and could see several rowboats and small motor boats all clumped together way out in the bay. It sounded like a party with shouts and laughter. The men seemed to be teasing each other about the size of the fish they were NOT catching. Their boasting and bragging voices carried out across the water so, while I could barely see them, I could hear them clearly.

"Hey, the really big one got away!" Or "This one's so big I can't reel it in!" Then it suddenly grew extremely quiet on the water and one of the speed boats turned toward shore and flew across the water. I went inside and forgot all about them.

II

Before dawn the following morning, we were awakened suddenly by voices and flashing lights. For a moment, I thought I was back at my father's house in Saint Paul, and ran into a wall where the door was supposed to be. I flipped on the lights and recognized my surroundings at last. A voice was indeed blaring instructions through a loud speaker somewhere close.

Dressing quickly, I left the dogs and ventured out. From the end of the dock, I could see flashing lights about a half mile down the shoreline. Out on the lake, there were more lights. Several large search lights sweeping over the surface of the water, accompanied by several voices. Then I thought of the fishing party from the night before. Did someone have an accident? Drowned? It was still too dark to see much. I took the dogs for a brief walk, fed them, uncovered Pearl's cage, and headed to Petersons store.

As soon as I walked in the door, I was worried. Selma, Myron, Robert, and Ray were talking with two state troopers. They all stopped and turned to me in unison.

Selma brought me a mug of hot coffee and said, "We need to tell you about Grace, honey."

She took my arm and led me into her parlor, followed by the rest of the family. The troopers left. When we were all comfortably seated in the cozy room, she began her story. Grace's story.

"Grace was Marie's sister. There were seven years between them, with Grace being the elder. Grace loved Marie with a passion. I think she tried to make up a little for Augusta's coldness. They were always together. It was nothing like the relationship between my girls, who were always arguing and bickering. Grace had the patience of a good mother where the life of her little sister was concerned. Grace taught Marie how to cook, you know. How to bake bread, too. When Grace went shopping for her clothes, she brought Marie along and outfitted her as well, since Augusta couldn't be bothered with the child's fashion needs.

When she turned eighteen, Grace fell in love with a local boy, Karl Musser. Augusta was livid. The boy wasn't Swedish, but Norwegian, and Augusta put great store in those things. Grace told her mother she would stop seeing him..."

"But she didn't stop, did she?" I truly hated Augusta by this point.

"No. They saw each other in secret. Often here because Augusta never came to the store herself. She would send Lydia. We, Myron and my children, looked out for Karl, as he had lost his family. He was nearly another son. Karl was a good boy, a kind man, and he loved Grace very much."

"Grace is in the pictures with my mother that are hanging in Grandmother's room." I suddenly knew this for a fact.

"Yes, I expect so. Anyway, one day Lydia happened to be here when Karl dropped Grace off after an outing. Lydia saw them together and reported to Augusta."

"I will never understand that loyalty!" Myron spat out the words in disgust.

"Nor will I, my dear," Selma agreed and patted her husband's knee. "The two families had been together for generations, you remember, and we don't know the entire history. Someone once told me that Rudolf's and Augusta's folks saved Lydia's father from prison, when they brought him to America. That could certainly account for strong loyalty."

"Rudolf?" I asked. Myron looked at me sadly.

"They haven't told you anything, have they child? Rudolf also worked for Augusta's family in Sweden. When they came to Minnesota, he married your grandmother. Why he did that is a wonder to me! Although, to be fair, Augusta was a different woman then. Not so single minded and full of hate. Rudolf was a good, gentle man. He died about this time. They found him in the woods with a tree across his body."

"Not exactly, Pop," Robert said. "The men were all out cutting trees and Rudolf's tree started to fall in the wrong direction. He had time, but Rudolf just stood there waiting for the tree to hit."

"Why didn't he run out of the path of the tree? Did he kill himself?" I wanted to know this, but all four of them just shrugged their shoulders.

"After the funeral," Selma continued, "Augusta forbade Grace to see Karl. She locked her in that night, but Marie let her out after Augusta was asleep. Grace left a letter that said she was happy with Karl and they were going to be married. She said she and Karl were going to have a baby, and Grace vowed to be a better mother to her child than Augusta had been to her and Marie. That same night, she and Karl both disappeared. We all thought they had simply run away......" Selma's voice trailed off. I abruptly stood and dropped the empty mug.

"Voices. Lake." I was stammering. I felt like I had been hit by a Mack truck.

Robert gently pushed me back into the chair and handed me some water, which I shoved away, spilling a few drops. Why do people always think water will help?

"The state men think it might be Grace and Karl at the bottom of the lake," he told me. The local police called in the state and they sent a diver up from Minneapolis early this morning. There are bits of a boat and some bones tangled in the remains of an anchor chain. One of the skeletons had a necklace." He fished it out of his pocket to show me. "This one. Mom gave it to Grace on her eighteenth birthday." I reached out toward the necklace, but did not take it.

"There was also an anchor," Ray joined in. "We all remembered it because Rudolf made it. It was from an old steel front tractor wheel. Some friends of ours were fishing last evening and one of them caught his hook on something that was hard to reel in. When he finally got it, it was a scrap of a heavy chain with a bit of leather bag which fell apart before it was lifted into the net. It had a corroded metal buckle, though, in the shape of the letters GLS. When he pulled it up, there was a human bone caught under the strap that closes the bag."

I remember purses like that. There had been an old American Indian who lived at Mille Lacs Lake when I was a child. He sold hand stitched leather bags and moccasins to tourists. Mom and I had both.

"None of us believed Grace would run away and leave Marie with Augusta." Selma was crying a little. "We all thought she would come back for her."

"Yes, and we sure didn't expect her to be at the bottom of the lake!" Myron wrapped his arms around Selma and just held her.

"I have to go home now." I stood and walked to the door. No one stopped me.

Back in Augusta's bedroom I stared at the photo of Grace and Marie. Tears slid down my cheeks as I thought of the aunt I would never know, and the mother I had lost.

I left the house that suddenly felt like a prison. Tired, dirty, hot, and sweaty, I stripped with a sense of freedom I hadn't experienced since age ten. I plunged into the lake and struck out for the island. Soon I realized I wasn't strong enough to reach my goal and, unless I wanted to drown in my frustration, I turned to head home. My limbs shown with a ghostly pallor under the darkened water. I appeared to be an alien creature as I dogpaddled and floated in the moonlight. The washed out lines of my body appearing and disappearing as I moved in the water.

The sun was gone replaced by early moonlight. Where had the day disappeared to so quickly? Hadn't I just gotten up? Time enjoys playing tricks on us humans. It must, as it does it all the time.

12

I was becoming obsessed with the need to understand what had happened to this family, to my aunt, my mother, and to me. It was time for lunch, but I wasn't interested. I climbed up to the second floor of Augusta's house to start yet another search. I knew there was a possibility that I would never learn more than I had already, and it wouldn't change my life in any significant way, but there was more, I just knew it.

I still didn't know how to get to the attic. First I looked at all the ceilings for a trap door. None. Then I looked in closets. Still nothing. Okay, they had to get up there somehow. I went to the grand stairway at the front of the house and slowly worked my way to the rear, checking every square inch. I even looked places that seemed impossible. At the rear, in what I was sure was Lydia's room, there was a closet next to the bathroom. At the back of the closet was another door. It opened to a short hall that led to a steep, narrow stairway rising to the attic. Finally, I was getting somewhere!

I promptly ran up these stairs and found a light chain. This room would hold some answers. After all, you wouldn't have several huge rooms full of boxes, crates, and trunks, which were exactly what I could see from the top of the stairs, and find that these were entirely empty of family secrets. In the movies the secrets are always found hidden in cellars and attics.

I decided to start in the farthest corner and work my way back to the stairs. It seemed like it would help with a chronological order of sorts as I supposed the oldest things would be the farthest away from the top of the stairs. The attic was one long hall with large rooms at either end and two smaller rooms at the center. Windows, large dormers, were on each side, nothing in the rear and only a small octagonal shaped glass at the front. At the dormers, were small bedrooms. Each had a narrow single bed, night stand with lamp and two drawer chests at the foot of the beds. Every surface was rough and unfinished and extremely cluttered. I marveled at the number of years that could be represented in these containers. The lives of my ancestors still lived in this attic. Probably of their servants as well.

I carefully picked my way to the edge of the floor and began. I would just make a pile of the most interesting things to study downstairs, and leave the rest. Sitting in the front corner were five or six ancient trunks. Two of them had "Svensson" stenciled on the top and sides. I knew enough history to know the double s came from "Sven's son," at one time, a Scandinavian thing. Immigration officials dropped an s. Two trunks were stenciled "Lundquist." I started there. One Lundquist trunk was obviously a woman's, the other, a man's. Period clothing from the late 1800s to early 1930s in varying states of frail condition. Some of it fell apart as I lifted it. Books written in Swedish, and that script I had seen downstairs, unrecognizable to my eyes. Letters, the same. The letters I set aside. There were also some infant clothes in the trunk of the woman. There was a marriage certificate in the name of Lundquist, Bertel and Irena, dated 1895. Augusta's parents? And two birth certificates in the names James and Myrtle. Where was Augusta's? I also found two heavy pieces of ornate jewelry that looked like rubies set in gold, but I wasn't sure. They looked to be from another time, anyway. The trunk belonging to the man held only a gold watch and clothing. There were molding leather shoes at the bottom. I put the engraved watch with the letters. The next trunk was quite elaborately carved. It had been painted at one time. A beautiful letter "A" adorned the inside of the lid. Ah, Augusta, I bet! Once again, clothing. But also, two birth certificates: Grace Lynn, 1951, and Marie Augusta, 1958. The wedding certificate was dated 1945 or 46, although that had to be an educated guess as I could barely read it, and issued to Rudolf Svensson and Augusta Lundquist. Nothing else. Had I expected love letters? A more human grandmother? As I closed the lid, my fingers caught and slightly ripped the silk lining.

I pulled out a heavy manila envelope sealed with wax. The documents inside were written in Swedish, but I recognized several names. There was a paper signed by Mr. Bertel Lundquist and Rudolf Svensson, which seemed to concern property, both in Sweden and Minnesota. Another lengthy paper stated the name George Olav Nelson in several places and was stamped with an official seal of the King of Sweden. Oh my! There was a mention of sums of money paid. What was this new mystery? I set this entire envelope aside. The remaining two trunks held what looked like bridal linen or hope chest items. Never used. There were bits of faded red scraps sprinkled on these linens. Maybe red rose petals. They crumbled to pink dust in my fingers. Some pieces of fine china were wrapped in fragile newspaper. Russian again? There were several wooden crates that held nothing significant, just more molding men's attire. Maybe Augusta had packed all of Rudolf and stuck him up here. I could see her doing that

The next carton held a beautifully colored hand-woven rug of an elaborate Indian design. When I shook it out I could see it was a woolen blanket for a child. There were tiny moccasins with beads and a beaded necklace. Also for a child. At the bottom was the softest woolen baby shirt trimmed in leather, beads, and downy, white feathers, and wrapped in paper. Whose baby and where was it? Okay, now I'm intrigued.

Next were several boxes of toys from around the 30s or 40s, I guessed. One crate held hand-carved wooden things. Someone had been quite artistic. A train set, trucks, a barn with several animals, and even a farmer. All were beautifully painted and looked totally unused. Another box held dolls whose faces were hand crafted, skillfully painted, and exquisitely dressed. Egg shaped wooden dolls, painted in bright primary colors and of several sizes caught my eye. Dressed in formal clothes, these dolls could fit inside of each other, one being slightly larger than the next. These toys had obviously been carried around for years and looked to be well-loved by someone.

There were dried up paint sets, jacks with balls, pick-up-sticks, Lincoln logs, and other things that I remembered playing with in the cottage. Several boxes of children's books written in both Swedish and English, others with notebooks of school studies and reports that were almost completely faded even though they were protected in the box.

The attic also contained bits and pieces of furniture, broken or simply discarded. There were a dozen rolled up Oriental rugs. I thought I would soon bring a couple to the cottage. Paintings, photographs, china, draperies, and many more outdated items one would expect in an attic. There was a huge hand-made roll top desk full of papers and accounting books and even a bottle of ink and a quill pen. Before I left I noticed other hand-made furniture that looked unused; rocking chairs, pedestal tables and an unusual small square table with a shelf under a tiny door. When I opened the door I could smell sweet pipe tobacco. In a narrow drawer was a hand carved pipe lying on top of two small notebooks, journals written in two distinctly different girlish scripts and, oh joy, they were written in English! I had hit the jackpot!

I took my small pile of interest and went back home to the dogs.

13

When I got to the cottage, the door was slightly ajar. Had I left it like that? I didn't think so. Pushing it open, I met a worried Lily pacing the kitchen.

"Oh dear! Oh dear dear dear!" Pearl was also very agitated. "Whatsa matter what are you doing to me?" His words tumbled out in his agitation and he paced back and forth on his topmost perch. He fluffed up his feathers and huddled in a corner, like he did when the dogs were overly excited or noisy.

"Sully?" I called, immediately realizing what must have happened. I hadn't closed the inside door tightly and the screen door, which had no latch, could easily be nosed open with just a gentle push. Sully, my curious, adventurous, naughty, and beloved pet, was not here. Without his excited and rambunctious usual greeting, the cabin was too quiet. I knew without looking, that he was gone.

Dropping the pile of papers on the table, I took off running. Check the dock, check the water, check the boathouse, and check the latrine. No dog! Run to Augusta's. Nothing.

"Sully!" I shouted over and over. Where are the retrievers and bloodhounds of the world when you need them? I ran into the woods, frantic with worry. He is such a little dog.

"Sully Sully Sully," I called

I ran through brambles, vines, thickets of birch and poplar, and acres of pines shouting loudly until my voice was raw. I ran through Jackson's piles, scattering the pieces without noticing where I was going. I waded through a swamp in water up to my waist until I remembered Sully hated the deep water. I ran until I was exhausted and it was dark. No sound or sight of the dachshund. Heading back before I lost my way, I was crying. It was entirely my fault. I was so careless. I shouldn't be responsible for any creature. Marcus was right about me. I was just a stupid worthless woman! By the time I got back to the cottage, I had come to my senses, but only partly. Still no Sully, though. I drove to Petersons store.

"My God, girl!" Myron exclaimed in distress as he and Selma jumped up from the bar where they had been drinking coffee. "You are all wet!"

I looked down unaware, and tried to speak. Selma handed me a mug and I swallowed the hot liquid not feeling or tasting.

"Sully, my little dog, is gone!" I finally got the words out, articulate enough for them to understand.

"I don't know how long he's been gone and I looked everywhere!" I was wailing again.

85

"Well, now," Myron drawled. "You haven't looked everywhere, or you would have found him. It's too dark to see now, but first thing in the morning we will all be over to help look." I was aware that this was the sensible thing to do, but I did not want to wait. Not for a second!

"Would you like to stay here tonight, Emily?" Selma asked gently. "This has been a long hard day for you."

"No!" I responded. Realizing how harsh that sounded, I amended with, "What if he comes back? I need to be there. I shouldn't have been gone this long."

"Will you promise to put on warm clothes and light a fire? Clean up all those cuts and scratches, too?" Motherly Selma was loath to let me out of her concerned sight.

"Yes." I was back in the car, driving slowly with my brights on and the window down, calling to my dog all the way.

I came back to a dark cottage and no Sully. Lily was clingy, winding her body around and around my legs, and Pearl quiet. I fed them and dropped to the sofa for a minute. I lit fires in the woodstove and the fireplace, but left the door open. I moved Pearl's cage next to the fireplace and covered it for warmth. I pulled a chair over to the door. Forgetting I was soaked to the bone, ignoring the casual pain from all the scratches and pricks from the woods, I eventually fell into an exhausted fitful dream. In this dream, Grace and my young mother were trying to pull Sully out of Grandmother Augusta's arms. But she was too strong and they couldn't get him. Augusta walked to the lake and held Sully under the water until he stopped struggling. Grace faded away before I could see her clearly, but my mother lingered, gazing with abject loss at my tear

stained cheeks. Augusta saw me and smiled. With an evil
chuckle she said "I have done this before!"

I woke with a start, sweating and shivering. It was
still night and the fires were out. Lily was sleeping at my
feet, but there was no Sully in my lap. I got up stiffly and
made more fires, put the kettle over the flame and cried. I
sobbed my way back to slumber. When next I woke, dawn
was in the window and Lily was whining to go out.
Apparently, she didn't realize she could simply nose the
screen open. I took her out on the leash this time. I
couldn't stand to lose both of them! The kettle was still
warm enough for coffee.

I drank several cups and waited for the Peterson clan
to show up, which they did, within the hour. Selma had a
thermos of real coffee and loads of food. She must have
also been up most of the night. If she noticed my still damp
and rumpled appearance, she made no comment.

Robert stoked the fires and added more wood.
"Okay, "he began. "What would you like to do?' Wow, a
man asking for my opinion. That had to be a first. I might
have really noticed if I hadn't been so distraught.

"All I can think to do is keep looking."

"What would interest Sully?" Ray also tried to be
helpful although I could see he was barely awake and
seemed a little confused about what all this panic was
about.

"Absolutely everything. Especially if it moves." We
split up and headed into the woods. It was decided Selma
would remain at the cabin and Myron would go to all the
neighbors and alert them. We looked and hollered for
Sully all day, but no one found any trace of the dog. Ray

found me when it was close to dark. I was shivering, and even I was aware that I was somewhat incoherent.

"Come on, Emily. That's enough for today." He took my hand and led me home. Ray's wife, Maryalice, was there. I hadn't met her before, but I liked her right away. She was beautiful like an actress from the 1940s. Straight black hair to the shoulders that danced when she moved her head, and crystal clear dark blue eyes. She wore a warm smile when she greeted me.

"You must be so tired and hungry." Her voice was accented slightly. Maybe Irish, I guessed.

"I suppose I should be hungry, but I'm not."

"I have been making friends with this large white creature." Her hand was caressing Lily's head as she looked up lovingly at Maryalice. "And Pearl, too." She laughed as Pearl squawked. "Hello, Hello, pretty Pearl! Pretty pretty bird."

"I wasn't sure Pearl was allowed out of her cage, though." She laughed her tinkling, lilting way.

"He", I told her, "can come out if the doors and windows are closed. Sully is gone because the door wasn't closed tightly." I began to cry softly. "I thought all my tears were used up."

"We women never run out of tears." She patted Lily some more. "How did a male parrot get the name of Pearl?"

I appreciated the distraction, wiped at my wet face and told her. "When Pearl was a baby, I bought him at a pet store. No one there could tell me what sex he was and the name Pearl just seemed to fit. By the time I realized she was a he, he knew his name."

"I love you, Pearl." He said to his reflection in his mirror. "How are you today?" We all chuckled at his vanity.

"Would you like us to stay here?" Maryalice looked concerned. I shook my head.

"No. I just want to sleep now." Everyone packed up and left me with promises to help again tomorrow. All the energy I had left was used up on Lily and Pearl. Again I lit fires, pulled the chair over, and opened the door. This time I was smart enough to grab a blanket. I knew in my heart that my little dog was gone. Drowned or eaten or lost in the woods. But I also knew I would wait for him anyway. Lily was still restless and nervous, so I sat with my hand resting on her head which seemed to help both of us.

14

I think perhaps I was too sad, or too wound up for
sleep. I believe a person can be so over tired, sleep will not
happen. I tossed and turned, as much as I could in the
chair, anyway. Lily got disgusted with all the movement
and went to the bedroom. I heard her jump up onto the bed
and turn in her customary circles before she settled down
for the night. I sat alone, kicking myself for all the stupid,
careless, and unthinking things I had done in my life. A
litany of all my faults and mistakes ran over and over in my
mind. Normally I didn't bother with regret, it seemed such a
waste of time, but I was hard-pressed to find a single good
thing about myself at the moment.

The marriage, most of all. I was in such a hurry to get
away from my father; I rushed off to college. The farthest
one he would allow. It was a "church school." At least
that was how I thought of it. It was associated with the
Lutheran Church, and our church in Saint Paul offered me a
small scholarship. In Iowa and away from home for the
first time, I threw myself into art classes with no thought to
future earnings. I met Marc my senior year and married

him so I wouldn't have to return home. Great reason, huh? Actually, I thought I did love Marcus. He often told me I did. I think it was just easier to believe that than to dwell on it. He did not want children, so I got pets. Then he did not want pets. I took my first real stand against him when I said the pets were staying. I thought he would argue, but he simply spent less time at home and made me miserable when he was there. It took me ten years to say, "This is so not worth anything!" and leave. I did not regret leaving at all, just the stupidity of marrying Marcus in the first place.

And now this loss of Sully. I knew he was curious. I knew he would run. I knew he didn't come when called. And still, I had left the door ajar! Eventually I cried myself to sleep.

Some time in the night I had the Augusta dream again. This time, as she was holding a tiny Sully under the water, it turned into a baby boy. Again the evil laugh and as she looked me in the eyes she said, "I was never happy! My daughters were never happy! You will never be happy!"

"No! Go away!" I jumped from the chair, knocking it over which started Lily barking.

"Hush now. Everything's fine." A voice in the darkness. Was I still dreaming? But it was a man's voice, and there had been no man in my dream.

"Who is here?" I heard the panic, barely contained, in my voice.

"Jackson McKenna." He responded softly as he turned on a light. Snuggled happily in his arms was my small red dog! I carried on like a distraught child. Sobbing until I got the hiccups, I held tightly to my dog. After his initial greeting, Sully wanted down and dinner. I calmed down some and took care of him. When I stopped crying, I looked gratefully at Jackson.

"Is this what all the fussing and yelling the past two days was about?" he asked cheerfully. "I thought maybe the world had come unglued."

"I thought maybe MY world would never be the same," I said. "I really love my dogs." Oh that sounded so inadequate! The past few days had all been too emotional and were taking their toll.

"I can see that. I found this little guy trying to get in to see Lydia." I stood for several seconds before that sank in. "Lydia? She is still living?" This was a surprise.

"She sure is, and she would like me to take you to see her. Can I come around this afternoon to pick you up? Maybe you'd like some time to be with your dogs and clean up a little?"

"Oh." I looked at myself in the mirror and was appalled at my appearance. "Good Lord, what a mess!" After Jackson had gone, I sat on the floor with Lily and Sully and was content just to be quiet and hold them close. Sully was no worse for his journey and I let him climb into my lap. None of us seemed able to keep our eyes open.

I slept without dreaming, and when I woke, it was with stiff limbs and achy bones from sleeping on the floor. I lay there momentarily confused. The day was over. There were fires in the cookstove and fireplace. Sully and I were covered with a heavy quilt. I sat up when I heard the quiet sound of pages turning. Jackson was sitting at my table reading in a dim light.

"Hey there, Emily. I hadn't the heart to wake you."

"I've slept all day," I said and sneezed. Oh no, my head was throbbing, my eyes were watering and my nose was runny. I sneezed again.

"I thought as much," Jackson said. "I bet you never changed clothes or ate." I couldn't remember, but when I looked under the quilt I caught a strong whiff of swamp.

"How long have you been sitting here?" My head was spinning and my vision was double.

"Long enough to know you were sick. After I left you this morning, I went to Petersons and told them you had the dog back." He held up an envelope. "Selma sent a note. I also told Lydia you would not visit today." I was now coughing.

"Listen," he said, "you go to bed and I'll feed and walk the dogs. Sound good?" I wanted to nod, but it made me too dizzy. Jackson gave me a hand up and propelled me to the center bedroom. The bed was made up. Real sheets, flannel, with pillows and quilts, and a flannel night gown lying on top. I was so grateful as I slipped off the disgusting swampy clothes, donned the nightgown, and crawled into bed. I was asleep again before Jackson brought the dogs back in.

It was mid-morning when next I opened my eyes. I rolled over onto a piece of paper: "Emily, I have the dogs with me. Don't worry, they have been fed and are on leashes. I promise not to lose them. Jackson."

This was good. I was very weak. I had to pee, but was sure I couldn't make it to the outhouse. I thought I had come across an old porcelain chamber pot with a cover under the sink. Mom had gotten it for me because I couldn't wait for morning light to go to the outhouse. Nor

would I go alone. Mom was tired of me waking her. Aha.
There it was. I nearly fainted when I bent over to pick it
up, but managed to get it to the bedroom, use it, and push it
under the bed. I saw a bottle of aspirin and water on the
bedside table. Taking three, I fell back on the bed. I must
have been completely wrong about Jackson. Good, I could
use a friend. Plus, it was obvious that my dogs adored the
man.

15

The next days were a blur. I think I mostly slept and dreamed. Terrible dreams that woke me in terror and chills. I remember being hot and freezing and wet. Once I heard someone say, "Your body isn't ready to be awake yet. Go back to sleep." I must have followed that sage advice. Eventually, I woke up in earnest to find a strange woman sitting near my bed. She was very tall and thin. Austere looking. Until she smiled.

"Good morning, young lady."

"How long have I been sleeping?" I felt completely unable to function for myself, weak and ill. I was surprised I could form sentences.

"Oh, about five days now. I haven't been here more than two. Selma sat with you also."

I sat up so fast I nearly blacked out. The dogs! Where were my dogs!

"Don't worry. My boy is taking good care of your pets. And you best not be moving so fast for awhile." This woman apparently could read my mind.

"Your boy?"

"My grandson, Jackson McKenna." She replied with pride and love in her voice. "I am your grandmother's friend, Lydia." Ah, just the woman I needed to talk to.

"Do you think you can eat anything?" I shook my head no, and that action made me dizzier.

"I expect you have a lot of questions for me." I was now totally convinced she could see into my mind! "You talked quite a lot when you were running a fever. I think I should just tell you the story and then you ask your questions. Fair enough?" I nodded and she began.

"My parents started working for the Lundquists back in Skone, Sweden. Augusta's folks were dairy farmers and land owners. They had many paying tenants and my family was one of them. They all had good and productive lives and farmed together until my father, George, got into some trouble. It was thought he stole two horses, but the horses were simply there when the family got up one morning. Of course no one believed an illiterate tenant farmer, and he was sent to prison. Not only did Bertel Lundquist pay the owner of the horses twice what they were worth," she took a deep breath, "but he returned the beasts. In addition, he bargained with the government to pay a fine and get my father out of prison. The official at the prison said they could only do that if father could get employment outside of Sweden." She stopped here for a moment, lost in her own thoughts. When I stirred restlessly, she continued.

"Mr. Lundquist purchased property in Minnesota to farm, and he sent my family here. He took care of us, you see. I was born in 1920, several years after they arrived in Minnesota. Augusta and her parents arrived in 1912 and built their house. She married Rudolf Svensson when she was about thirty-five. I married an Irish American, John McKenna in 1937 when I was seventeen. Augusta and I became friends and helpmates out of necessity. That grew into love and deep respect. There was so much to see to and children to raise. Do you understand?"

I did understand, and things were making more sense. "Tell me about my grandfather, Rudolf Svensson." I begged.

"Patience, Emily, is a virtue. Neither your grandmother nor your mother had much use for it either."

There was a loud knock at the door and Lydia left the room. Lily and Sully came bounding in and were up on the bed in a split second. I just love reunions! Sully buried himself under the quilts and went immediately to sleep. When Jackson walked into the room, I said "I think you must have worked the little guy too hard!"

Smiling really changed Jackson's face. He had a gorgeous smile. It lit up his entire being.

"He works himself too hard. He puts in ten miles for Lily's one." Well, I was sure that was true.

"Thank you," I began…

"No need, I figure I owe you after my initial rudeness. Lydia said she was ashamed of me."

"But I'm the one who nearly broke your arm."

"I was ashamed of you, too." Lydia was back. She directed her comment toward me as she held up a small stack of paper and a package.

"This all came for you during the last few days, but you need to rest for awhile. More story telling later." Jackson leaned over and brushed his lips over my forehead.

"Welcome back, Emily." Sully growled. "I guess he won't be coming with me!" But Lily jumped off the bed, eager to go.

"Always has had a way with the girls," his grandmother said, and Jackson had the grace to blush as he left me with a wave. Lydia said after he left, "Do you think you can get to the outhouse on your own?" I tried to stand and collapsed back, shaking my head. Lydia retrieved the chamber pot from under the bed and left me alone for awhile. Using it and getting back into bed was all I could manage. I went back to sleep wondering what I had done to deserve a kiss.

16

Late that afternoon, or maybe it was the following day, I woke feeling healed and hungry. Unfortunately, my body didn't agree with that assessment. My legs were too weak to get me very far from the bed. Thank goodness for the chamber pot. I heard low voices coming from the kitchen, so I called out. Selma and Lydia came to me.

"Oh my, look at her!" Selma said happily.

"I think she is much better," Lydia agreed. "Time to sit up and try to eat something?"

"Yes, please. I'm starving." The women brought in a large bowl of chicken soup and a slice of fresh buttered bread. Lydia propped me up against the pillows and I dug into the soup with gusto.

"Would you like a little more of the story while you eat?" Lydia settled back into the chair and Selma sat on the edge of the bed. I nodded my assent and kept eating the delicious soup.

"Let's see. Oh yes, I remember. When the Lundquists came to Minnesota, Rudolf and his family came with them. They all decided to leave Sweden because the economy was not good and so many were out of work. It was that way here, too, but we all knew how to farm, so we knew we could live well. And we did, for many years. Eventually, Bertel sold off all his property in Sweden except what he had given to his children who stayed there. Let me think a minute, James and Myrtle, I think were their names. He had also sold, or had given, Swedish land to Rudolf's folks who were not happy here, and went back home. He purchased more land here until it became quite a large parcel. He deeded most of it to Rudolf just after Rudolf married Augusta. We all assumed it was because Bertel felt he was becoming too old. His wife had died and he was frail.

"Many prosperous years followed, which you don't need to hear about. Just know they were good and happy years. Grace and Marie and my Ruth and Alice were great friends. My sons worked with Rudolf and my husband, John, until they joined the Navy. We had a small house of our own, but spent most of our time here. We all had rooms on the second floor to use as we wished." Lydia paused and said she was going for coffee. Selma and I wanted some too. When they returned with the coffee and freshly baked chocolate raspberry scones, Selma took up the story.

"One morning I was visiting Lydia. We were in the kitchen talking quietly about our children."

"As we usually did," Lydia interrupted with a fond look at Selma, who returned the look.

"There was a scream from upstairs and a sound of breaking china. We stood to investigate when Augusta stormed into the kitchen. She was limping badly. Her eyes were wild, her normally impeccably groomed hair was undone and trailing down her back and she was crying and screaming uncontrollably! Quite beyond reason. She collapsed in a heap at Lydia's feet. It took some time to calm her enough to hear her words. She held a crumpled paper in her hand, wet with tears." Selma stopped talking to wipe tears from her own eyes.

"It was a terrible day," Lydia said. "The paper was a legal contract between Bertel Lundquist and Rudolf Svensson. In short, it deeded this land and more land in Sweden, to Rudolf if and when he married Augusta. It looked like Mr. Lundquist had paid a bribe to Rudolf for the marriage!" Her voice shook with indignation.

"And Augusta knew nothing of this?" I was completely stunned by this news. "Surely she knew the property was in Rudolf's name?"

"Yes. But it was the custom then. In Sweden, in the Lundquist family, the men always owned the property. However, this was given to Rudolf ONLY with the condition he marry Augusta! She loved Rudolf with all her heart and she thought they married for love. Of course, the idea that the father she adored could treat her like property to be sold was just as devastating."

"My God," I stammered, "This must have destroyed her world!" This explained a lot about my grandmother.

"But," continued Selma, "that wasn't the worst of it." She looked to Lydia as if unwilling to continue this tale.

"Augusta was pregnant. She had fallen down the stairs from the attic when she found the contract." Lydia was unable to stop the flow of tears trickling down her face. "Augusta was so distraught, and with the fall, she miscarried the child right then and there! It was the boy they had both longed for and he was fully formed and perfect." We all sat in silence for a moment full of pity. Selma continued for Lydia.

"Augusta held the child tightly to her, sobbing beyond any grief I had ever witnessed. After some while, we were able to remove the stillborn baby from her arms, clean up the afterbirth and most of the blood. Augusta was passive now and we couldn't reach her with words. She gripped Lydia's hands to her as she had the child, moaning softly."

"Just then, Rudolf entered the room. Augusta flew at him screeching in words no one understood, Swedish, Russian, and English all jumbled incoherently together. She hit him over and over. Then, Augusta picked up the child and ran out the door. She ran to the lake and stood at the edge until Rudolf caught up to her. "This!" she screamed, "is what I think of you and our marriage!" Augusta bent over and held the dead boy under the water as if to drown him."

Oh my God! I knew this. It was in my dream.

Selma finished the story. "Something in Augusta broke. She was literally mad with grief and she never recovered. She withdrew from all of us except Lydia. She had all of Rudolf's things packed and put in the attic and she changed the locks on the doors, which had never before been used. No one was allowed to let Rudolf inside the house. We don't know where Rudolf went, but months later he was found dead in the woods under a fallen tree. He had tried to explain to his wife, but she would not see him. I think Rudolf truly did love Augusta by this time in their marriage. But the damage had been done and it was

102

too late for them. She would not see reason and she became a hard, lonely woman in a very short time, just days. Augusta even neglected the girls. Thank the Lord they had Lydia!"

17

The next morning found me bundled up in robes and blankets being slowly led outside by a patient Lydia. It was at my request as I needed the fresh air. The chair Lydia was headed for was next to the lake and in the full sunshine. It was an interesting piece of furniture: a wooded lounger with raised slats under the knees and a gently sloping back. I was settled in with a pile of things to look at, including an envelope from Anderson/Erickson Law Firm and another from Marc's office. I was interested most, however, in the journals of Grace and Marie.

Marie's notebook seemed to begin at about age seven. It was full of short sentences and tales of play and learning to cook, of swimming in the lake, and fishing with her father. The sisters had been home-schooled by a tutor along with Lydia's children. Marie enjoyed reading and her studies. It all apparently was a normal and happy childhood, but there was little mention of Augusta. Nothing really of interest until the last page. She wrote: "I unlocked Grace's door last night. She gave me her letters and diary. I was supposed to burn them or something. But

I couldn't and now Mother has them!" And that was it for Marie.

Grace's journal was more detailed. Hers started on her sixteenth birthday, but it didn't feel like it was her first journal. Perhaps Marie had succeeded in burning some of them before she was apprehended. Again it was a general description of a young girl's life full of friends and activities with several stories about Marie. For instance, the cooking lesson that began with an entire ten pound bag of flour in the mixing bowl, and on the floor, and on Marie! Even Lydia found that comical. Or the time the girls were reading under the blankets with a candle and the sheets started to smolder. My favorite is the entire day Grace spent teaching Marie how to ride a two wheel bicycle when Marie already knew how. I suppose she simply wanted the time with her older sister and neglected to mention that she had already learned.

There were stories of several outings with their father; shopping in the Twin Cities, fishing trips, picnics, learning to swim. No stories about spending time with Augusta, though. There were statements about how "Mother wouldn't approve" of one thing or another, or about her unreasonable attitudes. Grace wrote of how she was learning not to share her thoughts with her mother at all, to avoid trouble, arguments, fights, and being denied, arbitrarily, her freedom to come and go as she pleased or which friends she was allowed and those she was not. Grace mentioned, toward the end of the diary, that her mother was getting too interested in who she saw or talked to in a day, something she had not done before. And that Augusta touched and hugged her less and less the older she

105

became. One entry described meeting Karl Musser. She wrote that she knew it was real love within a half an hour of their meeting. She was, as they say, head over heels, crazy in love with the boy. Grace wrote of meeting him when he came to live with the Peterson family at the general store and how sweet he was to her. She wrote of her mother's objections to Karl and his family. That Augusta threatened to send Grace to relations in Sweden if she persisted, of the secret meetings with Karl, and finally of their discovery. She pleaded with Lydia not to tell. Lydia said she wouldn't volunteer the information, but if Augusta asked, she wouldn't lie either.

The very last page said that Grace was pregnant and in love and eighteen, so no one could stop her. She asked for Marie to forgive her for leaving and that she would be back. Once the newlyweds were settled, Grace would come and take Marie away with her. Her love for her sister was evident on each and every page.

I dozed in the warm sun thinking of what I had read and feeling extremely sad for everyone. Even Augusta. Lydia now didn't seem quite so blindly devoted to my Grandmother and I understood what had happened. I wondered about the dream I had of Augusta and the drowning of the dog-baby. It was all so distressing.

Dogs suddenly were upon me in a flurry of wet tongues and wetter feet and happy yipping!

"My babies! Hello hello. I love you, too." Sully couldn't find a spot wide enough to snuggle under the blankets and soon gave up lying on top of my legs. Jackson sat on the edge of the chair and asked how I liked it.

"The chair? I like it very much. I've never been so comfortable," I answered.

"It's one of my own designs. I'm thinking of marketing them. So you think maybe folks will like them enough to pay for them?"

"Absolutely. I sure would." I smiled, a little self-conscious when I thought about the tiny kiss. Of course it had been a chaste kiss, like one a brother would bestow on his sister.

"You look good," Jackson said.

"You look good, too." And he did. He looked relaxed, tan, healthy and very handsome, I noticed. "You must have finished moving the stacks of wood for your house."

"I did. Robert and Ray helped. So did Lily, but Sully was a little trouble." He chuckled. "Always underfoot, which should have been his name. Both he and Lily liked to take off running with a piece of the house. Lily returned hers when asked politely, but the red mutt refused to let go of his. I finally had to put him in the truck."

"Well, thank you for taking care of them. I appreciate it." He looked at me out of the corner of his eye.

"You don't remember do you?" He smiled.

"Remember what?"

"You asked me to baby-sit. You were pretty out of it, but I didn't realize just how much until the Doc said how sick you were. You had a fever of one hundred and three. For days! You said that you trusted me with them. But that you would hunt me down and drown me if anything happened to either of them. I just thought you were delirious, but you said it twice."

107

I realized then that I did trust him. I liked him, too. It felt good.

"Either me, Selma, or Lydia sat with you for a week. Then Lydia kicked me out, said you might not like me being there so much. She wouldn't let Robert or Ray or Myron in at all. That woman has a mind to her! I took the pets and stayed at Lydia's. Are you fine now? Should I leave the dogs and bring back Pearl?"

"You have a smart grandmother. Yes, I'm fine. I need to thank everyone."

"That can happen tonight. Maryalice is bringing supper and the clan will be here. Only if you're ready? They sent me to ask."

"Oh, I am more than ready. Every part of me is sooo tired of sleeping!"

"Okay, then. I'll see you later." I sat there for awhile, secure and happy, watching the dogs play in the shallow water, Sully on a long rope that Jackson must have made. They were greatly enjoying themselves. Even my shy Lily was getting noticeably braver and more adventurous. Although she did dash back to my side every few minutes, just to check in with me, I guess.

Soon, I made it back to the cottage and then to the outhouse without wobbling too much and under my own steam. I felt much stronger and ready to get dressed. While I waited for my company, I read and signed the divorce papers giving everything still in Iowa, to Marcus. I got to keep my Saab, Lily, Sully, and Pearl. Marcus couldn't even remember their names to list them in the contract. He called them "Spuds and that other one. And the bird, too." No problem. As there was no fine print, I signed them. Done!

I felt so liberated and free. For the first time in my life there was no one to answer to or consider in my decisions. My life was mine alone and I loved it. Wow. So much freedom. The next envelope was another "Wow!" It was from the lawyer, Mr. Anderson. Augusta had been a very wealthy woman. But then, she never spent her money on anyone, including herself. Mr. Anderson wrote that there was enough for me to live on without working, and that the principal amount would still grow substantially. Did I want the firm to continue to manage the estate as they had been doing for forty-five years? They sent me two check books, one for the estate and one for personal use, both in my name. There were three savings accounts and a stock portfolio along with money markets funds that could be accessed if needed. Grandmother must not have trusted the stock market much, though, as the bulk of the finances were in long term savings or CD's.

"Oh my God! I can do anything!" I spoke out loud even though there was no one to hear me, I was that excited. The only trouble, if it was a problem at all, was that I was already doing exactly what I wanted to do. However, it was a good thing I needn't look for work since I never held a job, and could do nothing useful. I was capable of learning, I was sure, but what did I want to learn? Simply put, what in the world did I want to do with myself? Now, with Grandmother's money, there was no end to what I might accomplish. Maybe I'd write a book. I always thought I could, but never had anything of much interest to write about. I did now.

I put all these financial papers away. I'll need a safety deposit box or something, I supposed. I signed the papers regarding keeping the law firm on retainer and added it to the outgoing pile of two. Included with the financial information was a sealed letter with my name on it in a shaky script, and a silver key. I set these aside for now because the company began arriving in ones and twos along with a mountain of food. Everyone had something in their hands and it smelled terrific.

Ray and Maryalice came first, with their children, two girls who were teenagers, and a young man who had just graduated from the University of Minnesota in veterinary medicine, and another boy, still in college at the University in Duluth. Robert came alone, followed closely by Selma and Myron. Last was Lydia with Jackson and Pearl. We feasted and laughed and all talked at once, just like I imagined a real family would do. I had vague memories of this sort of gathering when I was small, around Bengta's table.

I mentioned I would like to insulate the cottage and add a bathroom. Robert looked at Jackson with a question in his eyes.

"I have been sort of taking care of this place," Jackson said shyly. "I didn't know anyone would be coming after Augusta died and I liked this spot and thought I'd maybe live here." Oh dear, I thought. I wouldn't let anyone take this cottage from me, no matter who it was.

Like his grandmother, Jackson could read my mind. "Don't worry, Emily." He grinned at me. "I am not around most of the year anyway, and I can stay with Lydia when I am. I'm just happy someone will be here. It always seemed too sad to us when it was empty."

"Or," Ray joined in, "he doesn't take up much room..." He winked at me.

"Raymond!" Maryalice scolded him.

We had such fun. I felt like I'd always been a part of these lives. That I was important to these people. And loved. I felt loved. It was more than I could ever hope for.

18

Two mornings later, early, Jackson showed up with a thermos of Lydia's coffee and a full set of tools. Lumber, bricks, and insulation filed the back of his truck.

"I was planning on doing this soon, anyway. Now is a good time for me. No museum is waiting for me until spring. So, should we make a plan? Or, would you rather hire a complete stranger who doesn't know this place or you, when you are being irrational and unreasonable?" he teased me in a mock severe tone.

"Since you are the only person I know who makes me irrational, perhaps that's a question you'd rather not ask!" I shot right back at him. I sat at the table with paper and pencil, poised and ready.

"What exactly do you want to do? We can start with a list of everything you would like and go from there." Jackson lifted his expressive brows at me in question.

"I want to add insulation. I doubt there would be any, since this was only used in warm months. I suppose we need to cover the windows with plastic for warmth, but I sure don't want to lose the view. I truly hate to be cold, though. I'd like to put in a well and a bathroom." I thought for a few minutes while Jackson did some figuring.

"I think that's all."

Jackson looked up from his paper. "Wouldn't it just be easier to live in the house? Everything you want is already there."

"I suppose so, but I don't want to. It's huge and unfamiliar. I think it will always belong to Augusta. In my mind, anyway. Besides, I love it here, in this cottage. My mother is here somewhere. Sometimes I could swear that I've seen her out of the corner of my eye, or perhaps heard her laugh.... This cottage was really the only space we had together."

"Okay then. I wish I had a place I felt that way about."

He worked silently at his sketch again, then sat back and asked "How about this?"

He had drawn a stairway to the attic and angled it from the south rather than the ladder from the east. A compact bathroom with tub, toilet, sink, and medicine chest was tucked under and behind the stairs so it was against the inside walls, the tub at the lowest end of the staircase because one doesn't need to stand tall there. It was perfect. The sketch showed the remainder of that bedroom as a storage space with room for a stacking washer/dryer. Something I hadn't even thought of.

"I think I can use blown insulation. It would be easiest and I won't have to disturb the walls. Does the attic need to be insulated also?"

"I'm sure. Plus it would be nice to finish it off and make a dormer window facing the lake; there are just the tiny windows, one on the north and south. It could be a great painting studio." I was excited now.

"Robert said you liked to paint. Maybe you two can paint together?"

"Maybe." Right. Like the great R. G. Peterson would share an oil painting moment with me.

Jackson studied his sketch some more. "Hey," he said. "I saw some new windows that are pretty much like these." He gestured at the crank windows I loved so much.

"The insulation factor would be great. They have a double pane so no plastic needed." He looked pleased. "It's all going to be expensive you know. Is that okay? I don't want to get nosey but..."

I cut in before he got embarrassed. "Augusta left enough unspent money. It's time to use some of it. Do you think we can do all this before it snows and the ground freezes?"

"I have a friend who's a retired plumber so I bet I can get him here tomorrow to put in the septic system and we'll start with the windows. Those should be done first. Hey," his face lit up. "I read about this terrific water heater in one of my museum magazines. It's called 'on demand'. You'll love it. Only comes on when you need it. I'll find the article and show you." He was excited now, too. We worked well together when we weren't fighting.

"Listen, I'm going to town to see about these windows and talk to the plumber. Want to come?" I did, but I didn't.

"I think I need a nap. Plus, I'm not ready to go anywhere yet." Jackson nodded, measured the windows, and left. His mind was on working mode, and mine was exhausted.

"Good-bye-bye. Hi ya baby! Whacha?" Pearl said after he was gone. It takes Pearl awhile to articulate what he is thinking. His comments usually run somewhat behind the events that lead to his words.

I had just enough energy for one more thing before my nap so I opened the sealed envelope from Augusta. It contained a single piece of paper and another small silver key.

"Dear Emily Jane," I read. "Are you surprised I know who you are? It was your mother who kept us apart, not I. She felt I was not to be trusted and perhaps she was right. I certainly have not done well with my own children. But I am an old woman, now, with many regrets. I have tried to follow your life and did so until your unfortunate marriage. Has there ever been a fortunate marriage, I wonder? I may have kept your mother from one. Had I not done so, all of our lives could have been much different and I would not have spent my last years alone. Emily Jane, there are secrets to unfold and lies to be exposed in my house. I expect you are a clever woman and can uncover everything in time. Please do not think too badly of me. I was a broken and bitter woman and died with my sorrows intact as your mother died of her broken heart. Do not let this happen to you, Grandchild."

And that was it. I had so much to think about. I was overwhelmed and intrigued and very baffled. And, as yet, I did not know what to do with either key.

With all plans for napping gone from my mind, I pocketed the two silver keys and set out for Augusta's

115

house of secrets. Lily ran on ahead, seeming to know where we were going. Sully, on the extra-long lead Jackson had made for him, kept running around me in circles and tangling us both in the rope. He was delighted with this new game of "let's see how much trouble I can manage while tied to Emily."

We bypassed the front door and went around to the back. All around the house was a veranda, or porch, made of granite, stone, and marble. There must be a grander name than "porch" for such a structure as this, I thought. Trees had been cleared well away from the house and once there had been huge gardens here. Flower beds still were evident in places. Asters, daisies, and mums had taken over. Astibies and lupines in red and yellow stood in thick clusters, their faded color still somewhat discernable from the dried stalks, so thick in places no grass or weeds could be seen. Just spreads of purple, yellow, pink, and white faded to pale shadows of their former color. Even in the garden's disrepair, it was lovely. Tall "Kiss Me over the Garden Gate" plants were here and there on trellises, their long pink blooms swaying in the breeze. I knew this plant because they had been one of my Grandma Bengta's favorite and she planted them every year. Tall hollyhocks, her other favorite, were all along the sides of the buildings. At first I was surprised to see these blooms because they were considered to be annuals, until I remembered that many annuals are able to reseed themselves, if the seeds are left. There was a small shed off to one side of the yard, a long narrow greenhouse with several broken windows and, slightly into the line of trees I could see the outline of another building. I headed there.

It was a gazebo, ornately carved with flowers and angels, birds and butterflies. It was exquisite. The sides were screened and the roof solid, but the hinged door had fallen apart. There was some evidence of small animals nesting and burrowing here. Benches lined the circular interior and a round table sat in the center only large enough for a small meal for two. Perhaps there had been a little romance here.

I could hear the slight sound of running water and explored farther, until I found a spring flowing into a creek. Following this, we came to the lake. Turning back to the house, I walked through long grass and more asters until I tripped and ended up on my knees. What I thought was a large rock was a tombstone! Exploring on my hands and knees, I came across several more. I needed something to cut down this grass a little. I whistled for Lily, who was actually already at my side, and went back the way we had come to the house. In the shed I found several gardening tools and a pruning shears. That would work; it would take a while, though. Turning to go, I ran into Robert.

"Robert!" I squeaked. "You startled me." Then I giggled. "We keep meeting like this."

"I thought you were going to run me through with the shears." Robert steadied me. The dogs were squirreling around him acting like puppies. Neither had barked, which was odd.

"Dad sent me over with the gear you ordered. He thought maybe you had forgotten."

"Oh, right. Dog food. I guess I had forgotten."

"If dog food is all you think you ordered, you HAVE forgotten! It took me fifteen minutes to unload it all. I also came to invite you to see my studio, if you like. I'm working on a new series of paintings of this lake." I noticed a smudge or two of paint on his ruddy cheeks and he smelled of turpentine and linseed oil.

"That would be terrific, but I've just found a graveyard. I'd like to give it a quick look first."

"With the garden shears?" he joked.

"Of course not! The grass is just too long to see the stones."

"Show me," Robert said.

When I did, he got down on hands and knees and flattened the grass with the palms of his large hands. I realized what he was doing and helped. When we were finished we found ten graves marked with stones and a possible three more that were unmarked. The family cemetery, I was certain.

"I remember this place," Robert said and sat up on his heels. "I wasn't here when Augusta died, but I was when they buried the baby and Rudolf. I think these fancier stones must belong to Bertel and his wife. I don't remember her name. John McKenna is here, too. I bet George Nelson and his wife are here and one of Lydia's sons who died in the war. I have no idea about the others, but I'm sure my folks can tell you."

"Irena," I said absently.

"What did you say?"

"Irena. Bertel's wife was Irena. She was Jewish and from Russia. I found some of her religious books."

"Oh yeah, she was a beautiful woman. Sort of dark and mysterious looking."

"I suppose I should put Grace here." I sighed.

"What there is, anyway." Robert looked around this sad and lonely spot. "There isn't much left of them, you know." He had seen my stricken look. I hadn't thought, but of course the remains would be sparse after so much time in the lake.

"We can clean this spot up a bit. Plant some things."

I had enough of this tragic family for awhile and stood. "Not today, I'd love to see the paintings of R.G. Peterson." I gave him a hand up, and we left.

19

It was a short drive to Robert's studio, about one quarter mile past the General Store and overlooking the lake. It looked like a large remodeled barn/boathouse. White with chocolate brown trim, tall and narrow with three floors, the studio was an interesting structure. The ground floor was dug down and partly nestled into the ground. There was a boat ramp that led down to and into the lake. The entire front side was a heavy double door that swung open from the center out. A modest size speedboat and a two seater rowboat were tied to the dock which went straight out over the water about thirty feet or so. In the far corner, away from the water, stood a spiral metal stairway that went up. However, we entered on what would be the middle floor, from the back, into a tiny galley kitchen. Beyond that, was a wall of windows facing the water in a large living room that looked like it doubled as a bedroom. There was a table in front of the windows with two straight-backed chairs and dishes from several meals piled up in the center. Discarded clothing was draped across furniture and unmade daybed. No telephone or television was evident. It was definitely a man's house. There was nothing here that wasn't absolutely necessary.

"I've been so busy with the new paintings; I haven't cleaned up in a while."

He looked around, shrugged his shoulders, and led me back into the kitchen. On the far wall between counters was a wide door. It opened to a square hallway with steps going up and a smaller door opened to a minute sized bathroom of toilet, sink and tiny shower. The third level was all windows and all studio. Finished works were stacked against walls, some were packaged for sending, and some were hanging on the limited wall space. In the center of the room were half-dozen easels where ongoing works were displayed. They were marvelous! His style was realistic with, what I thought, was some fantasy in the mixture. But then, artists painted the way they saw things, not the way the rest of the world saw them. One of the works was of my cottage seen from out in the bay. I was so entranced I didn't hear Robert until he lightly touched my back. I jumped.

"Sorry, but I was talking and you were somewhere else." He smiled. "Where were you just now?"

"I was with Mom out on the water and we were heading home in the rowboat. We always knew where we were by the boathouse door," I told him.

"Should I paint the boathouse in this picture, you think? You might have to help me remember exactly how it was."

Before I could answer, my eyes were drawn to a portrait hanging at eye level with the easels. It was the only painting that wasn't of scenery that I had ever seen of

Robert's and I knew that face immediately. I turned to Robert with my mouth open but I couldn't speak. I looked at the painting again. He had captured my mother's face absolutely. She was happy and smiling and very evidently in love with the person she was looking at.

"Emily. I wanted to tell you about her, about us, but I wasn't sure how you would feel. My folks said you would understand. After all, it was before your dad. I loved her very much. Still do, really. Some things you can't ever forget. Marie was unforgettable."

"So, she obviously loved you too. Why didn't you stay together?"

Robert turned away from my eyes and gazed into those of the painting. He waited for several minutes before an answer came.

"My career was just taking off. I had to go to Chicago several times, and they wanted to send me to New York. I asked her to wait for me and she said yes, she would. We had a goodbye dinner in the gazebo and talked well into the night. I still go there to talk to her." He gave me a sheepish smile. "I left early the next day and when I returned, three months later, she was engaged to your father." The pain on Robert's face was as fresh and raw as it probably had been on that day.

"I asked her why and she told me that I never answered her letters, not one of them. I saw the hurt and bewilderment in her eyes. She said I must not have really loved her. Less than a week later, she was married and gone. She was screaming at me and crying and gave me no chance to say anything in response. It wasn't until later I realized I had never gotten any letters. But it was far too late."

"You never married." I didn't bother to make it a question, but he answered anyway.

"No. I couldn't. There never was anyone else in my life."

I hugged him tightly. "I can't forget her either," I said into his chest.

When I was young, I had this reoccurring dream of skeletons in holes in the basement floor. My mother would rock me and sing to me and tell me there were no skeletons in this family. She had been wrong. The closets were full of them.

20

Once again, the next morning, I was awakened by loud noises. These were just outside my window. Some very large engine and laughing men's voices. Lily stood with her front feet on the window sill wagging her tail furiously at whoever was out there.

Jackson! Oh my God, I had forgotten all about the construction. Hopping out of bed and pulling on jeans and a sweater, I leashed Sully and headed to the back yard.

"Morning, Emily. This is Adam Thompson and his brother, Ben. There is another brother, too. He'll be bringing the windows in a while." Hands were shook all around. I noticed the thermos of coffee in Jackson's hand and reached for it. Laughing at me, he handed it over.

"Our friend, here, has a serious addiction to caffeine."

"Don't we all." Adam said. "Coffee in the morning and beer in the afternoon. What more do we need?" Both of the brothers had hair so blond it was nearly white. The kind of color you see on surfers in California.

Jackson explained the brothers had a men-of-all-trades sort of business in Brainerd. Concrete, construction, lumber yard, garage, painting, roofing, septic systems, and more. Even some auto repair. The missing brother, Alex, did the bookwork, ordering, delivery, and finishing. Great guys to know, I thought.

"Sorry to get here so early, but it's going to rain and get colder real soon. Frost, too, and we have to get the septic system in. While the Thompson boys are doing that, will you help me take out the old windows?"

The backhoe was already digging and Lily was freaking out a little, so we went in and I fed the dogs and uncovered Pearl's cage.

"Whatsa matter?" he wanted to know, craning his neck out as far as possible he while he looked for the source of the noise.

"We are getting a new house," I told him seriously. I had to answer Pearl's questions or he would just keep asking the same thing over and over. "Whats a matter? Whatcha doin?"

Jackson was busy at work on the windows when I got back outside. It was a beautiful day. The sun sent its paler-than-summer gold through the trees. Like a painting from the impressionists, all was pastel and soft, hazy and calm.

"It sure doesn't feel like the weather is changing," I said.

"If it doesn't change tonight, it will tomorrow. Or the next day. Soon anyway. You'll see. So, do you know how to remove windows?" I shook my head no.

"Just follow me around, then, and do what I tell you." He patted my head like he patted Lily and Sullivan.

"Yes sir, bossy man!" I gave a crisp salute in his direction.

We worked at it hard all morning. By noon all the windows were out and piled on the grass. We cracked one and seriously broke another.

"They still look good," I said. "Can they be used somewhere else?"

"That, Emily, is the idea!" The Thompson brothers said in unison as they came around to the lake side with a basket.

"Time for some lunch, okay? Lydia packs a good one and we are starving." Adam rubbed his stomach in a gesture of extreme hunger.

We all plopped down by the lake and passed out sandwiches, salads, pickles, fruit pie, and hot tea. It was a feast. Food, I thought, always tastes so much better when eaten outside in the sunshine. It must absorb something from the sun's rays. Even potato chips have more flare at a picnic. Lunch inside is just lunch, but outside by the lake, it was special. Mom and I had eaten most of our meals at the end of the dock with our feet in the lake, dropping bits to the fish.

With lunch finished I was ready for a nap, but that was unacceptable to the crew. I yawned and Adam said "Hey you, none of that now!"

The hole for the septic system was about finished; Ben was cleaning up the edges. The spaces for the windows were ready; all we needed was for Alex to show up.

"Alex is the prompt one, so he'll be here shortly. We are doing great, though. Faster than I expected." Jackson sounded pleased, and I was thrilled at all of it. My own house for the first time, ever. I must have sighed heavily because I saw Jackson looking at me.

"Happy?" he asked.

"Completely."

"Most women wouldn't get so excited about windows, insulation, and a septic tank," Jackson pointed out with a smile.

"But it's a bathroom, too, and it's mine!"

Alex did show up on time, with a pickup full of windows and lumber. All the brothers were of different sizes and shapes, but all had white-blond hair, the same sunglasses, and baseball caps. I liked the way they were with each other, easy and joking, teasing and laughing with good humor. We really were lucky with the windows. In fifty years, the sizes of the crank windows were nearly the same. All Jackson needed to do was add some strips of plywood to make up for the difference in size and put them in. Alex had already finished them with lacquer. With four men, and me watching and handing over nails, screws, and hammers, the job was done in short order. I couldn't believe it! If we hadn't found the same windows, the job could have taken days, but these almost slid into place on their own. It didn't look much different, but I could already feel the difference inside. No drafts. It was late in the day and I thought the work was done for now, but three trucks put their head lights on high beams and shone them on the hole. The septic tank was lowered into its space and the backhoe pushed the dirt back in. I was shocked to realize it was after midnight.

"Sure beats an outhouse. You'll greatly appreciate it when the winds are howling and the snow is six feet deep," Adam chuckled.

"I once heard of a man who froze his butt to the seat and they didn't find him until spring, still sitting there with his pants down around his ankles," Ben said in a serious voice, while his brothers punched him and laughed at my expression.

"No, Emily, that never happened," Adam reassured me.

"Maybe not, but it could have." Ben was sticking to his tale.

Everyone promised to be back the next morning and they all left. Except Jackson. We took a bottle of wine out onto the dock to toast the cottage and the glorious night sky. I noticed a small aluminum Crestline rowboat tied to the dock and remembered what Robert had said about my deliveries. I loved it, it was perfect. I stepped down into it and grinned up at Jackson.

"Want to take her out for a spin?" I invited.

"You driving?" Jackson was definitely in the spirit of it all.

We rowed out to the middle of the bay and had our wine, the moonlight shown a clear path back to the dock, the starlight skimming the top of the water with their shadows dipping below the surface. It was like magic. I told him about finding the cemetery, my visit to Robert's studio, and the painting of my mother on his wall. I also related what Robert had said.

"I sort of knew," Jackson took my hand. "I wanted to tell you myself, but it wasn't my story to tell."

Then I told him about Augusta's letter to me. "It's just all so sad and unnecessary. Cruel woman, Augusta."

"Not always, Emily. She was like a second grandmother to me, you know. She often speculated about you when we talked, so I knew you were out there somewhere. Though I always thought of you as a little girl." He dropped my hand and rowed us back to the dock.

"We need to repair this boathouse, too, now that you own a real boat."

21

Jackson was wrong about the weather, thank God. There was so much to do! I was up and ready when the crew arrived. They had two extra carpenters and a plumber with them. Jackson got everyone working on one project or another. A delivery was made of cement blocks and roofing material. Another of rolled sod.

"I don't know if we'll get to the boathouse, but I thought we should be ready," Adam said. "Besides, Jax isn't always right about weather. He thinks he can smell it, but only Lydia can do it with any accuracy."

The man who brought the sod dumped a huge pile of black dirt on top of the septic tank sight and rolled the sod over the top.

"What's with the hill?" I asked him curiously. It looked very odd, this small hill behind the cabin. Like an Indian burial mound. I had seen many of them on my Iowa exploration treks in the past. Hopi, I remembered, these conical cone shaped piles of packed dirt.

"The dirt will settle over the winter. Be flat next spring, Miss." A man of few words.

Another truck pulled up. There was no room in the yard, so it parked on the road. Robert and Ray climbed out and started to unpack rolls of insulation. Lots of it. Jackson came out of the house to help them unload. "The stairs to the attic are about done. If you help me for an hour or two, we can put in this insulation," he told them. We had decided on the rolled insulation for the entire attic since it wasn't finished yet and there were just the bare studs and underside of the roof. Jackson told me it would be less messy, I think he was just worried about Pearl.

And that is how it happened. By the end of an amazing day, the stairs, insulation, most of the attic walls, and the blown in insulation were in place and finished. Except for the bathroom and boathouse, and dormer window the Thompson boys had for the lake side of the attic, it was livable. New flooring was stacked in the attic for future installation that would extend the floor all the wall to the outside walls and add a lot of space to the room. The space was transformed into something so much more usable. The dormer facing the lake would allow the glorious sunsets to decorate the room and delight those lucky enough to be there at that point in time. When the sunset was in the room.

"Hey, Emily!" Ray called up the stairs. "Come home with us, Selma wants to feed you supper." I didn't really want to leave, but I wanted to see Selma and Myron. I had a bill to pay and I was very hungry. Besides, my favorite food is a meal someone else has made. Especially Selma.

Maryalice and Selma had made another huge and satisfying supper. Stew, fresh bread, home made jam, meatloaf, mashed potatoes with gravy, and green beans from last summer's garden, and apple pie. I ate way too much. Jackson and Lydia were there also, and Jackson filled everyone in on the progress. We all had ideas and suggestions and talked for hours about the cottage. It felt like family again and I was so warm and happy. Lily and Sully had chew bones and were ensconced under the table, as satisfied with life as I was. Myron excused himself from the table and returned shortly with a cardboard box.

"I ordered this for Augusta years ago," he said, setting it on the table in front of me. "She didn't want it. Wasn't fancy enough, I suppose." The box held a light fixture. The glass was amber in color and shaped like a cube so the light would be fractured on the walls, like looking through a prism.

"Oh Myron! This is perfect for the new bathroom. I love it." And I did. Myron looked very pleased with himself.

"Knew there was a reason to keep it all this time," he said shyly to Selma.

Jackson and Lydia dropped me off at the cottage on their way home. Jackson walked Sully and me to the door where Lily was already wagging to get in, knowing already that this was her home.

"We will be back early tomorrow, Emily. I've got the Thompsons for another day. They'll work on the boathouse with Ray, who just built one for himself, and Robert and I will put in the bathroom. I've been talking to a plumber who is another good friend of mine. Owes me more than one favor. Anyway, tomorrow he'll bring his crew to put in a trench from the main house to the cottage to run water down from Augusta's well. It's pretty new, less than ten years, and cheaper than drilling a new one. Plus there really isn't time to drill. The weather is going to change one of these days. It really will!" He smiled at my raised eyebrows. "And, Robert's fishing buddies will be here to put in the dormer window, finish the walls and flooring in the attic so you can really use it if you want. It might be sort of cold up there this winter, though."

Well, the weather was changing. Jackson was correct. It was much colder the next morning. When I put my bare feet on the wood floor, I wanted immediately to pull them back under the blankets. Poor Pearl, he must be miserable. That got me up. I got a good blaze going in both the fireplace and the cookstove and set the birdcage as close to the stove as I dared. Pearl was all fluffed up for awhile, but soon warmed up enough to start talking.

"There you are sweetie! Good morning, how are you hello hello. Hi you baby," he chirped. I chirped back. I was on my second cup of coffee when I heard the first truck arrive. It was, of course, Jackson.

"Got something new for you to think about." He greeted me and handed me his thermos absentmindedly. "There used to be an oil burning heater in this cabin. As I remember, it heated the main rooms very well. Might be a nice addition to the wood. You'll need something to back up the fires to keep this place warm enough when the storms and wind hit. Can't let those pipes freeze."

I walked back into the living room and pointed to a spot in front of the middle bedroom, my room. "It sat right here. I remember. Is it still around?"

"Adam Thompson has it. Has for several years, since Augusta passed on before he rejuvenated it. He says he can get it done and over here by the day after tomorrow. Four days, tops."

Within the hour, one team was digging a trench from the house to the cottage, another was building a boathouse, and one more was putting in my bathroom. Ray had taken one of the claw-foot bathtubs and pedestal sinks from the house, and Jackson purchased a new low- water-usage toilet. All that was missing from my new/old bath was a pull chain for the toilet.

I went to the attic and sawed a square hole in the floor over where the oil burner would sit and realized I'd need to find a grate. I t had been a long time since I'd used a saw, but it was fun, and I enjoyed doing this small thing for myself. I left everyone hard at work, took the dogs, and went to ask Myron about a grate.

"Sure thing," he said. "Got two or three we used for Robert's place before he got a furnace." Myron was gone for only five minutes, bringing several grates back with him.

"I'd like to see this magic room you disappear to where you find all this stuff," I told him. "Must be huge."

He smiled his slow and easy smile and said you never know what might come in handy. Then he turned serious and laid a hand over mine.

"The coroner's office called this morning. You need to pick up Grace's remains."

Selma came in behind him and added "Karl had no family, and there are so few remains..." She hesitated, "I told the coroner to place them all together, after they determined for sure who they were. I hope that is fine with you, too."

It was.

22

The coroner's office was actually located in the hospital in Brainerd. The local doctors took turns in this office as there was no full-time coroner. Robert went with me and we were silent on the trip, both of us lost in our own thoughts. I was thinking of what might have been and how much I had missed being part of a family. Robert's thoughts were his own. Although the trip seemed to take forever, it was only about thirty miles.

We locked the dogs in the car and went in. A bright cheery receptionist greeted us. When we said what we wanted, she grew serious and quietly gave us directions. I produced some ID and signed papers, and a box was placed on the counter in front of me. I just looked at it. Two lives reduced to a box smaller than the size of a basketball. Robert picked up the box, took my arm and led me out to the car. We stopped at a small one-counter diner at the edge of town.

"I need coffee to warm me up," Robert grumbled.

I wasn't sure any coffee would be warm enough. The cold was in our hearts, not our limbs. We ordered coffee and hot sandwiches and waited. I looked around me at the diner. It was straight out of the 1950s: all chrome and glass and shining. The round seats at the counter were red plastic and you could twirl all the way around. I did this several times and felt like a kid out with her Dad when Robert put his hand on me to stop the twirling.

"You're making me dizzy," he complained. We ate, still silent, and drove home.

When we arrived at the cabin, I was amazed! The crews were loading up their trucks. The boathouse just needed a roof and a door. There was running water at the sink that we could actually drink, and the plumbing was done in the bathroom. Bits and pieces of construction left-over's, sawdust and small strips of copper wiring were strung about, but that could easily be swept up in minutes.

I was so pleased; I threw my arms around Jackson without thinking, and kissed him square on the mouth. Still not realizing what I had done, I ran around like a crazy woman, inspecting everything with delight. Robert took the grates upstairs and found two that fit. We chose one and he set it in place.

"Let's use this long one between the bathroom wall and the oil heater." Jackson was reaching for his power saw and screwdriver and heading to the bathroom. "You might still need an electric space heater when it gets too cold for the heater and the wood fires to keep up," he speculated. "Myron sells them at the store." This was no surprise. Of course he did.

Ray joined us and asked Robert if he was ready to leave. He was, and they left.

Jackson and I sat at the table where another basket of food sat. "Oh yeah," Jackson laughed, "Lydia and Selma were here to check on things. They were sorry to have missed you, but they loved this place."

"They knew where I was today, I think," I said quietly, sobered immediately by the thought of what was in the plain cardboard box. Jackson raised his eyebrows.

"Robert and I picked up Grace." That sounded so odd, so normal, like picking up a friend at an airport. I nodded at the box next to the door. "And Karl."

"We should have some sort of service. Lydia and the Petersons would like that."

"Now?" I knew he, or someone, had already dug the hole in the tiny cemetery. It was only a small hole, three feet deep and a tidy twelve inch square.

"Might as well. I'll pick up Lydia and call Petersons from there. It's my guess that they are expecting this today and are waiting."

Soon we were all gathered around the hole. Robert, Myron, Selma, Ray, with Maryalice, Lydia, Jackson, and me. Ray solemnly lowered the lonely box into the hole. Myron, Selma, and Lydia sang a song in Swedish, "Children of the Heavenly Father." I remembered that one from the Swedish church in St. Paul. The older folks each said how much they loved the two, and how sorry they were. I said nothing. What else was there to say? Grace was only a stranger and a vacant name to me. We all dropped a handful of dirt on the box and the women and I left the men to fill in the rest. We spent a very low key evening eating the basket of food. The Swedes seem to try and repair everything with tasty food. It didn't work on this tragic occasion. Even though it had happened so long ago, the old folks remember the two lovers well and their faces bore the trace of what had been lost.

Later, I wondered if what we had just done was even legal, but I didn't really care.

23

The next several days passed quietly. It got dark so much earlier. Each day was somewhat colder that the previous day and I had both fires lit and needed to turn on the oil burner at night. So we were toasty, if not a little lonely after all the flutter of people and activity. I slept when I wanted, ate when I wanted with no one to get in the way. I found a bundle of mail in my jacket pocket that I had forgotten about with all the turmoil with Grace and Karl. A letter from my husband's attorneys set me on edge.

"We have been informed that you have received a large property while married to our client, Marcus Wade. We must insist on full disclosure of all monies, properties, and goods so that an appropriate settlement can be determined."

Damn the man. He had a lot of nerve. The dogs were watching me as I crumpled up the letter and tossed it into the fireplace. The sudden spark of bright flame produced by the paper gave me some satisfaction, but just for a split second. I was determined to forget all about it until I next talked with Anderson/Erickson.

"We better get used to the quiet, puppies." I talked to them often. "I think winter is almost here and we aren't going anywhere."

Lily was stretched out in front of the fireplace on her side. Her gentle breathing lifted her flank rhythmically. If I stared at her long enough it would put me to sleep. It was almost as mesmerizing as counting sheep. It felt familiar and sweet, like I could imagine a mother would feel, gazing at her sleeping child..

Sully had climbed up onto her and slept with his nose tucked under her ear. At peace, both of them. Pearl was happily swinging with a slice of apple in his beak. So, I suppose it was just me who was lonely and restless. But, with some introspection, I knew I had always felt this way.

I brought all the art supplies down from the attic and closed off the grate for the winter. There was no sense trying to heat the attic. I set everything up in the kitchen and started a painting of the shoreline out my window. It occupied me for a couple of hours, but I lost interest in that as well. I never thought I would want a cell phone, but maybe…It probably wouldn't work in these woods, though. It was time for an adventure.

I walked and fed the dogs a very early supper, grabbed my car keys, and headed out. I stopped at Petersons to see if there was a short cut to the Twin Cities. I wanted to go there for an extended shopping trip soon. I needed a bookstore.

"Hello, Robert." I greeted him as he was leaving the store.

"Emily! I was just coming to check up on you."

"I'm okay, just a touch of cabin fever already, I'm afraid. Not a good sign, huh?"

Robert laughed and said it was a common ailment here in winter.

"So what do you do?" I asked, guessing the answer before he spoke. "You paint."

"Usually. Tomorrow morning I'm taking some paintings to Minneapolis, though, and getting supplies for my studio and some things for the rest of the family. Need anything?"

"I do. But mostly I'd just like to go along?"

"Sure. It will be a tight fit, though. Jackson will be in the truck, too."

"Hey, no problem." Jackson joined us at the door. "She's pretty small. Maybe we can talk about something more than fishing or the world of art!"

"Emily, we'll pick you up about seven. Okay?"

"I'll be ready."

When I got back home, I remembered I had no alarm clock. Back to shopping list making. I figured I would write down anything that came to mind as I wandered the cottage. I didn't know where the men wanted to go, so I'd come up with a variety of options. There is nothing more boring than shopping with a man who isn't interested in what you want, so I could list things that would be available at the places men go. Brilliant idea, but I was wrong about these men.

I still needed an electric space heater for the bathroom, shampoo, a few pots, and pans, and kitchen utensils. Mom hadn't been a cook either. But, the main thing was books! I loved to read and there wasn't much here. Mark Twain, which was what Jackson was reading while I was ill, my childhood mysteries, and novels about Scandinavian Immigrants, like *The Good Earth* and *The Diary of Elizabeth Koren*. All of which I had read many times over.

So, new books. I could hardly wait. Maybe it was also time for a cookbook or two. Never too late to learn. The recipes would have to be basic, with the wood cookstove. I was very basic, so simple should work out just fine. I needed to repay some of those excellent meals from Selma and Lydia. I was already tired of peanut butter sandwiches and canned soup.

Next, check out the art supplies: India ink and a thin pen point, Bristol paper, watercolor paper, new brushes, cadmium red (my favorite painting color) and Prussian blue oil paint. I had also always wanted to try painting with acrylic paints, so maybe I'd look at those. We needed new dog toys, as Sully was just now in the process of destroying his bear. Lily needed a couple of red balls, since we left those in Iowa.

"Oh dear," I moaned to Lily who was at my elbow. "Except for the art stuff, I bet the rest won't be at stores we go to! Okay. New list." Snow shovel, Sorel boots, heavy socks, oil lantern, coffee pot for the wood stove, soup pot. I dug out the original list and looked it over. I was able to cross off several things including sheets, blankets, pillows, and towels because Selma found those at Augusta's when she took care of me.

It was getting dark when I looked up from my lists. "Good," I told the dogs. "Closer to the adventure." The dogs and I went for a walk along the lake, and tucked ourselves in. The puppies tried to convince me they hadn't had their supper yet, but I didn't fall for their ploy of pleading eyes.

It certainly will be nice to have a good book and curl up in front of the fireplace in the evenings. I wondered if it was possible to make popcorn on the stove.

I was so keyed up about the next morning, I had trouble sleeping. I have always been like that. Whenever there was something exciting or worrisome the next day, sleep was hard for me to cultivate. As usual, eventually I did.

24

I slept, but not much. I was up, had coffee, and was bathed and dressed long before Robert and Jackson arrived. I was standing on the dock and daydreaming when Jackson touched my shoulder. I knew he was there so I wasn't startled.

"Somewhere else again, Emily?"

"No, I'm here and very happy." I smiled at him.

"Well, let's go. There is Lydia coffee in the truck. Ready?"

"You know, I think she puts something addictive in her brew," I stated firmly.

With me wedged in between the men, we set off. It was a merry trip with joking and stories. Robert had lots of stories about "Little Miss Emily" that Jackson had never heard. I remembered several. Like the time the dock was being repaired and Jackson pushed me in the lake and the dock pilings rolled off the dock and trapped me under the water.

"That was you!" I slugged him on the shoulder.

"I don't remember that. Anyway, Robert saved you," he tried to defend himself.

"Guess you do remember, then. Besides, it wasn't me so it must have been Myron or Ray." Robert kept his eyes on the road.

Come to think of it, I didn't remember ever seeing Robert at the cabin. Everyone else, maybe, but no Robert. I wondered why, but before I was able to ask, Jackson made an accusation of his own.

"What about the time YOU pushed me off the sofa and I bit a hole in my tongue." Jackson shot back. "They had to get the summer camp doctor over. Very bloody," he said almost proudly.

"Well, I don't remember that." But I did. "I didn't know these memories were of you, I guess. Just some unknown rude boy! Hey, did you teach me to shoot pool?" I remembered the short scene that flashed in my mind at the store.

"That was either me or Ray," Robert grinned. "We both played pool with you. Selma caught us, though, and thought we were a bad influence. You were kind of a rascal already, though."

"I wasn't! I was a sweet, shy quiet little girl."

Robert and Jackson looked at each other over my head and said in unison, "Sure you were!" We all laughed at that.

"Marie said you were quiet when your father was around, but when you were here, at the lake..." Robert said then, and his voice sounded a little strange. Wistful, maybe.

146

Damn, what had happened to me? How had I lost that spirit? I suppose between Dad and Marcus I let me disappear. Well, I'm back now, and it felt so great!

Robert drove past the exits for Minneapolis and headed for Saint Paul. We took the Snelling Avenue exit and drove into the suburb of Roseville, where he pulled into a Perkins restaurant parking lot.

"I'm hungry," Robert said. "How about you two?"

Oh yeah, we all were. We were seated in a booth and given coffee and menus. I must have grimaced with the first sip of coffee, because Jackson poked me in the arm and said, "It sure isn't Lydia's." The breakfast was tasty, though, so with stomachs full, it was time to shop.

"I have to go to the gallery, so can I drop you off somewhere? Or do you want to come with me?" Robert looked to us for answers. I had seen a Barnes and Noble bookstore from the parking lot and asked to go there.

"Me, too," said Jackson. "I'm starting to read Lydia's cookbooks; I'm so desperate for knowledge."

Robert dropped us off there and said he'd be back in an hour. I love bookstores. I could easily use up days just browsing the shelves. Fiction, non-fiction, biographies, big coffee table books of pictures, I loved them all. I liked the smell of books, the feel of their weight in my lap. Books took you places you would never learn about on your own, let you live other lives for awhile. Even fiction, where you could both go into someone else's mind and the places they wrote about. Books could broaden horizons, and make the world smaller at the same time.

But, with only an hour to shop, I got serious. Cookbooks first. I found one called *The Soup Bible*, by

Debra Mayhew. The cover said it "was all the soup recipes you would ever need." Sounded good, so I put it in the basket. I added an Italian, and a general casserole book to the basket. Like I said, basic was me.

On to the fiction section. On the way, I passed a sale table where the hardcover books were cheaper than the paperbacks. Wow, terrific. There were several authors I recognized: Amy Tan, a nice long novel by my favorite author, *The House of the Spirits* by Isabel Allende, Elizabeth Peters, J.A. Jance, and Barbara Kingsolver. I picked up novels by two somewhat lesser known, but tremendous Twin City authors, Erin Hart and K.J. Erickson. I found a special edition of Michael Crichton's *Jurassic Park* and *The Lost World* in one thick volume. Since I'd never read these blockbusters, I grabbed one. This was too good to be true! The basket was filling up quickly.

Jackson joined me with two books in his arms, poetry by Robert Frost and a thick novel about life in Ireland by Frank Delaney. On the way to the checkout, I picked up a copy of *Rebecca* by Daphne du Maurier and the sequel *Rebecca's Tale* by Sally Beauman. I'd read *Rebecca* at least six times in my life, beginning with the year my mother died, when I found a copy next to her bed. She told me it was probably the original gothic romance, the first and still the best. I never tired of it. I didn't think this was enough, but Robert was here and ready to move on. I was so thrilled with the books; I didn't care if I got anything else on my list!

Robert wanted several things for his mother, so we went to Target next. I got socks, underwear, and a soup pot. Robert talked me out of pots and pans and utensils, because Selma had so many. I found the pet section and picked up toys and big red balls. I looked at a small snuggle dog bed, put it back and laughed, "Like he'd sleep in that!" I announced to no one.

Robert bought quart canning jars for Selma, and an enamel vegetable canner. The old fashioned kind that are dark blue with white spots. Jackson bought a fishing pole and several strings of Christmas lights. Robert picked up the lights at the checkout, laid them back down and asked, "Christmas?"

"I like them!" Jackson blushed. "Besides, they're for Lydia." I believed him, Robert did not.

"Okay shoppers, where next?" Robert loaded our bags behind the seat or inside the large lock box that rode in the bed of the truck. It was getting so full of bags and boxes that the ride home was going to be tight.

"A grocery. Lydia wants dried fruit." There are grocery stores every few block in the Twin Cities, so that was easy. I picked up several things including the ingredients for Selma's scones. Jackson and I both bought several bags of different dried fruits, fresh vegetables, and a roast. Jackson said Yukon Gold potatoes were by far the best, so I got ten pounds of those as well.

"I need a sporting goods store and hardware," Jackson stated as he extracted a small note from his pocket. I recognized Lydia's fine printing.

"I need Sorel boots. Where do I get those?" I really didn't know: A shoe store, sporting goods? It was a mystery.

Robert and Jackson both said "Myron."

"Snow shovel?"

"Myron." The guys answered.

"Electric space heater?"

"Myron."

"Oil lantern?"

"Myron."

"Coffee pot for the wood cookstove?"

"Selma." This was fun. I liked shopping with these guys. Neither Dad nor Marcus ever shopped with me and both complained unendingly when I spent any money. Asking Marcus for money was impossible and I had dreaded it profusely. He always managed to wiggle out of the conversation before he actually gave me any.

"Okay then. Except for art supplies, I'm finished." Robert pointed to a store across the street, a Hobby Lobby. Never heard of it. The word hobby to me meant plastic flower wreaths, painted rocks, and crocheted hot pad holders or toilet paper roll covers. This store had all that, but so much more. I'd never seen so many tubes of paint or kinds of brushes. Every brand you ever heard of. There was nothing a serious artist could need that wasn't here. I went back to the front of the store for a cart when my arms were so full I was dropping items. So much for my list. I put a number of paint tubes in the cart, several packs of brushes, India ink in black and sepia, pen points, pencils, charcoal, paper of all types, and several pre-stretched canvases. Robert came over with a cart of his own, also full of paint tubes and brushes. He also had some turpentine that had no odor. I got some because Pearl was sensitive to odors and I always had to put him in another room when I used turpentine. Robert took the canvases out of my cart and picked up a heavy roll of plain canvas.

"I'll show you how to make your own, if you like. It's fun. Makes me feel more like an artist." He also picked up two gallons of Gesso, used in stretching the canvas over a frame.

"What do you think of acrylic paint?" I asked the artist.

"There isn't an art medium that I don't like." So, we ambled over to the paints again and I picked up several tubes of that as well. At the checkout, the clerk said a 50 percent off sale on paint would start in two days, if we would like to wait.

I groaned, "But we're from so far away."

"Just a sec." She smiled and picked up the store phone. The manager came over and she explained.

"No problem. Give them the sale price now," he said to her and winked at Robert. "Hi Robert, how are ya doin'?"

"Really great, Peter. I've got some new stuff you should see."

I was having the best time! There was no more room in the truck's cab or the lock-box, so all the packages went in the truck bed.

"One of us will have to stay with the truck from now on," Jackson announced to us.

The last stop had both a hardware store and one that sold sporting goods. I was exhausted and volunteered to stay with the truck. I fell asleep before we were out of the city limits. Which was somewhat disappointing as the one thing I had always liked about cities at night were all the lights and the patterns they made over the streets, people, and buildings, the almost science fiction atmosphere they created.

25

I was still in my clothes when next I was aware of anything. I didn't remember getting home or into bed or anything at all after shopping. I noticed my jacket and shoes in the middle of the living room. The dogs were not whining to go out or to eat, so someone must have taken care of that for me. Jackson, of course.

All the purchases were piled on the table and counter. Not only had I had gone a little wild with the checkbook, I raced recklessly ahead. Oh well, I noticed with a smile. I'd never shopped like that in my life!

A note was stuck to my painting: "Nice. Good composition. Love the colors. Keep up the good work." It was signed R.G. I looked at the painting with critical eyes. The views out the kitchen windows were some of my favorite anywhere. This lake is made up of several large bays that flow from one to the next. My bay was of the smaller size, but I could see directly across into the next, much larger bay. About half way across and to the right was a tiny island that held a summer camp in warm months. You could faintly hear the kids at play if the wind was from the correct direction. Farther to the right was a narrow channel, formed after the island had moved from being a peninsula and broke slightly away from the shore. It was shallow there and boats weren't always able to get through into another, small, long and narrow bay. At the end of this bay, was the General Store and Robert's place.

Also, Petersons had a dock where folks could get gas for their boats and bait for fishing. It was a good place to hang around and listen to gossip. There were sandbars in the channel but the current through it was swift and it was a dangerous spot. Most of the bays were lined with cabins, but they were usually occupied only weekends, holidays and maybe for a week out of the year. There were so many trees all around the lake; it was hard to even see the buildings.

Augusta had never sold off any of her lakefront property, or her woods, so I was fairly isolated. Several bays over, stood a turn-of-the-century resort with log buildings. This bay was more open and sunny. The lodge had a bar and fancy dining room with a deck that went out over the lake. It was a wonderful place to eat in the summer. You could watch the dare-devil water skiing and fabulous sailboats with their artfully designed sails from the tables. There was a nine-hole golf course, riding stable, and meandering trails through the woods

I remember some people showing up here, at the cottage, one day, all scratched up and hysterical. Bug bitten and bloody from scratching. They had left the trail, got lost in the woods, and been riding for two days. Tourists. The horses were fine. It was a shame the riders hadn't just trusted their mounts to return them all back to the resort.

The resort bay also had two islands that held one cabin each. I always thought it would be great adventure to live in a place surrounded by water. The only way to it was by boat. As a child I imagined all sorts of lives lived on these tiny islands, pirates, smugglers, run-away princesses, grand wizards who knew magic spells. These memories made me laugh now, but then, I was enchanted.

There were seven bays in all, each seeming like a different lake unless you knew the channels. I still knew them like the back of my hand. When I was very young, I thought some mysterious creature lived under the lake and, depending on his mood, could change the color of the water. Some things you remember, some you do not.

The fire in the stove was low so I picked up my saw, slipped on my shoes and went out with the dogs. Six feet from the steps, between twin poplars, sat a large pile of sawn wood just ready for the stove. There must have been at least a month's worth, for both the stove and fireplace. Ray and Myron must have been here while the rest of us were shopping. No wonder the dogs were happy.

I looked to the lake and saw the unfinished boathouse had a tarp securely tied over the building and my rowboat tucked inside. The grass had been cut. These were the kindest people I had ever known. My heart was so completely full. It was an unfamiliar feeling. I think perhaps the last time I felt this was here, with Mom, held securely in her arms as she read me a bedtime story.

I filled the wood basket and went inside. There now was a wooden open bin, a tinderbox, next to the stove and one next to the fireplace, both full to the brim. I guess I don't have to worry about being alone here.

After breakfast, I inspected the purchases. Unpacking it all was as much fun as buying it had been. I cleaned out the nearly empty cupboard under the toaster and stored art supplies there. I moved some things off the mantle and lined up the books. The brightly printed jacket covers added a spot of color. I chopped up vegetables and filled the new soup pot, then took a bath and dressed in warmer clothes and new thick socks.

"I'm going to Myron's for a few more things," I announced to the dogs. Sully was too busy with his new toys to look at me, but Lily perked up and ran to the door. I took a leash just in case and we left Sully to his own devices. I checked the door twice to convince myself it was closed securely. After closing Lily in the car, I returned to the door for a final check.

There were several cars in the gravel lot at the store, so I put Lily on lead and entered. Several fishermen were seated with coffee at the bar. They stopped talking when I entered. I simply smiled at them and went to the store. The Petersons were both behind the counter.

"Heard you had a busy day!" Myron chuckled. "Couldn't stay awake. The boys said they half carried you into the cottage."

"Myron!" Selma chided. "She isn't yet fully recovered from her illness."

"Enough about me. Who do I need to thank for all that was done at my place yesterday?"

"That would be Ray and his buddies out there." Myron gestured with his head toward the bar.

"Be right back," I told the Petersons and took Lily back into the bar.

"Hi guys. I'm Emily Lind and this white cloud of a dog is Lily." I introduced us to the nodding and smiling group.

"We knew you twenty-some years ago," one of the men said. "It's nice to meet you all grown up and back here again. It will be good to get some life back at the Svensson place."

I recognized that voice. "Were you one of the men who found Grace?" I asked him.

"We all were." He looked at the group.

"We were all pretty sorry about what we found," another said, "But I suppose it's better to know than to wonder. Grace and Karl were both friends of ours. But it was all so long ago."

"I want to thank you for all the work you put in yesterday. It sure was a nice surprise." I didn't want to talk about my family any more.

"We had fun doing it. Our kind of project, easy and quick. Besides, we want you to feel welcome."

"I do, and thanks again. Stop by for coffee."

"Anything else you need, just tell Ray."

"Nice guys," I said to Myron back in the store.

"Yep. That's the way we raise 'em here!" He had a space heater, kerosene lantern, and coffee pot on the counter waiting for me. "Rest will be here Friday. What size boots?"

"Seven."

"You want liners that come out of the boot or not?"

"I have no idea," I answered and looked down at the light weight leather shoes I had on. "You tell me."

"I like the removable liners best. You can dry them out."

"Great. I need matches, too, long and short," I added before he could ask. We said good bye and exited through the bar, where everyone had to pet Lily.

"Good thing this isn't Canada," one of them laughed uproariously, "Might think she's a polar bear and shoot her!"

"Then I'd have to return the gesture and shoot you as well." My tone was just serious enough to give them pause before they laughed.

Back home again, I stirred the soup and worked on my painting for what remained of the afternoon. I realized I still hadn't gotten a clock, when my stomach started to growl and it was turning dark. Thinking there were likely some left-over's at the main house in the huge freezer, I walked over. I heard Selma telling Myron to cart several packages to Augusta's for said freezer. She was always trying to feed me.

The phone was ringing when I went in the back door. I had almost forgotten what that sound was! By the time I got to the library, it had stopped. In Augusta's bedroom, I took an electric clock off the wall and a small bedside clock from the table. I also looked at the pictures again. We all look so much alike, Grace, Marie, Augusta, and me. I jumped when the phone rang again. When I picked it up, I could hear someone, but they said nothing. Had it simply been a wrong number? I set the receiver back with a frown. I felt uncomfortable for the first time since arriving more than a month ago.

Back at the cottage, I guessed at the time, set the clocks, fed the pets, and ate my wonderful soup along with Selma's bread from the freezer. Picking out a new book, I settled next to the fireplace with a quilt and a dog in my lap and another at my feet, and read until I could no longer keep my eyes focused on the words. It was exactly as cozy and wonderful as I thought it would be.

26

Before I even opened my eyes to the day, I sensed things were different. I could hear tiny beads of ice pellets hitting the window over my head. As I slowly stirred, I listened to the wind blowing itself all around my small home. It sounded like a hurricane with tree branches hitting the outside walls and windows. In a town or city, you can never really appreciate the howling that wind can make. It is a terribly lonely and isolating noise. It absorbs all other sounds, until it makes a home inside the brain. The appetite of storm winds is insatiable, unrelenting, and without mercy. I'd always suspected this but, until this morning, never experienced it firsthand. Thinking Pearl was probably cold, I got up and stoked fires and turned on the oil burner. It was a dark, heavy day. Foggy over the water and ice covering the ground. I set up the kerosene lantern just in case, because the lights were already flickering. Having never been here this late in the season, I didn't know what to expect. It was lovely outside, though, in spite of the weather. Lily absolutely refused to go out and Sully peed extremely fast, he neglected to even lift his leg, but squatted like a female. He barely got himself off the steps before he was returning to the safety of the overhang above the steps and door. He growled once at the sky and the ice pellets bouncing off his head.

I lingered over my coffee for a long time and didn't bother to get dressed. I wanted a sweet roll with my coffee, but didn't want to go out, so I tried Selma's scone recipe. She said you could put any fruit in them, so I tried dried cherries. They smelled like Jacobsons Bakery in St. Paul, and I was hard-pressed to wait. I am not known for my patience. I'm the kind of woman who devours half the batch of cookie dough, before it makes it to the oven.

The scones were much lumpier than Selma's, and a very odd shape, but I didn't mind that. The flavor was great. I was enjoying the smell of fresh baking in my home, and was starting on my second scone and more coffee when there was a knock on the door. I threw a sweater on over my pajamas and opened it to Jackson.

"You are soaking wet and have ice in your hair," I told him.

"Maybe you should invite me in then." He grinned at me and patted Lily. These watchdogs were no good when it came to Jackson or Robert! I opened the door wider and gestured him in.

"There are coffee and fresh scones. I'll just go and get dressed."

"Don't do that on my account," he grinned wider. "I've seen you in less." That stopped me dead in my tracks.

"What are you..." I started.

161

"When you were sick. Someone had to take care of you. Until the ladies kicked me out, of course."

Oh, that. Okay then. I sat at the table and sipped my coffee.

"What's up?" I asked.

"Nothing. I didn't want to follow around after Lydia all day and I thought maybe you'd be more interesting."

"Not today, I'm afraid. I'm going to sit around eating, drinking coffee, reading, and maybe trying to cook something."

"Need any help with those?"

"Jackson, you must really be bored! Sure you can stay. My house is your house, so help yourself." He took off his jacket and cap, picked out a book, poured coffee, and sat next to the fireplace. We spent a quietly companionable several hours just like that. I took the dogs out, he took the dogs out. Pearl asked "What are you doing here?" several times, but Jackson ignored him. Pearl then tried a different tactic with "Oh, there you are."

"Hello Pearl, pretty bird. How are you today?" Jackson whistled at the parrot.

I stood up and stretched. Time to move around a bit. "Fancy a walk?" I asked him.

"Better get dressed first."

"Got it."

We took the dogs and went over to the lake. Ice was just beginning to form at the edges. I wondered if the lake would freeze over completely. It was amazing to see my favorite place in a different season. We walked in silence along the shoreline for about a mile. Sully's feet couldn't

162

take the cold ice pellets stuck between his toes, so Jackson carried him.

"Okay, this is where Augusta's property ends. By the lake, anyway. It also goes another mile past your cottage in the other direction."

"I had no idea she had so much!"

"What will you do with it?" Jackson inquired with interest as he sat on a fallen tree trunk and set Sully down. I looked out over the still foggy water and thought about it.

"I expect I'd like to leave it the way it is. For now anyway."

"I'd do the same." Jackson started walking back the way we had come. "Too many people here already."

Back at the cottage, we both grabbed wood and went in. I picked up the *Easy Italian* cookbook and leafed through the pages. It all looked like too much work for this lazy day.

"I'll make scrambled eggs." Jackson offered.

"Great, I can make toast." So we did. After our late lunch, Jackson looked thoughtful. He stood by the window for awhile and I watched him, wondering. Finally he asked, "You were married, right?"

"Still am, I suppose. I haven't heard. And anyway, I was married, he wasn't. Does that count?"

"Do you love him?" Oh dear, where was this going?

"I don't think I ever did. He was too much like my dad." I told him about Marcus and Dad and how much happier I was now.

"I think I am just beginning to know who I am. I spent a lot of years being who they wanted me to be until that just didn't work anymore." I glanced at the dogs and the cabin and Jackson. "I like all this so much better." I smiled shyly at Jackson and decided to take a leap. "You are nothing like I thought you were."

"Is that good?" he was serious so I answered in kind.

"That is very good. I really like you, Jackson." I didn't want to give him time to say anything so I went on. Have you ever been married? I don't think you are now, or you probably wouldn't be here."

"No, close though. Twice. Came to my senses when I realized they were big city women and I basically was not. When my job takes me to cities, I forget who I am. Do you understand that?"

"I think we are alike that way, then. Some people just belong in the woods. Not really hermits, but not easy in crowds or noise, either."

"Let's take your boat out one last time, before the ice prevents us. I want to show you someplace special." Jackson began pulling on his boots. "Dress really warm."

Out on the water I lost all sense of direction in the fog. Jackson seemed to know where he was headed so I relaxed and went with him. He rowed for what seemed like a long time, but refused when I asked if I could row for awhile.

"Nearly there." Soon he pushed into shore. We got out on frozen mossy ground, as there was no beach here, and pulled the boat out of the water.

"This way." Jackson took my hand and tugged me up the slope. We trekked through dense pine trees and it was rough going although not slippery under these thick trees. We trudged up a hill and down into a narrow valley and half way up the next hill, where he turned toward the lake.

Through trees I could make out a log cabin and the lake behind it. The cabin looked like it had been built yesterday. Like the Scandinavian immigrants had just arrived in Minnesota and were beginning to settle in.

"What is this place?" My interest was definitely in high gear.

"Let's go in." The cabin was one room with a ladder off to one side leading to a second floor, a loft, really. A bed was built into one corner. A small table and three chairs were in another. A fireplace, in another. The door was in the center. There was new cement between the logs and some of them looked new. Glass in the windows, too.

"This is where Lydia's folks first lived when they came from Sweden. Lydia was born here. I decided, some years ago, not to let it fall apart. Lydia hasn't seen it yet, so please don't tell her. It's a surprise for her."

I looked out the window at the lake. The sleet had stopped a while back and sun was trying to break through without much luck. The ground in the open space around the cabin was covered in shattered diamonds made of ice.

"This is beautiful," was all I could think to say.

"I'll bring you back in summer. It's great to sleep here. All you can hear is the wind in the pines and bird calls." Just at that moment, a lone loon called from out on the water. I laughed and turned to go. As I passed Jackson, he abruptly pulled me to him and kissed me hard. He slightly moved away, looked into my eyes, caught his breath, and kissed me again. This kiss was exploring and long and oh, so soft. It was like satisfying a thirst I wasn't aware I had! I held on to him so I wouldn't fall.

"I have wanted to do that for weeks," he whispered, his voice full of emotion.

"Well then, why didn't you?" I rested my cheek against his chest.

"Good question," he laughed. "I'm shy?"

"Me, too."

"No, you are not shy!" Jackson looked at me with astonishment.

"With men, I am. Dad and Marcus taught me to be leery. I trust you, though, and my dogs trust you. Everyone I have met here is wonderful and they all trust you."

We kissed once more and Jackson whispered in my ear that we should go as I was turning blue. Back to the boat and back to the cabin. There was a note on the door.

"Took the dogs. Come to Selma's for supper. I'll get Lydia."

"From Robert. Look at that neat printing," Jackson pointed out.

Selma's table was set and everyone was waiting for us. After a brief welcome from the busy dogs, we sat, too. Myron poured wine into our glasses.

"Where have you two been?" inquired Robert.

"We took the boat out for one last ride till spring." I winked at Jackson who winked back.

"Uh huh," said Lydia, and Jackson blushed a little.

"We did, Gran! We rowed over to our land."

"You were so close and you didn't bring Emily to see me?" Lydia was teasing him happily. She was so cute.

"Dig in everybody, I'm starved," demanded Myron as he started with the mashed potatoes. Later, Jackson drove me home, dogs and me in the back of my Saab and Lydia in the front. He walked me to the door while Lydia got into his truck.

"I have to fly to Boston tomorrow for a few days."

"Don't forget you belong in the woods!" I kissed him goodbye.

27

I felt like I had known Jackson for many years. It was
so odd, I never knew Marcus. And I was married to the
man! I think I just saw someone who wasn't real. Or
maybe I invented who I thought he was, because I didn't
spend enough time with him to know him. I did not miss
Marcus at all. It was such a happy relief to not have to
wonder how he would be when he eventually did come
home. Should I speak to him or not? Should I straighten
the rooms one more time? Were they clean enough? Was I
dressed properly? Would he still want the meal he'd asked
for? Actually, the biggest question was what the hell was I
doing there? It is no wonder I took nothing from that
house! Everything there was cold and empty, like my heart
used to be. My life at this moment could not have been any
more enriched. I felt renewed, renovated, just like my
cabin. In all this happiness, I felt so completely whole. If I
never discovered Augusta's secrets, I don't think I would
have cared anymore. It seemed I knew enough.

I left the dogs and walked to Lydia's. She would be
lonesome with her grandson in Boston. At least I walked in

the direction I thought I would find Lydia. All along the lake shore ice was slowly growing thicker, a sheet of opaque frosty-milky white. The water would lap up over it, and it would dissolve the edges only to form again, this newer ice leaving a small ridge on top of the old. The dim, washed out sunlight still sparkled on the water. It wasn't nearly as diamond-like as during the warmer months, but it was evident. Life here was tranquil, soothing, and peaceful. That very calmness was rubbing off on me.

On the walk, I heard bird calls every so often. Squirrels would dart out of my way with acorns and other seeds carried in their tiny jaws, sitting upright every so often to munch on a nut held between their front feet. Once, when I was about six, I had made a pet out of a chipmunk. My only childhood pet. I named it Sweet Pea and loved it dearly. Every morning I would hand feed it dry breakfast cereal. At summer's end, Mother made me leave it. I never saw it the next summer, and was so devastated, I didn't try again.

I was glad I had dressed in the Air Force parka. It was colder than it looked next to the water. Sunlight is always deceiving. I thought I should have found Lydia by now. I had been following the lake, assuming she lived on the shore, but I really had no idea. I cupped my hands over my eyes and scanned the lake front. A fraction of a mile farther on I could see a jut of land that held a tiny cottage in its middle. A thin stream of smoke rose straight upwards over the chimney. That must be the place! As I got closer, it looked more and more like those pictures you find in antique shops of rustic stone cottages with cobbled pathways and overhanging thatched roofs. Vines and willow trees surrounded it. There were still flowering red geranium plants on the inside sill of the front windows which were framed by lace curtains. I knocked with the old fashioned brass handle in the center of an arched door. Lydia, in starched apron and pink dress, opened it. She looked very pleased to see me.

"Do come in, Emily, my dear. How nice it is to see you." I felt guilty for not coming sooner.

"Well, you are here now, aren't you?" This ability of hers to read my thoughts was disconcerting, but no longer uncomfortable. We sat in front of windows that let in every speck of sunlight, on chintz covered matching chairs. The sort of chair that held your entire body in its arms. Crocheted circular rag rugs covered the floor, and there was a basket of ongoing work at her feet. She pulled it out and resumed working.

"I thought you might come today, so there are fruit tarts in the oven." This woman was everyone's idea of the perfect Swedish grandmother. She was tall and thin, but warm and comforting at the same time. She reminded me very much of Grandma Bengta, except for the height. Bengta was tiny. Lydia had twinkling blue eyes and curly white hair that liked to escape from its knot at the back of her head. She had a direct way of looking at you, and seemed to always say what was on her mind, which she did now.

"You like my Jackson, very much, don't you." It wasn't a question.

"Yes." I decided to be just as direct, as she probably knew anyway.

"Good. He likes you, too. And that is hard for him."

"It doesn't seem that way." I was surprised by her comment.

"Maybe this time, it isn't."

A timer went off in the kitchen and Lydia set her crocheting in the basket and rose. "Follow me to the tarts," she invited. Her kitchen was light and airy in spite of its small size. I could see a bedroom off to one side and a bathroom on the other. That seemed to be it.

"You are surprised at this tiny place," Lydia stated with a smile. "You must remember that we lived in the main house while I raised my family. The Lundquist family was very good to us. They never treated us like servants, even though that is what we were. Augusta and I were very close. Most of the time, anyway. She was family. My husband, John, and Rudolf were in business together. They developed some of the lake properties and built many cabins. They built additions on the resort on the big bay. Did you know? It was Bertel's business originally. My father, George, cleared several acres and farmed. He had no head for business, just earth and animals. Jackson is like him, more than his own father, I think."

"Jackson is very fond of you, too," I told her, although I knew she knew that.

"He is my only close family now. My children are far away or have died. My John died at a young age in an accident while building a house." She gazed out the window and smiled as if she could see him standing there. Maybe she could. It would not surprise me.

"Life was shorter and harder then," she went on. "It was too easy to die." She shook herself slightly and turned back to me. "You did not come here to listen to an old woman rattle on, though, did you?"

"That is exactly why I came!" We both laughed.

"Okay then. What would you like to know? Everything, I'd guess, although I think I have already told you most of it. I expect you have explored the house by now?"

"I have. It is amazing. I have two keys…" I fished them out of my pocket to show her. "And I don't know what to do with them. I haven't found anything locked." Lydia took the keys and examined them.

"They appear to be the same," she noted. "You will have to keep looking." She handed the keys back. "I have no idea." But her face told a different story. Lydia knew something!

"Did Augusta have expensive jewelry? They look like keys for a jewelry box."

"Why, yes, now that you mention it. I expect they are in the house somewhere. Most of the things were her mother's, so they are old and quite beautiful as I remember. Irena came from Russia and her jewelry was heavy, large, and ornate. Augusta didn't wear many of them. Just a cameo brooch which she wore all the time."

We talked for most of the afternoon, about gardens and flowers and cooking. Woman things. She told me about the beautiful gardens that everyone helped care for, and the picnics by the lake and in the garden. About playing croquet with the children and swimming lessons and boating. It sounded ideal. Until Augusta went off the deep end.

I hurried walking home as it was rapidly growing dark. As I neared the main house, I could see the door was wide open. I didn't think I left it like that. Calling out as I entered, and looking around, I saw nothing a miss and it was quiet, so I assumed that I had indeed left the door open. I need to be more careful. I pulled it closed and locked it. I went around to the back and found this door open as well. This was very odd. I was more than a little frightened now. Back at the cottage I looked in the attic and all the rooms. Nothing. The dogs didn't seem worried, so I locked the cottage door for the first time and settled in for the night thinking it would be hard to sleep. It wasn't.

28

Each time I opened my eyes it was still dark. When
Lily finally had enough of this lying abed, she pulled off
the blankets. Exposed to the chill of the room, my warm
body reacted as if poked by a sharp stick.

"Okay, okay. I'm up!" I told her.

It was dark because it was snowing heavily. From the
look of outside, it had been snowing for several hours. I
had never seen such oversized flakes. It was a magical
view. I dressed and took the dogs out. From the end of the
dock, we could see nothing, but water and snowflakes.
When I turned around, the cottage was barely visible. I
suppose I should have dismantled the dock before now, but
it was in such bad shape I decided just to put in a new one
in the spring.

The snow was getting thicker and heavier as I stood
there. Even Lily was ready to go in. She made several dog
snow angels on the way and inspected each one with her
nose. I joined her until she sat on my chest and knocked all
the breath from my body! Then I filled all the wood

baskets and stoked the fires. Uncovering Pearl, I was greeted with "What are you doing here?" Good question.

"Living my life," I told him as soon as I realized that was exactly what I was doing. My life. I surely loved the sound of that.

There was no doubt I was cabin-bound for the day. I wasn't even sure I could find my way to the house in this storm as visibility was less than two feet. It was very strange, though, absolutely silent. I swear I could hear individual flakes hit the ground. Soft rounded mounds of the white fluff were piling up against the trees and cabin. It was precisely like watching a silent movie. I stood with elbows resting on the window sill and just watched the flakes disappearing into the black-as-tar lake. The dark lines on the birch trees stood out like neon signs. My entire world was black and white. Eventually I picked up my book and settled in my fireplace chair. I realized I hadn't had coffee yet, and laughed. Jackson wouldn't believe it!

By mid afternoon, I was restless. The snow had stopped and I wondered what it was like in the woods. Leaving Sully, who would just want to be carried home, Lily and I set out. We got to the spot where the stovewood house piles had been, and I sat on the same downed tree. The snow seemed deeper here. Every once in a while I could hear snow sliding off a tree trunk and hitting the ground with a soft plop. Dark green pines, white and black birch and soft clean snow would make a lovely painting, I thought. If you didn't freeze first. The birds and squirrels were beginning to move around a little but there were far less of them. My toes and fingers were cold, so time to go home. Off in the distance I heard a loud crack that sounded like gunfire. Lily was instantly on her feet with hair raised. I was sure it was simply a branch breaking under the weighty snow, but I was also uneasy. We were nearly a mile from shelter and it would soon be dark. Sometimes I have the intelligence of a rock! We headed back the way we came, both of us glancing around with vigilant eyes. It seemed I was a little jumpy lately, beginning with the open house doors. Spooked by everything and nothing. I needed to stop that. Behavior like that belonged to life with Dad or Marcus. There was no place for that here.

Snug and warm, tucked in my beloved cottage, I decided to continue the family tradition of keeping a journal. I rummaged around and found an old notebook and pencil. When I opened the spiral notebook, the front page said "Thoughtbook #8" in my mother's neat hand. What's this? It was full of sentences, thoughts, and poetry. A snapshot of me at four or five slipped out from the pages. I started to read.

The first few entries were about being pregnant. She knew I was a girl. She knew I was Emily, because that was the name my father and she had decided on when they were young. Wait, that's wrong! I didn't know why, it just felt wrong to me. Dad would never have picked out a girl name, he only thought about sons, even after I was born. There were several comments about his grey eyes. No, that was wrong also! Dad's eyes were blue. When she wrote about thick wavy hair, I knew it couldn't be my Dad she was thinking about. His hair was short and very straight. Always. What is happening here? The journal was blank for several pages, as though they were meant to be filled in at a later date. Then her happy mood stopped, she was lonely. Sad poems that actually brought tears to my own eyes, took over the pages. Like this one:

"Alone in myself
I dive into the oriental,
Usually under my feet.
And watch the colors
Come together over my eyes.
I pretend to
Evaporate
Like waves of time
Like moisture on skin.
Like you."

There were dozens of them, poems, and sentences, simple thoughts. All of it spoke of her despair, like this last one:

"I have become a shadow
I am a whisper. I am invisible.
No one hears me, no one sees me.
I have nothing to say.
Emptiness in the lake looks back at me
I have no reflection
I have no weight, no substance.
Just this longing
In my naked heart
That follows me

Always and everywhere
And it will never go away."

Somehow I was sure she was not writing about my father. And I remembered the portrait I had seen at Robert's studio. And his admission of his love for my mother and I knew who she was dreaming of. Robert. So, why did he leave her? Was it because of me? Did he not want to raise another man's child? The remainder of the notebook was empty. She had run out of things to say.

I no longer wanted to start a journal of my own. My mother's despair had rubbed off on me. I was having difficulty understanding how I could not have realized the extent of her depression. Did my father know? Did Robert? I did not know who to blame for her unhappiness.

It took me several long and lonely days to put my mother's last journal notes in perspective and behind me. I realized that no one can really be to blame for another's depression. Or for their happiness, for that matter. We are responsible, ultimately for ourselves. Grandmother Bengta once said to me, when I did not want to go to school, because a friend was angry with me, "You are only responsible for your own actions and responses to people, no one else's." It's amazing how often that memory comes to mind. Bengta had many helpful sayings. One I never understood until recently was; "Do not wish your life to go faster. Every year will move faster than the one before." Smart woman, Grandma Bengta.

29

"Shouldn't Jackson be back by now?" I asked Lily. "He said just a few days."

It had been over a week. I wasn't waiting or counting the days. Not exactly. Well, perhaps I was, if I admitted the truth of it. I was missing him, though. That didn't take me long. And I didn't think I would be interested in a man for awhile. He was unusual, not like any men I had known in my limited experience. All the men I met here at the lake seemed unusually nice. Nice is such a bland word, until it fits. I liked to talk to Jackson and he liked to listen. The dogs liked him, and I believed the dogs. They are so much wiser than people. More honest.

Maybe the snow held him up. I should try to get to Petersons store today. I shook my head to stop this mindless meandering around. I was babbling and I wasn't even talking.

I made coffee, got dressed, fed the pets, and headed outside. Sunlight, though dim, was trying to brighten things up. The snow was deep and I didn't have a shovel yet. I brushed snow off the car and started it so it could warm up some while I played with Lily in the deep white stuff. She loved it! We made snow angels and I watched her try to leap rather than walk. She resembled an oversized rabbit. God only knew what I resembled as I tried lifting one foot then the other through the snow. It was exhausting work, so I plopped my butt down on a drift for a rest. Sully was already waiting at the door. Caked in sticky snow, his ears were stuck to his body and snow was packed tightly between his toes. He flipped over on his back, held his feet in the air and looked pathetically helpless.

"We aren't going anywhere today!" I shut the car off when I realized my small car didn't have enough oomph to move forward in the snow, and in we went for a warm breakfast. I made enough eggs, toast, and bacon for a family of four. Good thing I like leftovers. The dogs begged for bacon and I relented. Shortly after, I heard the rumble of what I sincerely hoped was a snowplow. It was the next best thing, Ray in a large truck with a blade on the front. He did a thorough job of plowing out the lane all the way to my door, and to the main house as well. To thank him, I made fresh coffee and heated up the remainder of breakfast, which he polished off in seconds.

"Thanks, Emily. But I can't stay. Got lots of folks to dig out today. You should go see Ma. She's waiting for you. You've got to get a phone!" And he was off and running. I followed him out the lane. Ray turned right and I went left to Selma.

I hardly recognized the road in all the snow. It looked like Ray had plowed out everyone who lived on the lake year round. The other places, he left snowed in. The lot at the General Store was full and folks were talking and drinking coffee from steaming Styrofoam cups. Selma and Myron were busy behind the counter. Robert was stocking shelves. Everyone needed supplies, it seemed. Or maybe just the companionship.

"Hello, Emily." I was greeted when it was my turn. Myron reached under the counter and pulled out several envelopes addressed to me. "Mail doesn't get delivered to the cabins this time of year, so everyone just picks it up here. Selma likes to sort it all and the postman likes the help."

I nodded and thanked him, then went to sit at the bar to wait until they weren't so busy. I looked at the mail while I helped myself to a cup of fresh coffee from the pot that sat on the bar for anyone who needed a jolt. Two envelopes from Anderson/Erickson, one from Marcus' office, a forwarded card from the dog's veterinarian, and one with no return address, although I recognized Marcus' scrawl, and a postcard from Jackson, which I read promptly.

"Miss you," he wrote, "We need to take up where we left off. Got a surprise for you. Hope you like it. Jackson." Hmm, I didn't know what was more intriguing, the surprise or the taking up where we left off.

The dogs were due for vaccinations and check-ups. Okay, find a new veterinarian. Anderson/Erickson sent a monthly statement of my accounts and a letter telling me of the expenses for the main house which they took care of directly from their office. Did I want that to continue? It seemed to be heating, electricity, phone, and money paid to Mr. and Mrs. Henry Neilson, who went in once a month to dust and check up on things. They sure didn't charge much. Perhaps it was the Neilsons who had left the doors open? Maybe something had happened and they had to leave in a hurry and intended to return?

I guess, for now anyway, Anderson/Erickson may as well continue to pay the household bills. I wasn't sure what I wanted to do with the house. Only that I did not want to live in it.

I opened the letter from Marcus, thinking I shouldn't bother: "We have to talk. NOW!" That was it. I laughed until I got the hiccups and dropped it in the trash.

The Petersons looked like they were going to be busy for awhile, so I waved and left. When I pulled in behind the cabin, Jackson was leaning against his truck. I think I was nervous, then excited, then thrilled as I flew out of the car and into his arms.

"I guess I don't have to ask if I was missed!" he laughed after we kissed. His arms were wrapped tightly around me.

"I think there has been too much time wasted in this family, too many secrets left untold, too many emotions left unexpressed. I think I just don't want to waste any more precious time since you never know what will happen in life. Plus, I never was good at playing coy or hard to get. It's pretty much 'what you see is what you get with me.' I told him and kissed him again.

"It's good that I like what I see then! I missed you too. Now, close your eyes and let me lead you inside," he ordered. I did.

When we were in the kitchen he slid our jackets off. The dogs were wild to see him; jumping, whining, twining around our legs. "No peeking!" He turned me around to face the table. "Okay, open." On the table was the most beautiful old fashioned bird cage. You could tell much of it was handmade. There were beautifully carved ladders and swings with tiny birds etched into the wood and fancy windows and a snug woven metal sleeping pouch. It looked very Victorian English. I loved it.

"Jackson, it's wonderful!"

"I was cataloging a collection of things a member had given to the Boston Historical Society. She had a number of things like this that she and her husband had collected over the years. We talked for hours. Actually, she talked and I listened and recorded her stories for the museum. You'll have to listen sometime. She was old enough and observant enough of the culture of the Eastern US during the depression. Anyway, she gave me this."

"Let's see what Pearl thinks." I said getting Pearl out of his cage.

"What's a matter? No! No!" said Pearl, running up my arm and flying to the top of the refrigerator where he promptly turned his back on us. "What are you doing here? No! No!" He screeched. We both laughed at his antics.

"Oh well, "Jackson shrugged, "No matter. Close your eyes again." He left, taking the dogs with him. It sounded like he went into the back room. When he came out, he didn't bring the dogs.

"Hold out your hands. No, cup them," he ordered when I just stuck them out palms up, pushing them together into a bowl. My eyes flew open when he placed a small warm bundle of feathers in my hands. It was a very tiny parrot, green with a beige-green-brown striped neck, velvety, slightly flat brown head, and a maroon tail that was longer than the bird itself. His bright inquisitive eyes were circled in pure white, and there was just a hint of pink on his belly. He was adorable!

"This is Tinkerbell. He came with the cage."

I was speechless. He was so small. He also seemed quite at home in my hands and totally at ease. He let me examine him thoroughly for a few minutes, then climbed up my chest and hid under my hair. I smiled delightedly at Jackson.

"He is a green-cheeked conure, about a year old. Mrs. Hendricks asked if I could keep him, but I told her I was on the road too much. I also told her I had a friend who would take great care of him for her. You."

"How could she manage to give him up?" I wanted to know.

"She's going to live with her son, and he is allergic. So, will you keep him?"

"No! No!" Pearl complained. "Whatsa matter with you?"

"Yes! Yes!" I replied.

"What are you doing to me?" Pearl wasn't going to give up yet. He was not a happy parrot at this moment.

We sat on the sofa for a time, watching the birds and petting the dogs. Pearl settled down a little when he realized he didn't have to do anything with Tinkerbell except tolerate him. Tinkerbell could say his name and "good morning." The dogs hardly even noticed the new-comer although they did thoroughly investigate his cage.

"So, tell me what you have been doing while I was away. God, I wish you had a telephone!"

I brought Jackson up to date. I showed him Mom's poems and told him about the open doors. He looked worried.

"Emily, I need to go back to Boston for awhile. The museum asked me to set up an exhibit of Victorian England crafts. It could take awhile. I will probably be gone until Christmas." He sat closer and put his arm around my shoulders. "I must admit, I'm worried about those open doors. I doubt you left them that way."

"I must have." I really shouldn't have told him. To change the subject, I mentioned Marcus' "letter." It did not have the desired effect.

"Do you think he could be dangerous?"

"Marcus? No, he's just a bully who needs to think he's in charge. He used to push me around, but I will not let him do that any more. I'm stronger now."

"Does he know where you are?" Jackson asked.

"I don't know. I guess his lawyer has Augusta's address, and maybe the phone number, if they have caller ID." Suddenly, I remember the ringing phone.

"Even if he does, what would he want with me? He could hardly wait to get the divorce."

"And are you divorced?"

"Well, not yet I guess." He looked at me for several seconds.

"Just be careful," he said.

30

The weeks after Jackson returned to Boston kept getting colder. It snowed some every day and sunlight was scarce and dim. Even first morning light looked more like late afternoon. I tried painting, reading, and cooking, but nothing satisfied me. I had one excellent result from cooking experiment, potato soup with cream cheese, because I didn't have sour cream. It was wonderful. "Company good", as Mom would say.

The dogs were restless, too, so we took many short walks during daylight hours. Lily headed first for the rear of the cabin searching for Jackson, I was positive. Her tail sagged considerably when she found his parking spot vacant. Poor little Sully would get cold feet and lift one up, then another until he was flat on his back giving me his pitiful look, and I would carry him in. Eventually he refused to go more than two feet from the steps. I shoveled a flat spot for him to use.

Lily, in complete contrast, loved the cold. So much so that it was hard to get her back inside. She would run out on the now frozen lake and skid on the clear ice. She'd scrape the snow from the ice with her front feet; look deep down through the ice, and bark. I think she knew the water was under there somewhere. And the ice was keeping her from minnow chasing.

Pearl continued his best to ignore Tinkerbell, who imitated everything Pearl said, which drove Pearl into a bad temper. Sully taught Pearl to bark, the funniest sound I think I ever heard. I wasn't always able to discern whose voice I was hearing, Sully or Pearl. When Tinkerbell was particularly offensive, Pearl barked at him. It made me laugh out loud, and I was cheered up considerably.

One afternoon I decided, with some reluctance, that it was time to explore the house some more. I had almost decided to try the basement, but was loath to do that alone. I left the dogs napping and trudged over. The phone was ringing as I went through the front door. This was beginning to make me nervous as it seemed to happen too often. I hesitated, but picked it up. Just before it disconnected, I heard Marcus say "She's there." I truly did not think Marcus was dangerous, so I relaxed a little. But who was he talking to? It sounded like there must have been another person with him. And why didn't he talk to me? I dialed the number for the house we had shared, but that phone was disconnected. I locked myself in, and went back upstairs.

I sat in Augusta's small parlor to try to think like she would, while I studied the silver keys. They did look like they would open jewelry cases but I hadn't found any. While I daydreamed, I remembered a movie I had seen where someone had hidden things behind a strip of decorative molding. There certainly was no shortage of that here. I started with this room and went over it all slowly and carefully. This is nuts! I needed to talk to Augusta's friends, and decided to begin with Selma.

Selma was baking as usual and welcomed me cheerfully.

"I'm getting a start on Thanksgiving," she said.

"Thanksgiving! Already?" I was surprised. "Have I been here three months?"

"Nearly, dear." She responded absentmindedly, while tending to the cookies.

"Well, it sure doesn't seem that long to me."

"Of course not, dear, you have been busy. Will you come to us for Thanksgiving Day?" She looked at me and smiled.

"I hadn't thought… but sure. I would like that." I remembered the potato soup recipe. "I can even bring something."

"Wonderful! Jackson and Lydia always come too." She set coffee and a plate of ginger cookies, still warm, in front of me and sat. I sipped and took the keys out of my pocket.

"Can you tell me anything about these?" I asked.

Wiping her hands on her apron, she picked up one of the keys and examined it closely.

"Augusta wore this around her neck," she told me. "See, you can see where the chain rubbed on the silver."

Sure enough. I hadn't noticed before. The other key was unmarked.

"Anything else?" I wanted to know.

"Sorry, Emily. I have no idea. You should ask Lydia." Of course I would do that.

We drank our coffee, ate our cookies, and talked about the holidays.

"Long ago, we all gathered at Svensson's for each holiday. The house would be decorated so fine. Especially at Christmas time. Greens, holly, even mistletoe. It was so jolly. Myron would play Santa for the children and Rudolf, tall and thin as he was, was his elf. The children knew, of course, but it was such fun. There were decorated trees in several rooms, and presents everywhere. We all contributed, and many other families would come for dinner and to spend the day with celebration and song. There used to be a fair number of musicians in this neck of the wood, fiddles, flutes, penny whistles, banjos and a guitar or two. Augusta played the piano, you know. And she had a strong, lovely voice." Selma's gaze drifted off, lost in herself and her memories. "I thought those days would go on forever." She said this sadly.

"But, they didn't" I added.

"No." That was all she said.

31

Lydia was also baking for the upcoming holidays. After leaving Selma's toasty warm kitchen for the icy cold of the road, I arrived at Lydia's, where I was invited in for more treats. I told her I couldn't possibly eat anything or drink any more coffee.

"Not even MY coffee?" Her eyes twinkled.

"Well, maybe half a cup with lots of milk," I weakened, as she knew I would, and was already getting a cup. I took out the keys again and laid them on the table. Lydia sat and stared at them.

"I wondered what had happened to those," she said. When she looked back at me, she had tears in her eyes.

"I want you to know that I loved your grandmother," she began. "But, I often did not like things she did. I tried to talk her out of doing them, but she was very stubborn." Lydia hesitated. "I don't want to tell you about this."

"But Lydia, I need to know about my family."

She sighed and whispered, "I suppose…"

She stood and automatically refilled our mugs with steaming brew and wrapped her hands around hers tightly, as if she needed that small warmth.

"Marie and Robert were inseparable. They were the same age and grew up together in school and at home. You never saw one without the other. Even when they were in grade school and the other children would tease Robert about playing with a girl. We all assumed they would marry. Except, of course, Augusta. She wanted more than a "lake boy" for her last daughter. Marie was sent away to school and for awhile she stayed. Until she was seventeen. But by that Christmas she was back home and refused to leave. She, like Grace, would meet Robert away from the house. By this time, I understood what Augusta was doing, and I helped Marie. I think Augusta knew I was interfering, and she was angry. Robert had to go out east for a time, and the next thing I knew, Marie was engaged to your father, Howard Lind."

"The keys?" I prompted her.

"Oh yes. This one," she picked up the one that had been on a chain, "opens a wooded box about six inches by twelve. In it are several letters that Marie wrote to Robert."

I was confused. Why did Grandmother have Robert's letters?

"In the front foyer, there was a table where we all put things to be posted. The mail man picked them up daily. Augusta took Marie's letters to Robert before the post was taken." Lydia shook her head. "I didn't know this until years later, or I would have done something."

I was so stunned it took a moment for it to sink in. My god! What had Grandmother done? Oh my poor

Mother. I was angry in every fiber of my being. I was shaking and if Grandmother had been alive, I could have killed her myself!

"No one else knows this." Lydia continued. "I couldn't bear to tell Robert, or even Selma. I am so sorry. I do not think Marie was very happy after her marriage to Howard. Perhaps she still loved Robert."

I know she loved Robert! I understood more than I wanted to about my parents at this point. Did my father know? Did Robert?

"I always thought Mom died of a broken heart." I sobbed on Lydia's shoulder when I simply could not hold back the tears that had been threatening to flow since arriving.

"Yes, I think she did. It took ten years, but I think she did." We held each other until I stopped crying.

"Where is the box of letters now?" I asked her.

"I have no idea. I never saw them, but you should ask Myron. He cleaned up some after Augusta died, and he is the one who buried her."

"When is Jackson coming home?" Suddenly that seemed most urgent.

"He hasn't called me." Lydia finally smiled.

"Well, he just better hurry." I smiled back.

"Yes, I think he better."

So, back in the Saab and back to Petersons General Store. I found Selma and we looked for Myron for some time before we found him at Robert's. I was leery to speak in front of Robert, but he knew something was up when I hesitated. Perhaps I simply saw him differently. Anyway, he said he had errands to run and left us.

"Myron, do you know what these are for?" I again took out the keys.

Myron touched the keys in my hand, but didn't pick them up. He started to shake his head, but Selma stopped him.

"You tell her what you know, Myron Sven Peterson! There are too many unanswered questions and we have had enough!" She took my hand.

"I made two boxes for Augusta years ago. I don't know what she kept in them. I do know they are hidden somewhere in the house or on the grounds." Myron promptly answered his wife.

"Myron..." Selma started in.

"I swear, woman! I do not know!"

"I know what is in one of them." I told them sadly. "Lydia told me. This key, the one from the chain, locks a box full of letters from Marie to Robert." Both of the Petersons caught their breath and Selma paled visibly. Myron helped her into a chair.

"Did Lydia know what was in the letters?" Selma was finding it difficult to speak.

"No, only that Marie grew more withdrawn and dejected with each passing year. Until she finally seemed to give up on life and tragically died."

"I wonder if Robert knew?" Selma was having trouble breathing normally, so I did the sensible thing and got her a glass of water.

"Lydia said no."

"This explains so much. We couldn't figure out what went wrong between the children. We were expecting a marriage between the families, you understand." Selma was better. Maybe there was something to this water deal after all.

"Marie went to the Twin Cities several weeks after Robert went to New York, and when she came home she was engaged to your father. Augusta was so angry! She refused to have the wedding, so the children eloped to Saint Paul, where Howard lived. Nine months later, Lydia said you had been born and Marie was bringing you here for the summer." Selma and Myron exchanged another of their private glances. "Robert never told us anything and we didn't want to upset him any more than he was. Besides, I don't think even he understood what had happened."

"Now, I think we all know. Augusta, once again ruined lives." I was bitter, and I felt sorrow for all three of them, Marie, Robert, and Howard. It was unrequited love all around. Because of my selfish grandmother. My father surely realized his wife did not love him. I doubt anyone would have acted differently than he did. Maybe he even wondered if I was his. Maybe I should be wondering that, too.

We all walked back to the store and sat around the table. The kitchen was so cheerful; there were no sad stories or secrets in *this* kitchen I thought. As I gazed fondly at these two people I had come to love like family, I had a brilliant idea.

"I know what we all need!" The idea was so perfect and so sudden, that I nearly shouted.

"And what might that be, Little Miss Emily?" chuckled Robert as he came through the door with an armful of firewood.

194

"Let's have the traditional holiday celebration at the main house! You know, decorate it all up and invite the neighbors, just like you used to do. God knows the place is just going to waste all empty."

"Yes!" Selma was excited about the idea. "That is a wonderful plan." She grabbed a pencil and piece of paper and began writing names on it.

"Hold on, girls." Myron looked skeptical. "There's a lot of work to do on that place. The water isn't running in the house, and..."

"Yes it is."

"Well, The Neilsons haven't been there since Emily came and it's probably filthy and..."

"Come on, Pop!" Robert looked excited too. "Ray and I can get the hard stuff ready, Maryalice and her girls will help, and these two aren't helpless." He gestured at Selma and me.

"Jackson will be back soon, too. Oh, this will be so perfect!" I was completely caught up in the plan. "We need a real stove and oven, though. Robert, can you take me into Brainerd in your truck?"

"First thing tomorrow, if you can wait that long," he teased.

32

Robert picked me up at 8 a.m. With fresh cinnamon rolls, which I eyed with suspicion, and a thermos of coffee we started out. I was already gaining weight and, while a small gain was acceptable, all these treats were dangerous. So far I had worked it off, but I was sure the winter would be long and not hold much chance of strenuous activity. Especially if all these kind people kept doing things for me!

The sun was in full bloom this morning and our spirits were high. Robert talked a little about what life was like when he was a boy, and how much fun the big holiday gatherings were. The Petersons often spent the night with the McKenna's over the holidays, and the house was full and happy.

"After us children were sent upstairs to bed, we would go back down the stairs to the halfway landing and watch the festivities. Or we'd hang over the balcony railing and listen. I think Pop and Rudolf knew we were there, but they kept our secret." He was smiling. "On Christmas Eve, one year, we waited up for Santa Claus on that balcony and fell asleep. In the morning, we were covered in quilts and had pillows under our heads and there were presents on all the steps, leading all the way to the decorated tree!" He laughed. "Ray couldn't figure out how Santa's reindeer got past us."

"Well, I think it's time to make new memories and traditions," I said with firm conviction.

Robert put his arm around me and pulled me to his side. "Emily, you are good for us. I'm so glad you're here," he said.

I found what I wanted at the first appliance store. It was a large stove with six burners on top instead of the usual four, and the oven was wide enough for two, twenty-five pound turkeys. At least that's what the sales woman told us. I'd never cooked a turkey. It was a good thing I had Lydia, Selma, and Maryalice to cook. I tried to remember a single holiday I'd spent with Marcus, but I was drawing on nothing, neither happy nor sad, just a vast nothing. The store promised to deliver the stove the next afternoon, so we were done.

Robert dropped me off and I went to the house. Selma and Myron were there uncovering the furniture and airing out the downstairs rooms, so it was frigid in the house.

"There you are!" said Myron. "I can't find the vacuum cleaner."

"You are asking the wrong person. I don't know where anything is," I shrugged my shoulders.

Selma came out from the kitchen pushing an antique looking vacuum in front of her. She also had a damp mop and dust rags which she handed to her husband. She pulled a bottle of lemon oil from her apron pocket and gave it to Myron also.

"I think we can close the windows now." Selma was all business this morning. "And let's get hopping!" She plugged in the vacuum and began.

"Jackson is waiting for you at the cottage..." Myron began, but I was already on my way. Jackson's truck was behind the cottage and the back end was full of boxes, but I ran past it and up the cottage steps. All the pent up loneliness and vague fears suddenly caught up with me and much to my surprise, I burst into tears.

"What's wrong Emily?" Jackson folded me into his arms and led me to the sofa, not letting go. "Is everyone alright?" He shook me a little when I wasn't able to answer right away. "Tell me!"

So I did. "We are all fine," I sobbed. "Everything is great. I'm just so happy you're home!"

He laughed. "This is happy?"

"Yes. Really happy." And he kissed me on my tear-stained cheeks, then my swollen eyes, and finally, my lips.

"I missed you, too," he murmured. "You have to get a telephone."

I pulled his head back down to my lips again and held him there. This kiss was long and slow and intense. Somehow our jackets fell to the floor and bothersome buttons became undone. He pulled back a little and looked into my eyes. "Em?"

My answer was to kiss him again. He picked me up and carried me to the bedroom, kicking the door closed before the dogs could follow. We both lay on the bed and slowly undressed each other, caressing and kissing.

Exploring each other's bodies was more exciting than I could have imagined. This was a totally new experience for me. Marcus had never bothered. Sex with him took all of two or three minutes. When Jackson's fingers lightly touched my nipples, I moaned, and arched my body to his. He entered and held me tightly, as we rocked each other. Fourth of July fireworks exploded between my legs all the way to my brain, and we collapsed back onto the bed.

"Wow. I need to go away more often," Jackson grinned. Then he got serious. "Okay. Now tell me."

I told him about the letters and what Augusta had done to the young lovers. Again.

"It was just like Grace and Karl! This is so despicable. And I thought about all the secrets and the lies and how if Marie and Robert only believed in themselves more, it never would have happened. It seems to me that most people are afraid to put themselves out there. You know, tell each other what they are feeling rather than hide behind their fear of rejection or betrayal or whatever it is."

"And you don't want anything like that to happen to us?" he asked gently.

"I don't want to waste any time! Life is short and opportunities are so easily missed, because people are too afraid to admit who they are or what they want!"

"I'm not like that." Jackson held me closer. "I love you already, Emily. Well, except for that explosive temper, anyway!"

I started to tell him the same, but my words were lost against his lips and we made love again. I had never felt this with anyone. Certainly not Marcus! This was intense and free and uninhibited. I fell asleep with one of

Jackson's hands tangled in my hair and the other between my legs.

The dogs were whining at the bedroom door and it was almost dark. Jackson was propped up on his elbow watching me. He had pulled the quilts snuggly over our bodies. He felt so comfortable next to me.

"So, when can I move in?" he chuckled when I woke enough to see him clearly. "In keeping with your not wasting time theory." He added, seriously.

"I thought you just did." I scampered to the door, naked still, to let the dogs in before they destroyed the woodwork. We all dove deeply into the quilts for some active dog play.

"They don't like to be left out." I spoke from under the quilt.

"They'll have to get used to it."

"I suppose we should get up, but I feel so lazy and comfortable." I groaned as Jackson kissed my neck and nipples.

"Hey," he whispered hoarsely. "Did you happen to notice the size of the bathtub I put in your new bathroom?"

"Oh, you mean the one big enough for two?"

"That would be the one." We raced for it. Sitting with my back up against Jackson in a tub full to the brim with hot water and soap bubbles was one the of best moments of my life to date. He had lit several candles that I didn't even know I had. The dogs were happy someplace else, so we were alone. Soon, the cozy, wet nest turned into something else, and the splashing water doused most of the candles before we were satisfied. This whole togetherness thing was so new to me, but it somehow felt familiar. Almost like we had done it all before.

After we cleaned up our mess, Jackson made sandwiches and canned soup, which tasted better than steak. We took coffee outside with the dogs, to let them run off steam, too. It was dark and very romantic. The wind had intensified and was howling over our heads through the very tops of the pines. Yet we could feel none of it at ground level. It was quite odd.

33

It had been many years since I woke up with a man I loved next to me. I couldn't even remember the last time. I was acutely aware of Jackson's body stretched up against mine. With Jackson on one side and Sully on the other, I couldn't move. Jackson was stirring, too, and Sully growled. I tried to be quiet, but I just couldn't hold back the laughter.

"What's up?" Jackson mumbled grumpily.

"I see you and Sully wake in the same mood." I thought this was very funny. Jackson slid his arm over me to pat the dog into wagging his tail.

"Sully is as easy as you are." Jackson kissed me. "Good morning my sweet one," he said.

"I have been wondering what's in the packages we left in your truck last night."

"Oh yeah, those." He nuzzled my neck and kissed it. "They can wait." He gently put Sully on the floor and his hands began to roam all over me; which, of course, gave me ideas of my own. We were already learning what each of us liked. Jackson liked to be kissed everywhere, and fondled slowly. His penis fit so perfectly in my hands, mouth, and body. It was like he was built just for me. I loved to make him groan. He just couldn't stop himself. I liked everything he did, my body responded to his touch like it knew what he was going to do before he did it, and was very ready. It was another blissful union.

"I could get so used to this," Jackson said after. "On the other hand, I think we need more practice!" He rolled over on top of me.

"We will have to practice later. I have pets to feed and walk and uncover."

"And I suppose I have food to cook and fires to tend."

"Yes, you do! Unless you'd rather do the pets?" I asked him.

"Can you cook?" He responded doubtfully.

"Sure, if you're not fussy...actually, not too well."

"Okay then, I am hungry. So I'll cook and you can learn." We had fried egg sandwiches on powder-milk biscuits, bacon, and coffee. The dogs even had some, and the birds had bits of egg and toast, which Pearl loved and Tinkerbell shredded and dropped down to the waiting dogs.

"It's pretty hard to resist Pearl when he keeps asking 'Is it good?' while I'm eating," Jackson complained.

"You just need to learn to share." I laughed at his disgusted look. "And now I really want to know what's in the truck."

"Help me unload it, then." So we put jackets and boots on and did just that. The boxes were full of turn-of-the-century things: lampshades, dishes, picture frames, leather bags, and, best of all, Christmas decorations. They were brightly colored fragile things. Bells, balls, spirals,

Santa Claus', angels, icicles, reindeer with red ribbons, even a tiny red dachshund.

"This is great!" I hugged him. "I don't have any decorations of my own any more, and I love to make the house festive and colorful. It was something Mom and I did together and it was always so beautiful."

There was another box with several strings of colored lights. Both the oversized ones that I remembered from childhood and newer, tiny things that looked like fairy lights when they were lit. Grandma Bengta had wee candles on her trees and, even though they were family tradition and lovely, I always opted for electric lights. I had a fear of fires and had visions of burning pets that stopped me from taking chances. My rule was no lit candles unless I was actually in the room with them. I didn't even leave the fire lit in the fireplace, unless I was there. I would wait until it was out, or very nearly so. Even then, I was always so happy to return home and find everything fine.

"I talked to Lydia day before yesterday, and she told me about your plans for the holidays. One of my museums had just gotten a truckload of these things for a new wing on decorative arts, and this was the leftover stuff. They were going to stick it in the basement, so I talked them out of it. Nice, huh?" Jackson was proud of his acquisitions and pleased that I liked them, too.

"They are so very perfect for Augusta's house." I told him.

"I think it's time to call it your house. We need to forget about Augusta. As much as we can, anyway." He took a large box out of the cab of his truck and handed it to me.

"This is especially for you." I opened it to find a velvet dress, long, with a tight-fitting bodice and flowing skirt. It was a deep blue and soft as silk.

"Jackson! This is stunning!"

"It will be, with you in it." He smiled. "It's from a vintage clothing store in Boston. It's my favorite color."

"It's the color of the sky just before it gets dark," I said.

"Exactly."

We took the decorations up to the big house, I wouldn't have been surprised to see the crew hard at work already, but there was no one there. The house was immaculate and smelled like fresh lemons. They had finished cleaning and there was nothing left to do, but wait for the stove to come.

We piled the boxes in the library. I wanted to decorate immediately, but it wasn't even Thanksgiving yet. The long elegant dining room table was set, as was the table in the kitchen, with all but the plates. A note on the counter from Lydia said we would set it up as a buffet and people could sit where they chose. Serving spoons were piled next to a huge stack of plates. This would be such fun! Another note, from Maryalice, told me she would take care of inviting everyone, and asked if there was anyone I wanted to ask. I didn't even have to think about that, everyone in the world I now cared about lived on this lake.

"While we're waiting for the stove, I want to show you something." I took Jackson's hand and pulled him to the foyer. Pointing to the oddly carved wall, I said: "Do you remember this?"

"Sure. Augusta had a man from Minneapolis come up here to make it, oh, I don't remember exactly when, but some time before she died." He looked at it more closely and traced a line of carving with his finger.

"Hey, I think it's a map. This line is the creek that flows past Lydia's log cabin into the lake. And this smaller bump here might be the gazebo. And this," He ran my hand over a row of even smaller bumps, "is the cemetery."

I was getting into this game. "This bigger knob is this house." I touched a rough square clump. "And here is my cottage, by what must represent the lake, large expanse of flat with no protrusions. It is a map of Augusta's property. And a very clever one at that! No one who didn't already know it would guess." I traced all the lines and turned to Jackson.

"But why? What is its purpose?"

"Knowing Augusta, she is trying in her odd way, to tell you something." Jackson still studied the map. "Have you been to all these places?" He gestured at the bumps.

"I don't even know what they all represent." I took the keys, which were still in my jeans pocket, out and held them in my palm. "I just have these. One for a box of letters and the other for a jewelry box, according to the Petersons and your grandmother."

"Which you haven't found yet."

"Right."

We heard the appliance truck at the rear of the house. My train of thought was broken now anyway, so I went to open the door and let the delivery people carry in my new stove.

34

Thanksgiving Day dawned without sun, two days later. In fact, it was nearly a blizzard. It's a good thing everyone lives close, I thought. Jackson hadn't spent the night and it was very cold in the cabin. I was already used to him getting up before me and stoking the fires. But, I couldn't be lazy this morning. I had made the potato soup the day before and it was in the refrigerator at the main house, but there probably was still more to do, so I dressed and dealt with my babies and went over.

It was early yet but of course, the Peterson and McKenna clans were already busy setting up. People I hadn't met yet were dropping off covered dishes for later, and it was as busy as Grand Central Station on a Friday afternoon.

I got a quick kiss of welcome from Jackson, which everyone smiled at, and was handed a dishtowel. Several hours later, we were ready. I happened to glance out a window and noticed that the fury of snow had trickled down to just a flake now and then. Much better for traveling these narrow country roads. Ray had plowed out a large parking spot for cars earlier that morning so we were even prepared on the outside.

The turkeys were perfect and I now knew how to cook them, well, mostly. Sweet potatoes, squash, corn, biscuits, gravy, several salad dishes and casseroles, more vegetables, soups, and homemade pickles. Pies, cakes and cookies, too, all were coming in the door along with the families who carried them. The Petersons had all dashed off to change clothes and I went back to the cabin to put on my new/old dress and get Lily. I left Sully, my manner-less puppy, behind as he would just be underfoot and trying to escape. I still had not relaxed my vigilance where he was concerned as I surely never wanted to go through that experience again.

I stood at my bedroom window for a time, just watching people arrive. It seemed we had a lot of neighbors. I recognized the group of fishermen who had found Grace. They had each brought their families. Everyone who came was carrying something: food, wine, instruments. I was a little nervous at meeting so many new people, and I felt like the Grande Dame, which frankly, I did not want to be. Suddenly, I felt Jackson behind me. He wrapped his arms around my waist and ran his hands up over my breasts.

"Umm," he said. "I knew you would feel like this under this dress."

I turned and kissed him, hard. "Hold that thought!" I ordered, and we left for the party. My leather boots were very slick on the new snow, so Jackson picked me up. We were laughing merrily when we arrived.

What a party it was! It lasted well into the night. Without the football games on television that captivated all the men in my family, these men and women remained in the same room. I always hated that football tradition in my dad's family, the separation of the sexes with the women in the kitchen and the men glued to the television set. It seemed to rob us of what holiday get-togethers were supposed to be about.

This holiday was like a Norman Rockwell painting. Laughter and candlelight filled the place, sparkling on the glass cupboards in the dining room. Bottles of wine were passed up and down the tables, and we ate until we could hold no more. The adults swapped stories and recipes and the children played on the grand staircase, and hide-and-seek everywhere. We finally had to restrict this game to the main level, as no one could find each other. But then, Lily found the children much too quickly. They could not believe how she was able to locate them so fast. One small girl got lost in the attic and we all had a time trying to locate her calls for help. Spirits were high and everyone liked being together again.

After eating, the tables were shoved against the wall and the carpets were rolled up. All the musical instruments were retrieved from the corners, where they had been temporarily stored, and dancing began. The musicians played dance tunes for hours. Selma, Lydia, and two of their friends from Sweden sang a song 'from the old country' they said. I never had so much fun!

"We have missed these gatherings," an old woman told me as she left with her family. "Thank you for starting the tradition once again." She kissed my cheek. More than one person told me I looked like Marie.

"Why, it's almost like having Marie back again." a friend of Mom's from school mentioned to another as they left the house.

When most of the families were gone, the rest of us cleaned up. There was so much food left. I insisted no one could leave without taking something with them. Selma packaged up leftovers for all of us. And several packages, labeled and dated, for the freezer.

"I know how you feel about cooking," she told me. "So now all you have to do, is heat it up. It takes but a minute and you'll have a real meal."

I hugged each of them at the front door when they left. Lily and I looked for Jackson as I turned out lights and locked doors, but he wasn't there. My Sorel boots mysteriously were sitting by the door, however, so he'd been back to the cabin. I kicked off the leather dress boots and put on the Sorels and happily walked home in the moonlight with Lily dancing in the snow all the way.

My cottage was dark except for twinkling gold and white lights in all the windows. A large candle, too, lit the kitchen. There was one tall glass of wine on the table.

"Jackson?"

"In here." I picked up the glass and the candle and followed his voice to the steamy bathroom. Jackson was in a bubble bath with his glass of wine and a silly grin on his face.

"You did tell me to hold that thought!"

211

I chuckled as I slipped off my clothes and joined him. Sully barely bothered to lift his head as I entered the room. He was stretched out in front of the space heater.

"I wore him out, so he wouldn't bother us." And, he didn't.

I loved making love to Jackson. It was like a dance so private and intimate that I could lose myself completely and not doubt it for a second. Every part of my body responded to his touch in ways I didn't know were possible. All he had to do was smile at me, and I was ready. Parts of me that had long been dormant were now alive and tingling. The heat between my legs was so intense I thought I could burst into flame. I pulled him into me and held him there tightly. Later, we left the mess in the bathroom, blew out the candles, kept the twinkle lights on, and moved to the bed, where we made love once more.

"Happy?" Jackson whispered in my ear.

"Supremely. If I were any happier, there would have to be two of me to handle it."

"Now there's an interesting thought." We fell asleep breathing hard, our bodies intertwined so that I couldn't tell who was who without touching. Sully had wormed his way to the bottom of the bed and Jackson didn't seem to notice, so I let him stay.

I realized I had never trusted anyone like I trusted Jackson. I didn't know this kind of relationship was possible for me. My life is complete, I thought as I finally let myself fall into sleep.

212

35

I was out on the lake; it was night and very windy. I was barefoot, but didn't feel the cold. The sky was clear and thousands of stars were swirling around and falling on the ice where they fractured into a million pieces and slipped under the lake. Then the stars turned into a blizzard and I couldn't see. A huge black shadow was coming at me across the ice, rapidly, but I was trapped on this spot and couldn't move my legs. The ice was rapidly turning into a vast black hole under my feet and the water was rising about my ankles. Someone was calling my name, and someone else was screaming, a loud unpleasant sort of shriek, rising and dropping and rising again. I knew I had to run, but where? The ice held me captive. And from whom did I need to run? Then the ice was reforming and caught my ankles in its tight icy cold grip. I woke in a sweat, heart pounding and confused, frigid chills traveling up and down my spine. Sunlight was streaming in the window, so it had to be mid-morning. The dogs were both with me, but no Jackson. This was the kind of dream it would take all day to shake, I knew, as I got up and dressed. No one seemed in a hurry to go out or to eat, so I assumed Jackson had taken care of those chores already. I automatically began to make coffee, and then realized it was done. Sipping a cup, I wondered about the vivid dream that held me in its frightening shadow. For some reason it made me think of my childhood nightmare of skeletons in holes in the basement floor.

I put on my Sorels and parka and took the dogs out on the lake ice, testing it as we went. It was solid. So, we proceeded over the ice to Robert's. It was a shorter walk over the ice, than if we had taken the road. In about a half hour, we were knocking on the door. Robert wasn't at home, but we needed to warm up and went in anyway. I was sure Robert wouldn't mind us being there. I went up to the studio and sat on the floor and just stared at the portrait of Marie. The carefree look of her in that picture was exactly the way I liked to remember her, young and full of life. So completely lost in my thoughts, I didn't notice Robert until he put his hands on my shoulders.

"Hello, Emily," he said quietly, respectful of my mood.

I looked at the fawning dogs in disgust. "They don't even attempt to warn me of you or Jackson!" I complained. Robert sat on the floor next to me and tried to hold one hundred pounds of Lily on his lap with Sully trying to get to his face.

Laughing, he said "I like that about them. I also know how fierce they would be if I had intentions to harm you. Jackson told me about them when you first met. In the woods," he reminded me when I looked confused.

I laughed too. "Only for a second! They were losing interest in the protection thing much too quickly. They would have been in love with him in a second or two more."

"So, Little Miss Emily, what can I do for you today?"

I told him what I now knew about Marie's letters to him and what Augusta had done to them both. He actually had tears in his eyes when I finished.

"I wondered if something like that had happened, when Marie mentioned my failure to respond to her letters. If you ever find them…"

"Oh, I swear I'll find them!" I interrupted. "And you will read them all. It will be over twenty years too late, but you will get your letters." We sat in companionable silence for awhile, both of us looking at Marie's face. Someone's stomach growled and I looked at Robert in surprise.

"I didn't think I could ever eat again, after yesterday," I said.

"I think that was me, but I'd agree with you. Let's go see what Selma's got cooking." Robert stood and pulled me to my feet and off we went to Selma, who was more than happy to feed us a huge country breakfast. My God, but I was going to become very plump, if I kept on eating the way I had been the past few months.

I wanted to go look harder for the letters, so I could make good on my promise to Robert, so I asked him to drop the three of us off at Augusta's. I also showed him the map-carving.

"Any ideas?" I asked.

"Not off the top of my head, but I sure will think about it." He left me there to ponder. I felt all around the wall, pushing, pulling, and turning knobs. Nothing did anything. Too many mystery novels, I laughed at myself. There wasn't room enough for a secret room in the wall. I even watched the dogs to see if they were more interested in any one spot, but they were sniffing the grubby children's handprints on the stair railings, tails wagging wildly. Then they took off at a trot to find those mysterious children.

I thought the secret room idea was a great one though, so I headed upstairs. Starting with the attic, I carefully looked at all walls, closets, any place for a clue. A few cobwebs were all I found up there. On the second floor, I found a few pieces of broken jewelry in Augusta's room. A single small opal and a scrap of silver that looked like it had been in an earring were stuffed into a crack in the old wood floor. They were beautiful, but not any help. I put them in my pocket. I didn't even bother with the main floor, as we had done a thorough cleaning job before the Thanksgiving feast. All the dishes had been washed or dusted and put back in their cabinets. But, as I went down the rear staircase, I noticed one of the steps was a tiny bit wobbly. Sure enough, the top of the step could be lifted. It was a hiding place for a small boy's treasures. Marbles, tops, yo-yo's, a baseball, an ancient half-empty pack of cigarettes, that sort of thing. I put them all back and closed the step. Jackson would like that. Some of it probably belonged to his father. Tired, dirty, and discouraged, I trudged home.

36

The week after the holiday, things slowed even more. The bustle of Thanksgiving preparations seemed almost a dream. But the weather was calmer and warmer and there was even a little sun. My mood cheered also. Having Jackson around was good for me and the birds and dogs adored him as much as I did. One day, over another candlelit dinner, he informed me of a change in his plans.

"I have to go back to Boston." He sounded dejected.

"I thought you were free until the end of the year."

"There are some problems with the Victorian exhibit. Some doubts about authenticity, I guess. It should only take two or three days." Then he brightened. "You could come with me."

"And who would take care of these guys?" I gestured to the room full of pets. "Robert is in New York for the opening of his new works, remember?"

"Yeah, I do. You'll be fine, anyway, right?"

"Oh course I will." Right.

He left before I was up the following morning, but fires were burning and coffee already made. I went to

Petersons for a few supplies, had more coffee, and helped Myron fill shelves, which was usually Robert's job.

"Have you heard from Robert?" I asked.

"Selma talked to the boy. He sold several pieces, and a wildlife print shop is asking for the right to copy a few more. So, he's happy." I chuckled inwardly at the "boy" reference. Robert was fifty-one years old. But then, I was still "Little Miss."

"When will he be back?"

"Two or three days. He's promised to take the ladies Christmas shopping."

I dropped the box of cereal I was stocking in surprise. Christmas shopping! I hadn't even thought about it. I hadn't actually purchased a Christmas present for anyone since I was in college. I better get on it soon.

"Say, Myron, tell him I want to go too, okay?" I went home to make one of my unending lists. Try as I might, I couldn't come up with any great ideas. Except maybe one. I noticed Robert gazing fondly at a Golden Retriever puppy, walking on a leash with a young boy at his side. I asked Robert why he didn't have a dog and received the standard reason: "I'm just gone too much." Well, that was before he had me to babysit. Okay, one gift down, several more to go.

I went to bed with Christmas on my mind and dreamed about terrible choices. Like skis for Myron, or a motorcycle for Lydia. Sometime during the night I was awakened by a thump against the rear of the house. Both dogs were growling low and deep in their throats. I shushed them and listened.

"Damn you! Don't push me! Watch where you're going! I think somebody lives here!" A voice whispered harshly.

"So what?" Another voice said loudly. "What the fuck do I care?"

"Do you want them to call the police?" A woman's voice this time, thin and whiny.

"No phone lines, idiot!" The loud voice again. "Besides, they probably don't even have cops around the woods."

"Enough arguing!" That was the first voice once again.

"That's her car over there by that big house. That has to be the house she inherited. So let's go find her." Oh no! That was Marcus talking.

"We already tried, you dolt! She isn't there tonight." The voices moved on, but I was shaken. I heard a car start up somewhere down the lane, before I could breathe. What was going on? I spent the remainder of the night waiting for dawn. This was too much for me to deal with on my own. There were at least three of them. One had sounded really tough and mean. At first light I took the dogs out and they immediately ran to the rear of the house. Just below my window, the snow was covered in footprints and a few cigarette butts. Lily's fur stood up down her back and she started to trot to the lane with her nose on the ground.

"Lily, no!" She lifted her head and looked at me. "Come!" I ordered, but she was on a mission and too far from me to care what I wanted. I picked up Sully and ran for the car. As soon as she heard the engine, she was back.

I knew that would work. She loved riding in the car more than food. At Petersons, Ray, Selma, Myron, and Ray's two sons, Philip and Greg were having coffee at the bar.

"Emily!" Ray came over to me. "We were on our way to see you. Is everything okay?" I told him about my night visitors.

"They were here before we opened." Myron was angry. "Wouldn't stop pounding on the door until I opened it. Very rude about it, too. Said they needed gas, but they only got two dollars worth!"

"Pop was worried so he called us to come over. The biggest guy wanted to know where you lived."

"Big guy?" I asked.

"Yeah. Huge. Linebacker big. Mean look about him. Told him I never heard of you." Myron spit out the words.

"I think one of them is my husband. I have no idea who the others are or why any of them would be here."

"I don't like this," Selma said quietly. "I want to get Robert and Jackson back here and call the state police."

"And tell them what, Ma? That we think there is a boogieman in the woods?"

"There is, isn't there?" she demanded.

"Here's what we'll do, park Emily's car out of sight and the boys and I will take her home and stay with her until Jackson returns." He turned to me. "Okay with you?"

"Yes, but I feel a little guilty, taking you away from home."

"Don't. I'll bring most of them with me." He grinned. So that was what we did.

The cottage was full with these sturdy, happy men, and I felt better immediately. It's pretty easy to be brave when you feel safe. Phillip, the youngest, was very interested in painting, so I got him started on a canvas. Two or three hours later, I could see that he had inherited some of his uncle's talent. Ray and Greg were ice fishing just off shore where they could keep their eyes on us. Maryalice came and I asked for a cooking lesson. We had a great day. Sully was in love with Phillip and slept on his feet. Anyone who has ever owned a long-haired dachshund knows two things for sure. They love to be warm, very warm, and they have to have a pillow. Even if it is just a sheet of paper or a wrinkle in a rug. Phillip's feet were perfect.

After supper, both of the boys wanted to stay, so we sent Maryalice and Ray home. I saw Ray hand over a rifle to Greg at the door.

"That makes me nervous," I told him, uneasy.

"It's more for show than anything else," Ray reassured me. "It's just like a BB gun."

I started to protest, and stopped when I looked at Ray's eyes.

"Please, Emily," he said, and I nodded.

The boys and I spent the evening playing Monopoly, an old board game that had been here since my childhood. All three of us took the dogs outside for their last run, and I settled them down for the night with blankets in the other bedroom. Sully refused to leave Phillip. I stayed awake listening for hours, but heard nothing other than the usual creaking of the tree branches against the house. Before I fell asleep, Sully joined me under the covers, and we drifted off.

Ray came again, very early the next morning and was visibly relieved, I think, to find us all in one piece. There were no new footprints or tire tracks on the property. It was a sunny day with milder temperatures and I felt no fear. I sent them all home. Greg needed to get back to his veterinary practice and Phillip, to school. Greg vaccinated the dogs before he left and neither of them even noticed what he was doing.

"You are good at this." I smiled at him.

"I love it," he responded, blushing a little.

Ray also needed to get back to work, but promised to be back before dark.

"I'll probably be at the main house," I mentioned as he left.

37

Sometime, in the middle of doing something completely unrelated, I remembered that I had yet to check out Augusta's Bible. I also wanted to look around more closely in the library. It took me longer than I expected at home, so I didn't leave for the house until mid-afternoon. Walking over, I was glad to have the dogs along.

When I unlocked the front door, Sully took off like a rocket with Lily fast on his heels, knocking me into the map-wall, as I had come to think of it. I fell hard against one of the knobs and knocked it off. Sliding down the wall with pin pricks of bright light sparkling in front of my eyes, I sat still until my vision cleared. The knob my head had dislodged had wooden screw threads at the base. Odd, I thought as I stood again. It had been covering a small keyhole! The screw perfectly fit into this. The largest of the knobs had been situated over what Jackson thought was Augusta's house on the map. Checking my jacket pockets, I found I still had the keys. The silver key, that had been on the chain, slid into the keyhole easily and popped open a small, flat section of the map, cleverly hidden amongst the knobs and carvings and impossible to discern from the remainder of the map. It was about seven inches wide and twelve high. Tucked tightly behind this space of the map-wall was one of the wooden boxes Myron had described. I removed the plain, flat box and found the key also fit this lock and I lifted the lid. As I expected, it held a bundle of letters tied together with twine. All of the envelopes were addressed to Robert Peterson, from Marie Svensson. They were written on the old-fashioned air-mail paper, thin and nearly transparent.

At first the letters were numerous and dated about a week apart. Later, only one every May, until they stopped the year she died. Underneath this bundle, was a smaller one: three unopened letters to Marie from Robert. There were several cards and letters to me from Augusta, as well. It appeared to be one every birthday, stopping by age ten. But I had never seen them. These, like Mother's, had never gone through the mail. Wrapped up in Marie's letter bundle was a fragile, white hankie with a wide lace border. It still carried a whiff of her scent. I clutched it tightly as I read.

Mother's first letters were all about missing Robert. Filled with day-to-day trivia and pleas to come home soon. She was pregnant. Very excited about the baby she and Robert had made together, she was already calling it Emily. This, according to the letter, was the name she and Robert had decided on for a daughter in all their planning and daydreaming of their future life together. Marie could not wait to share this with Robert, get married and live happily ever after. I was so confused! A baby named Emily? Was Robert truly my father? I sat for a long time simply dwelling on that possibility. I didn't think my Mother would name another's child what she had chosen with a first love. In fact, I was sure of it. My poor mother.

Soon, the tone of the letters changed. She didn't understand why he was not responding. She knew he had received the letters, because they were not returned to her. Next she wrote,

"Robert, I am desperate to hear from you! Do you not care for me or the baby at all? If you do not write soon, I will do something terrible. I cannot raise this child without a father."

And, I guess she did. This letter was dated April first of the year I was born, and she married Howard the end of April. I was born the end of October. Well, I now knew for sure. Robert was my father. *My God!* Robert was my father! What had Augusta been thinking! I could hardly take this information in. I had a father. Robert.
One letter simply broke my heart.

"My Dearest Robbie, Do you remember when you whispered to me that I was marrying the wrong man? It was the day of the wedding and I was leaving for Saint Paul. You stopped me at the train. The second you said those words, I knew you were right. I was a fool, though, and

so caught up in my own hurt I couldn't do what my heart told me was right. I married Howard anyway. My pain was so great, I couldn't see past it. I was also a coward. I had learned throughout my life, never to care to deeply for anyone. People leave you. But you, dear Robert, broke down my defenses and I loved you with all that I was. I do still. But it scared me to death, and I married a man I couldn't be hurt by, someone who would never get close enough. I needed a father for Emily. I have made such a terrible mistake! Please, come Robbie. I will be at the cottage all summer waiting for you. Love, Marie"

The next nine letters were a variation on this theme. Some mentioned me and how fast I was growing. Some told him of my painting talent, or of seeing his work on the pages of magazines or at small galleries. All were sad and lonely. The letters grew shorter as she was sinking into an abyss. The very last letter said,

"Robbie, I think of you every day. I have waited for you for ten years and I know now that you will never come to me.

226

I have missed my chance with you because of my foolishness and I am heartbroken. I love my daughter, our daughter, but it is not enough. Without you, I have no heart, no life. I have tried, but I have no will left. Please take our child. And please forgive me. Know that I have always loved you and I will forever, but I will not return here. This must be what poetic justice feels like. Marie"

I was sitting in a daze in the middle of the foyer floor and hating my grandmother with a new intensity. How could she have done this to her own daughter! Both of her daughters. As surely as if she used a gun, Augusta killed my mother! I was sobbing uncontrollably, when Robert came in. He stopped dead in his tracks when he saw the letters in my hands. I wasn't able to speak, so I just held them out to him. Robert took them and left me. Sully followed him to another room, and Lily lay with her worried head in my lap. I realized I still held the hankie when I reached out my hand to stroke Lily's head. I had held it so tightly the lace pattern was imprinted on my palm.

It was fully dark when Robert came back. I sensed him behind me. He turned on a light in the parlor so it wasn't too bright and sat beside me on the floor. Taking both my hands in his he pulled me closer. "We are family. You are my daughter. I have wondered about you ever since I first heard your name. I am so sorry, I should have known this. My heart knew, but my head was too stupid."

"Do you think we should have our DNA tested?" I asked him, knowing I didn't need it to satisfy my own mind.

"I absolutely trust these letters." Robert was firm. "She wrote just like she talked."

"I don't remember much about her anymore!" I sobbed. "And I loved her so much."

"Well then, I'll just have to tell you everything I remember," he laughed. "Almost everything. Emily, I'm so happy!" He hugged me again. "It's like a second chance, almost, isn't it?"

"It is definitely a new beginning for us," I agreed wiping my cheeks with the hankie. "Now tell me something about her."

"You have only to look in a mirror to see her. Every time I look at you, I see her. But it doesn't make me sad," he said when he saw the look on my face. "It makes me remember all the love. She was smart, like you, and she laughed easily, like you. She was creative. She would draw me little pictures and hide them in my room. It was like a game. She was easy to be around and I could tell how she was just by looking at her. And she could do the same. Even when we weren't together, we sort of were. I can still feel her, you know. Some days it's like she never died."

"With love like you two had, you were foolish not to declare it, in spite of everything. What could have been worse than what happened? You could have waited to go east, you could have defied Augusta." I shook my head.

"I didn't think she wanted me," Robert stated flatly.

"How can you say that after what you just told me!"

"I don't know. She married someone else?"

"You should have gone to her! In spite of the marriage. She was young and afraid and she hadn't heard a word from you in all that time. Love that intense doesn't change in such a short time, no matter what a person does or doesn't do. You should have told her."

"Yes." His voice was thick with unshed tears.

38

Robert was my father. Robert was my father...It was hard to absorb this amazing truth. Soon, both Robert and I had told whatever parts of the story each of us wished to share. Robert had dozens of photographs of a young Marie, a teenager, that I had never expected to see, or knew even existed. He showed them all to me and told me story after story about their lives as children. Mom had sneaked downstairs to the library to call Robert on the telephone, long after Augusta had gone to bed. He said they often talked until morning but, when I asked what they discussed all those hours, a blank look came over his face and he wasn't able to remember.

It seemed that both Myron and Selma had suspected our blood connection for some time. Lydia said that she suspected when she saw us together and noticed the many resemblances and identical gestures. Jackson wasn't home yet, and didn't know. As for me, I was reveling in my new found family. I felt like a mystery I never knew existed, was now solved. The Petersons wanted to be Grandma and Grandpa, so I tried to please them. I couldn't have hand-picked a better situation. I had felt welcome there since the first day, so I knew I belonged. I wanted, with all my being, for my mother to be here. My wishing for her was so strong, it was a physical pain. Her face and body appeared to me out of the corners of my eyes and in my mind on a daily basis. She was my shadow. I had long ago learned to live with it, and expected it never would leave me completely.

When we all were settling down from this astonishing turn of events, planning got underway in earnest for the Christmas festivities. It was decided by Myron, Selma, and Lydia that Christmas Eve would be a family affair held in Augusta's parlor. Although, they all carefully called it Emily's parlor, and Christmas Day would be another celebration like Thanksgiving Day. Robert insisted that I was to be reintroduced as his daughter, no matter what anyone thought about it. His parents approved, as did I.

With only a couple of weeks to go, we started collecting greens and I picked out two beautiful trees for decorating. The tree for the cottage, Ray helped me set up, but I left the decorating to share with Jackson. The pine smell in the house was glorious. When we set up the tree at the main house in the parlor, Ray and Robert thought we needed one for the living room as well, since there would be so many here to celebrate. Lydia remembered packing several boxes in the attic with decorations of all kinds, so we went to look.

"Look at these!" Maryalice exclaimed. "They are so beautiful! Colors and glitter and lights. It's wonderful."

"There is enough here to fill a shop." Katie, Ray and Maryalice's youngest, noted with glee. "They are so fragile and old-fashioned and elegant. Some of these have got to be from Europe. This Santa looks more like an ancient Father Christmas from Russia, don't you think?"

"Yes I do. You know, I have been thinking, we should all stay here on Christmas Eve. Together. The entire family. There's more than enough room and the house will be warm and toasty. It is going to be so beautiful; we need to look at it for more than one or two days."

Maryalice and Katie loved the idea too. "Some of us can stay all week."

"Yes!" joined Bettyanne, Katie's sister. "It will be like we rented a whole resort for a week's vacation."

All joyous about our plan, we lugged the boxes downstairs and started to unpack them. Most of the ornaments were the traditional balls, icicles, garlands, large colored lights, Santa's, angels, animals of all sorts and a few dogs and cats with red bows around their necks. There were incredible hand-painted bells that were so fragile we were afraid to use them. On the inside edge was hand printed "Saint Petersburg." So these were Russian then. Some of the Santa's had an old European look about them as well, especially the ones riding reindeer with tiny bells on the saddles. There was another box filled with candles of all sizes and candle holders to match. Maryalice unwrapped a box of exquisite balls with "Marie" etched on one and "Grace" on another. Others had Lydia's children, "Ruth," "Alice," "John Jr.", and "Mark". Another had "Lydia and John" printed in script with the date 1938. The box also contained several broken balls, whose names were unreadable, but I could guess them.

Myron, Selma, and Robert joined us for a late lunch. Lydia had set out sandwich makings and we all made our own. Of course, there was lots of coffee. I cornered Ray and Myron as the others were cleaning up.

"I have been thinking of getting Robert a puppy for Christmas. What do you think?"

Myron looked skeptical. "What will he do with it when he's away?" He asked.

"I'll take care of it. I'd love to." I laughed at his look. It told me that he was afraid that task would fall to him and his wife.

"You know," Ray was thoughtful, "He's been eyeing that Golden Retriever we see around once in awhile."

"That's what I thought. Do you think Greg could help me find one?" Ray said he'd get Greg's phone number and an hour later, he slipped me a piece of paper.

By evening, everyone was ready to go and I was ready to make that phone call. The house had never been so fragrant or lovely. I was beginning to love it almost as much as my cottage. We had wrapped tiny lights around the green pine garlands and hung them over doorways and down wall edgings. Jackson's Victorian decorations were on the tree in the parlor and Augusta's on the tree in the living room, so we could close that fragile room off from small children's hands when we weren't watching. More tiny lights were strung across the china cupboards in the dining room and the glass behind them magnified both their beauty and number.

Mom would have been proud. She had been the queen of Christmas for me. Every year she outdid the one before. I definitely got my love of this holiday from her.

233

We would shop and wrap many small gifts for each other. We baked several kinds of Swedish cookies like almond spritz sugar and butter cookies, pepparkakor, a snappy ginger cookie, and Christmas bread with cardamon. My favorite was fattigmands with a small amount of brandy mixed in the dough. Mom said these were known as the poor man's cookie, but I never could find out why.

We also made traditional things like decorated frosted sugar cookies which Dad could eat by the handful until I told him they took too much time to fashion for him to eat so fast. He tried to eat them slower when I was watching. I guess I still thought of him as Dad. Strange to realize he wasn't. Had he known? Was that why he seemed so distant with me? Probably. It certainly would explain the life we shared. Or didn't share.

Mom always made us matching dresses for the holiday, too, with a tie for Dad. Once she even made a matching dress for my favorite doll, a "Sweet Sue" doll. She was much larger than the popular "Barbie" dolls, and much more reasonably proportioned. Dad actually wore the tie a few times, although he thought everything, but the tree, was a waste of time. The tree, he loved and it often took the three of us hours to pick out the best one. We had these paper hearts made from old Christmas cards or wrapping paper that were braided together and hung on the tree. Grandma Bengta had made them and tried to teach me, but my results were so clumsy, she would remake them. I never minded though, as she made it all such fun. I remember one year I was driving them all nuts in my excitement. Grandma Bengta tied me to the staircase with a dish towel so she could set the table without breaking dishes by tripping over me. She had a lovely way of wrapping gifts with another, smaller gift, wrapped up inside the first or tied on the package with a bow. Ah, as a child it was all such an adventure.

Even the midnight church service at our Lutheran and very Swedish, church was special. Everyone would dress in their absolute best and the church was lit only by candlelight. I always loved the carols, and even Dad would sing. Often as we were leaving the church, it would be snowing and it was like specially ordered magic for me.

All that changed of course, the year Mom died. No more enchantment. Christmas turned into just another day. Dad had no interest in the holiday after his parents died, so even the tree became a thing of the past. I was usually home alone on Christmas Eve and on Christmas Day; Dad only watched football games on television.

So, this year was even more special, and I intended to enjoy every second of it with my new family. My real family. I called Greg to see what he could do to help with the puppy.

"I think it's a terrific idea, Emily. Uncle Robbie always seems sort of lonely, don't you think?"

"Yes I do, and I want to do something about that. Did he tell you…"

Greg interrupted with a whoop.

"That you are his daughter? You bet! I think he has told half the state by now!" Greg gave me several phone numbers to call about puppies and we said good bye. I started with the closest place and got a young boy.

"Greg Peterson told me you might have a litter of Retrievers," I started in.

"We only have two left and Mom said we could keep them." Then, with the phone somewhat removed from his mouth I heard "But Mom, you said!" The boy's voice was replaced by a laughing woman.

"Hello? You are calling about the puppies?" she asked me.

"Yes, but I certainly don't want to upset your son." I was laughing, too, as I could hear his arguments in the background.

"My son has two adult Golden's and if he keeps one puppy that will be plenty. Although I'm sure he won't agree."

They didn't live very far away and we agreed to meet at their home the following morning. This was going to be fun. Being a somewhat reasonable person, I had only the two dogs, but I often found myself eyeing puppies with speculation.

As it turned out, they lived only two miles farther down the shore from Robert's place. So these must be the dogs he often admired. Perfect. Karen Anderson answered my knock and several barking voices accompanied her. Her son, Matt, was about six and an active little guy who needed to know all about me before I would be allowed to view his puppies. He felt much better when he knew I had two dogs already.

"Can I come to play with them?" Matt wanted to know.

"He's been lonely this winter," his mother said. "He misses his school friends, who live in town, and his dad is off in the Army Reserves for a month."

"Dad will be here before Christmas!" Matt happily informed me. Taking my hand, he led me to a large playpen filled with shredded paper and two yellow fluff balls. My god, but they were cute.

"This one is Butterball, and he's a boy. This one is Angel and she's a girl." Matt was as proud as the beautiful adult Goldens laying next to the playpen wagging with satisfaction. The pups were identical.

"Which one do you like best?" I asked Matt while we cuddled the pups.

"Sometimes I like Butterball and sometimes I like Angel." He told me with a serious face which then broke into a huge smile. "But Butterball's a boy, like me."

"Okay then, it's settled and I'll take Angel. But, Matt, this is a present for Robert Peterson, and he will most likely name her something else. Will that be okay with you?"

He nodded sagely and said "I can keep a secret."

"Good boy." I paid for the puppy and Matt agreed to keep her until a few days before the holiday. His mother promised to keep him away from Robert and I invited the family to come on Christmas Day. Matt brightened considerably.

"Okay! Then I can see Angel again. And play with your dogs, too." He trotted off making plans for the visit out loud with the two adult dogs.

39

One gift taken care of, several more to go. I was gazing at the decorated trees at Augusta's the next afternoon, admiring the hand painted balls with the names etched on the sides and thought I could maybe do something like that. I used to be good at calligraphy back in school. I plucked several light colored plain balls off the tree and put them in a box to carry home. If it didn't work, I could paint them a solid darker color. Practicing on paper first, I decided I liked the painted names better than the ink ones. The ink names were neater, but the painted ones were more colorful and cheerful. Plus, they were easier to make as I was handier with a paint brush than a narrow ink pen.

By the end of daylight, I had finished Selma, Lydia, and Katie. Maryalice and Bettyanne would take longer. I was quite happy with the results so far. I painted dark green holly with red berries, then the name, then more holly and berries with my tiniest brush. It was such a good time that I finished my painting of the lake as well.

As I cleaned up, I happened to look out the windows to see the most glorious northern lights. Aurora Borealis, what a lovely name. I hadn't seen them in real life before, just in movies, so I was stunned by their magic and beauty as they danced their ballet across the sky, stretching and condensing as they went. Without really thinking about it, I began to paint. By three a.m., I was done. I had painted a dark calm lake with pines on the opposite shore in a thin strip at the bottom of the canvas, and wavy strips of green, purple, silver, and pink with bits of yellow woven in, with some visible stars. I loved it! Sully had given up and was sleeping at the door. But Lily was pulling at my pants and whining, so out we went. I sat on the dock until dawn was dimming the waves of color. By then, I realized how cold I was, even with two dogs in my lap. I went to bed with an empty stomach and most of my clothes on, dreaming of swimming in a lake of northern lights.

As I began to wake up, I saw Jackson's sleeping form next to me. His arm was draped over my clothed body and I remembered the lights over the water. I kissed him awake so I could share.

"Jackson, wake up!"

"I am awake," he mumbled and turned away.

"No, you're not." I climbed on top of him to find his lips again. This time he kissed me back and wrapped his arms tightly around me and we flipped over.

"Yes, I am." And he proceeded to prove it.

After I had been soundly kissed and gently undressed, we made love. Jackson trailed his fingers up and down my legs, then my body and when he cupped my breasts and lightly nipped at my nipples, I was so ready! Pulling him deep inside, his penis filling me exactly, I looked in his eyes, not knowing which of us was moaning. We kissed as we climaxed and he relaxed against me. I clamped my limbs around his glorious body and held him to me, never wanting to move, running my fingertips over the muscles of his back and shoulders. As we lay there lost in each other, he began to stir inside me again and I rocked my body to his rhythm until the sun exploded in our heads and we sank back onto the mattress. As I was coming back to normal, I looked at the doorway and laughed. Sully and Lily were sitting there with their heads cocked and ears up. Jackson laughed, too, and sat up.

"Guess I forgot to close the door this time." Both dogs seemed to know they were now invited and leapt onto the bed with us.

I pulled him down and back under the covers for a bear hug. "Welcome home, my love."

We kissed for a long time, sweet and slow, with none of the urgency of before. Just the comfort of togetherness, and love, and complete trust. Jackson said the most wonderful thing ever. Something I never thought I would hear from another person.

"Emily, you are my home." He was propped on his elbow, smiling down at me, and the blankets somewhere at the foot of the bed. "My God, but you are beautiful." His fingers playing with my navel. "Especially this little dab of blue paint."

"I'm surprised there is just a little paint. I've been working."

"Yes, I saw. I thought it was Robert's." I looked surprised, I guess because he continued. "Really, it looks like his work, Emily. I can tell you were painting something you were very involved in."

"It was the first time I had seen the northern lights. I was entranced and sat out on the dock 'til dawn."

"Ah, that explains the clothes." Time to get up and get on with the day. I slipped into clean underwear and the same shirt and jeans.

"Jackson, the most amazing thing has happened. I found Marie's letters. I read them and…"

"Robert is your father."

I stared at him surprised yet again about this talent he and his grandmother possessed.

"Gran and I have been speculating on this ever since you arrived."

"It seems we all have and no one was talking with anyone else about it." I added.

"No one wanted to hurt you or Robert in case it wasn't true. I sure am glad it is true though. If I'm not enough to make you stay here, maybe together Robert and I are."

"Oh Jackson, you are my home now, too. I am not going anywhere."

The dogs were very antsy, so we went out. It was snowing again and colder as well. The sky was heavy with clouds, so much so, that I couldn't see across the bay. I told Jackson he got home just in time for a major storm.

"Yeah. I heard about it and took an earlier flight. This storm could close the airports for awhile. I think the northern lights always tell us when this will come. It's my theory, anyway." He chuckled at my skeptical expression. "I said it's just a theory," he defended himself.

"Well, I believe you. Let's feed the pets and go to Petersons for supplies." We took Jackson's truck because the snow was already too deep for my little, low-to-the-ground Saab. Ray was plowing out the parking lot, but it was filling right back up. Inside the store, people were gathered in the bar talking about the weather, all excited like people get when it's a real storm. A bag of groceries at everyone's feet. I left Jackson to greet his friends and went to see Myron and Selma.

"We saved you some milk, bread, and eggs, Granddaughter." Selma loved using that title. She hugged me and laughed. "I can't get used to that," she said.

"Call me Emily. We all know I am your granddaughter. Besides, I might not know you're talking to me." She handed me several loaves of homemade bread. Rye, wheat, and Swedish Christmas bread with cardamon. Yum.

"It smells like ginger cookies, too." Jackson took a whiff of the sack.

"I've been baking." Selma smiled at him fondly. So what else is new, I thought. Jackson piled some canned foods, cereal, and crackers on the counter and I added chocolate, peanut butter, and several cheeses. Myron picked up another large bag and set it on the counter as well. "I took the liberty of getting you some fresh fruit and vegetables." He smiled shyly. "I know it's good for the birds."

"Myron, you've been studying!" Selma was laughing at him.

"And here is Lydia's order." I think he wanted to change the subject to avoid more teasing from his wife.

"We'll see that she gets it."

Back out in the truck, I was shocked at how fast the weather was worsening. Ray had given up and parked the plow in an open shed. We headed slowly for Lydia's. I think Jackson drove by instinct, because nothing was visible.

"Em, I'm going to drop you off on the way. I think I should stay with my grandmother."

Not wanting to lose him so fast, I made another offer. "Let's pack her up and bring her to us. She can give me cooking lessons."

"Not that you need them, of course. It's just to make her feel needed, right?" We were both chuckling until we nearly went off the road. At Lydia's, the snow was already half way up to our knees and just below the running boards on the truck. While Jackson tried to clean off the windshield wipers and put heavy chains on the tires, I went to get Lydia. She had a small case packed and was watering her houseplants.

"I knew you would come," she said as she donned her heavy coat and boots. "I'm ready." Handing me a bag of baking supplies, she picked up her suitcase and we trudged out to the truck. Jackson helped with the bags and got Lydia into the truck and we crawled home. Literally crawled. The ten minute trip took over an hour. This was going to be a true winter storm!

40

We got Lydia settled in my room since it was the closest to the heat and Jackson and I took the larger bedroom in the southeast corner by the fireplace. I was going to strip the bedding, but Jackson simply switched the mattresses. It's good to have a strong man around once in awhile, I teased him.

Jackson went out to try ice fishing for our supper and took the dogs with him. Lydia was going through my cupboards and taking things out for soup. She was tsking and making a list as she sorted through the cupboards.

"It's no wonder you don't cook, child! There is nothing here to cook with."

She quickly put me to too work, chopping onions and peeling potatoes. From her own supplies, she took carrots, celery root, spinach, and turnips. We chopped those together in companionable silence. I liked the way she chopped the vegetables without ever lifting the knife from the cutting board. With a measured movement, she advanced the knife down the neat pile of vegetables and sliced through.

"Hot vegetable soup is what we need to go with the fish Jackson will catch." She started simmering it.

"If he catches, you mean," I said.

"Oh, he will." And, of course, he did. We had a savory meal and watched the fire for a time, took the dogs out for a last run, and went to bed. I lay in Jackson's arms for a long while, listening to the wind play around the cabin and feeling snug and very lucky.

The storm hadn't let up at all during the night. There was a half inch of frost and ice on the inside corners of the older windows at the rear of the cabin. Jackson and crew had run out of fine weather, and hadn't replaced them yet. The new windows were still piled in the attic along with the lumber.

It was actually difficult to get the door pushed open enough to let the dogs out. We didn't even bother to leash Sully. He couldn't run away in this deep snow. He never even got off the step, and he sure did not like the cold snow tickling his bottom. Jackson shoveled off the steps and gave up on the rest.

"We must have four feet by now, including what we already had," he told us when he came in, shaking his body, not unlike a dog, to rid himself of the clinging flakes. "Probably more, really. And it isn't slowing down any."

"Well then." Lydia was tying an apron around her middle. "Let's make coffee and breakfast, shall we? What would you like?"

"Swedish pancakes," Jackson answered, without mulling it over. Lydia got out flour, milk, sugar, and eggs.

"This is an old favorite family recipe," she said to me. "You might want to write it down." She cracked three eggs into a bowl and whipped them up until they were thick and creamy. Next she stirred in one and a fourth cup of milk, then one tablespoon of sugar and a dash of salt and stirred some more. Last she added three fourths cup of flour and mixed it all until it was very smooth. She set a large cast iron griddle on top of the fire in the cookstove and buttered it liberally. When it was hot, she poured a thin circle of batter the size of the griddle. "When the underside is light brown, we'll flip it over," Lydia lectured, smiling.

Jackson got out jam from the refrigerator and Lydia put it back in.

"Use this." She took a jar of shiny maroon colored jam from her bag of supplies. "It's this year's lingonberries," she told us. As the pancakes were done, she piled them on a plate and stuck them in one of the warming ovens at the top of the woodstove until all were finished. Then we each took one and spread the jam over the cake, rolled it up and devoured the treat. It was an extraordinary new taste sensation for me. It somehow even tasted Swedish. Rich and sweet.

We three spent the rest of the morning and most of the afternoon decorating the tree and wrapping gifts. Lydia had brought some of hers along with her and closed herself in her room for a time. The remainder of Jackson's Victorian ornaments looked so wonderful on the tree. There were strings of tiny silver foil stars, so fragile and sparkly when they caught the light. More strings of silver beads, and glass icicles, and small white angels riding reindeer. Several antique old-world Santa's that looked like ancient Russian grandfathers, or maybe Father Time from Fairy Tales, with huge bellies and stern expressions.

My favorites were the china painted dogs of all sizes and types. Some had red caps on between their ears, and some were frolicking; one that looked like Sully, was napping under a tree and flat on his back. Another riding in a red wagon. A larger, gold dog was poking his head up out of a huge canvas bag full of wrapped gifts.

Myron had even thought to add cranberries to the supplies, so we popped popcorn and strung it with the cranberries and hung that on the tree as well. Pearl and Tinkerbell flittered around, and Tink sat in the tree. Pearl thought the tree was too scary and flew back to his cage. He sat on top and scolded us loudly, though. "Whatsa matter whatcha doin what are you doing here what are you doing to me good morning I love you!"

There were also a dozen more words we had never heard before. All were out of sequence and made little sense; "fish, tools, darn, water and sweetheart." We had to put Tinkerbell back in his cage when he started to eat the popcorn. He gave a very loud wolf whistle when Lydia walked by his cage.

"Don't get too excited Gran, he does the same thing to me." Jackson and Lydia shared a smile.

We had leftover pancakes and soup for supper and when the electricity went out, we stoked the fires and went to bed. The dogs decided Lydia needed them more than we did, and she was delighted when they snuggled up against her. Oh well, I had Jackson. I knew sometime during the long night, my Sully would come back.

41

It took a couple of days, but finally the snow stopped. It was still heavy and grey, but there was no new snow. The electricity was back, and we could hear Ray on the snowplow, which sounded like it was working harder than usual. I looked out and saw that it was a state plow, and much larger than Ray's. Within minutes, we were dug out except the plow had just gone down the lane and nowhere else. The driver had cleared the way to the front door of Augusta's house, leaving high banks of the white stuff that walled in the lane. We had breakfast and coffee and cleaned up as Ray came and finished the work. Jackson joined him in hand shoveling until the walk and the vehicles were free. He had already been to Lydia's, he said, and the way to the store was clear. Lydia came out to hand him a thermos and he was on his way. Jackson and I took turns shoveling from the lane to the big house, only a few feet the state plow hadn't been able to get to, and went in to check on it. After resetting the clocks and relighting the pilot light on the furnace, I led Jackson through the house to show off all the decorating we had done. He loved the idea of an overnight with the family. We were planning our shopping trip to Brainerd, when there was a loud knock on the door. No one ever knocked; they simply walked in calling out as they came. Jackson motioned me to stay where I was, but of course I followed him to the door. We opened it to see Marcus standing there with a look of total disgust on his otherwise handsome face.

"I figured if I was going to get any response from you, I'd have to come up here. Do you have any idea how bad the roads are?"

"Then perhaps you shouldn't have driven here," I told him firmly, with my hands planted on my hips.

He shouldered his way past us and dropped a box on the floor, ignoring me as per his usual. He acted as if I hadn't spoken a word. Also his usual.

"This is some of your junk." He pointed to the box. I hadn't thought I wanted anything from his house until I opened the box. My laptop computer, a few books that had been my mother's, some pictures of Howard, Bengta, Algot, and me, and, best of all, a box of Christmas ornaments my Mom and I had made together. I was surprised and even a little touched by this gesture. But, I was also sure this wasn't why he had come. I looked up from the box to find Marcus and Jackson sizing each other up.

"Who is this guy?" Marcus asked in his usual insisting manner. I ignored the question. I could play this game, too.

"What do you want?" I asked as I stood to face him.

"It's freaking cold; can I have a cup of coffee or something?" I started to say there wasn't any, when Jackson smiled with malice at Marcus and answered.

"Sure, I'll make some." He sauntered to the kitchen.

"This is quite the house." Marcus was looking around. "Give me a tour." There he goes again, I thought. Demanding, not asking. Only I was stronger now, and did not want him here, not in my house!

"No."

He started to push past me anyway, but I moved to block him. "No means no, Marcus." He just shrugged his shoulders and turned toward the library.

"The lady said no, you idiot." Jackson was at my side immediately, sensing trouble. Marcus smirked.

"Where is that coffee?"

"I changed my mind." Jackson was very still. "Why don't you get to the point of this unwelcome visit?" he stated flatly.

"This is no concern of yours, bud." Marcus was getting angry.

"I'm making it my concern. *Bud*."

Marcus backed down like I knew he would. Jackson was bigger and Marcus only bullied people who were smaller than he was, like me and all the other women in his life. He turned his back on Jackson as much as was possible, and faced me.

"If you want this divorce, Emily, and I can see you do," he gestured to Jackson with his head. "I need something from you. This house and property is worth a lot of money and you," he pushed his finger into my chest, "are holding out on me!" I shoved him back so hard he almost lost his balance. His face reddened and his eyes glared into my face.

"You shouldn't have done that!" Marc glowered, eyes shooting arrows.

"No Marcus, it's you who shouldn't have come. Now leave." I could tell he still didn't know how far he could push this new Emily. He looked confused for just a second and then was ready for combat, until he remembered Jackson. As he backed toward the door he said, "This isn't over!" But I slammed the door as soon as he was through it, without answering.

"We will have to deal with him sooner or later." Jackson said.

"I'll call Augusta's lawyers and ask them what the legal aspects are. Now, where were we?"

"Making coffee, I think," Jackson answered as he kissed me.

42

Before long, Lydia was ready to go back to her own house because, she said, there was still so much to do for the holiday and she was way behind. She didn't like being away from her geraniums more than a few days, she said. Jackson drove her and I went back to the main house to the attic. My intention had been to call the Anderson/Erickson Law Firm, but I got distracted as usual by exploring. I thought maybe I could get some ideas for more presents. When I spied the old roll-top desk, I knew it was perfect for Jackson. He was always spreading his papers and plans for museum projects all over the table. Between that and all my painting supplies, it was hard to find a place to eat.

I found a carton and began to empty the desk drawers and cubbyholes. When I pulled out the center drawer I found, stuck in a crack on the underside, a photograph. It was very old and frayed, with a sepia tint. But I could see it was of a young curly haired man in a suit and a lovely young woman in Native American dress. It was quite a formal pose. I stared at it for a long while before I realized it was a wedding photo. It was like all the early 19th-

252

century wedding pictures I had seen, with the man seated and the woman standing next to and slightly behind him. I always thought it was very sexist, until Grandma Bengta said it was because the bride didn't want to wrinkle her gown. That made sense. Something about the woman's face looked so familiar. I took the photo downstairs to the hall of ancestors, as I called it. There was no match. Still… I put it in my pocket for later speculation. As I turned to go back to the attic one portrait caught my eye. I had been looking for the wrong person! The young man in the photo was a dead ringer for Bertel Lundquist. Oh my! The woman was not Irena, his wife. Irena had a Mediterranean look about her, this woman was Native American. I took a closer look. Or was she really? Then it hit me like a slap in the face and I literally ran to Augusta's bedroom. Now I was completely dazed. She looked like Augusta, Grace, and Marie. She looked like me. The photograph had obviously been hidden. From whom? Not Bertel of course. I went back to the roll-top desk.

I carefully sorted through the papers I had tossed in the carton and then the remaining drawers. All there was to be found were old receipts, bills, bank statements, and the like. I started a list of what I had noticed that made no sense: this photo, the box of Native American Indian baby clothes, no birth certificate or passport for Augusta, the unused hope chest items in the trunk.

I was too stunned to be thinking clearly, so it took a few minutes. Obviously Augusta was this woman's child and most likely Bertel was her father. People had been telling me how much all the women in my family looked alike, and not one of us looked the tiniest bit like Irena. It seemed odd to me now, that I hadn't thought about that before.

I thought about it while I finished with the desk, oiled it, and threw a blanket over it until later. I was expecting Jackson soon, so I went downstairs to the library. I again went through the desk there but there wasn't anything hidden away, no new-found secret to unravel. But this was Rudolf's desk not Bertels. I found a leather bound ledger and took the Swedish dictionary off the shelf. I didn't need the dictionary, though. When I opened the ledger, everything was written in English. What a relief. Most of the entries were of acres of land both bought and sold or bartered. Only one seemed pertinent. In 1893, Bertel sold over one thousand acres to the Ojibwe Tribe of Mille Lacs Lake for one dollar.

43

I remembered there being several families of American Indians around here the summers Mom and I spent in the cottage. She called them the Chippewas and I learned later, in a class in college, that Chippewa was a name the white settlers gave to the local Ojibwe tribes. I couldn't remember why. There had been several children that I played with and the man with the pony rides was also Ojibwe. Garden produce and eggs were delivered to us, as well as, occasional gifts from a man who had been warm and friendly both to my mother and me.

We went fishing together. He took me and several other children on walks through the woods. He told us stories and the Ojibwe names for everything we saw. I thought, if I tried hard enough, I would remember some of them. I grew up thinking he was a nice man, but what if he was more? What if we were related? The more I thought about him, the more I remembered. In fact, I think he was the person who taught me the game of leaving me behind and becoming something else! I remembered playing the game with the old man and a young boy. Sam, maybe?

The object of the game was to learn about the world and other ways of viewing things by totally being another. Using only my imagination, I would become an eagle, a muskrat, a sunfish, or anything else. Once, I became Sam and he became me. After that, we became best friends. Sometimes we would play the part for hours, sometimes for days. I would always be in character at this time. I would try to think like what I was becoming; respond to the outside influences in kind. Poor Mom! She finally had to ask; "Am I talking to my daughter, Emily? Or to Sam?"

Of course, there were limits to this game, physically. I never did really fly. But, I think the real purpose was to stretch my imagination and it surely did that. It was easy for a child to learn this. I tried to teach my mother and she did try. We drove my father crazy with it. I learned respect, tolerance, and appreciation that are still with me today.

I was pretty sure I could find the house of the old man. I needed to check something back at the cottage, a secret hiding place I had made as a child that I had completely forgotten about until this minute. I put on Sorels and parka and headed out the door only to see Marcus sitting in his car directly in my path. God! I assumed he had gone back to Iowa.

"Marcus. Go home."

"Not until I get what you owe me."

"If I owe you something, and I'm not sure I do, you will get it. But not from me, from my lawyers. You haven't given me time to contact them yet."

"Where is your friend?" Marcus looked like he already knew Jackson wasn't here and it was just little

Emily again. The woman he could push around. I walked around his car and continued on my way. When I realized he probably didn't know the cottage was mine, I stopped and went back to the car.

"I will call the lawyers today. Okay? Now will you go?" I guess Marcus took that as a sign I was weakening, because he got out of the car and grabbed my arms.

"What else are you hiding from me, you bitch!" He shook me and my footing slipped as I fell backwards. I thought Marcus was reaching to help me up, but I never got the chance to find out. Jackson came out of nowhere and shoved Marcus back against his car. He had me up on my feet before Marcus could recover.

"Unless you want a fight right here and now, leave." Jackson was dead calm and quiet. A sign I had come to know as dangerous to anyone who was trouble. Marcus seemed to understand it too, and got into his car and backed it nearly into us as he started down the lane. At the end, he stopped and threw several handfuls of what looked like cloth, out his window. He took off with such anger and speed, he almost drove into a tree.

"Thank God he didn't hit that tree." Jackson was laughing. "It's always been my favorite."

We walked down the lane to see what Marcus left us. My clothes, shoes, jewelry, and makeup were scattered over the ground. Good grief! Had I ever dressed this way? Spike heels, cheap satin, low cut dresses, tight sweaters, and very short shorts. I started to laugh until it turned to tears. Jackson held me until the storm subsided.

"Are you okay, Em?"

"Oh yeah. I am more than okay. Let's get a garbage bag and get rid of all this junk."

We got a large garbage bag from the cottage and I didn't even look at my things as I stuffed them furiously into the bag. Done! If only getting rid of Marcus was so easy.

"What do you want to do with the rest of today?" Jackson was still somewhat quiet and careful with my feelings.

"I want to see if my old hiding place is still in the cottage. Want to come?"

Jackson grinned at me. "Oh yeah. Childhood secrets of yours have got to be interesting." We went back inside and to my bedroom. I pushed the bed to the wall and checked the floorboards for the loose one. It was still here. I lifted it and peered inside the hole. The old shoe box was on the verge of complete deterioration, but the contents were there. I gently lifted them out one by one and handed them to Jackson. My first pair of moccasins, hand stitched by the Ojibwe man, and beaded on the top with likenesses of local flowers. My mother kept throwing the ragged things out, but I would save them. The stitching was unique. After all this time, the puckers all around the edges were evident. I remembered the old man telling me that one word for Ojibwe was "puckering." There was a necklace made from antler bone and shells and shiny agates from Mille Lacs Lake, which my friends and I had found on an outing with the old man. There were several arrowheads and bits of flint, a knife blade, that looked more like a rock than a blade as it had been my first attempt at knapping, a small leather beaded drawstring bag, that needed to be oiled and softened up again, and the "special thing." I looked up with awe and understanding. Jackson appeared puzzled. He didn't understand yet.

"What is all this stuff?" he asked me. I told him about the things I had found in the house.

"You think you are related to this tribe?" Jackson looked stunned.

"I remember more and more about my childhood summers every day. And yes, maybe. But anyone who would know is dead." I showed him the photo of Bertel and the woman.

"Wow. She could be you."

Then, I picked up the special thing and held it out to him. It was a carved picture of Bertel and the Indian woman holding a baby. Behind them, were shadowy figures of several other Indians, but no Swedes. Above the people flew a small hawk and an eagle. There was a log cabin off to the side of the people and Jackson nearly dropped the carving in surprise.

"That is Lydia's family place!

"Could it also have been Bertel's first home in Minnesota?"

"It's possible."

"I think I might know where to go for answers. If I can find it," I announced with excitement, as I was eager to discover more.

"Can we wait until tomorrow? If we get lost, or even if we find it, night is coming," said my rational Jackson.

I certainly did not want to wait, but Jackson was right. Besides, it wasn't very likely that anyone would still live in the tiny house by Lake Mille Lacs.

44

We made a quick supper of fish, canned beans, and
fried potatoes with green peppers and cheese. It doesn't
sound like much, but it tasted delicious. I was standing at
the sink daydreaming about the past and washing dishes
when Jackson came up behind me and wrapped his arms
around my middle and hugged me hard.

"I love you, did you know that?" He whispered in my
hair, his voice husky and his breath warm. His hands slid
under my sweater and cupped my breasts. He was kissing
my neck, my ear lobes, and then his hands slid under the
waistband of my jeans. He slowly moved them, caressing
softly, down, down until his fingertips found what they
were seeking. I sighed and arched my body back into his
as his fingers entered me and we were both rocking back
and forth. Jackson turned me to him and unzipped my
jeans and they dropped to the floor. He pulled off my
sweater, bra, and panties and kissed everything he could
reach. He knelt down in front of me and slightly separated
my thighs to reach inside me with his tongue. As I cried
out, Jackson lifted me and I wound my legs around his

waist and guided him inside as we slumped to the floor together.

"Bed?" He whispered on my lips.

"No time." I whispered back.

We lay in a sweaty tangle of limbs, until the cold of the floor reached our subconsciously stupefied minds.

"Fancy a hot bath?" I asked.

"Great idea. We do think alike." The dogs came racing into the kitchen as we stood. Sully was in such a hurry that he ran straight into my legs. It seems they knew when to leave us alone and when it was okay to come back. I slept, warm from the bath and the love-making, dreaming of Indians and families and making love.

The next day was gloriously bright. Sun sparkled on the deep snow and made it look like the snow piles were coated in diamonds or crystals. It was cold though. I dressed in my warmest clothes and still Jackson asked me to put on more.

"I won't be able to move," I complained. "I can't bend over now!" And I proceeded to prove it.

"At least, put on another pair of socks." He handed me a pair of woolen ones that looked hand knit.

"Lydia?"

"Yep."

"Well, okay then." And I pulled them on. Surprisingly, my feet still fit into my boots. Jackson picked up some sandwiches he'd made and a thermos of coffee, and we were off. I was very excited. Perhaps also somewhat nervous about who or what I might find out. Another adventure.

We drove to Mille Lacs Lake and turned off the highway onto a thin gravel road that went all around the lake. There were no summer cabins here, no fancy boats or water toys. Small, neat houses stood scattered at the edge of the woods, some with cars at their sides, others without. There were several fish drying racks and the whole area smelled like hickory wood smoke. A few children played in the snow and sunshine. They stopped and watched us pass. A snowball struck the truck and I looked, but saw no one. We passed a woman outside shaking a rug and another sweeping snow from her steps. It was eerily quiet and the tires sounded like thunder on the crisp windswept snow. After another mile, things looked more familiar to me and I asked Jackson to stop. I got out of the truck and slowly approached a tiny house with smoke coming out of the chimney. I was uneasy. I hadn't thought what to say, or how to explain myself. All I had was a single photograph and a feeling. With a suddenness that stopped me, a red tail hawk swooped down at my side to grab a field mouse out of a ditch, as though he didn't even notice me. It was gone in an instant with a wild screech, but it shook me. Was this some omen? I felt I was standing at the edge of the world and I was alone here. Jackson may as well have been in another country.

The door of the house opened as I stood there and a man about my age came out on the step.

"Are you lost?" he asked me.

"I don't think so," I answered.

We looked at each other for a minute. Then another minute. The name from the past came to my lips.

"Are you Sam?"

Before he could answer, a gravelly voice called from inside the cabin. "Samuel! Bring the girl and her friend inside before you all get frostbite!"

We were gestured inside without a word. Samuel looked somewhat disgruntled at this command, but stepped aside for us.

When I was a child, I was addicted to a British television show called "Dr. Who." It was a tongue-in-cheek, slapstick drama that took place in both the past and future. The Dr.Who, and there were several who played the part, of the day traveled in the TARDIS. It was a bright Christmas red telephone booth that when entered, suddenly was huge and filled with wonders and many rooms. That was this house. It was sturdy logs, stone, and glass. The front, where we entered, had a single window and door, but inside was airy and light with a solid glass wall facing the deep woods. A fire was lit in a central fireplace and a very old man sat hunched in front of it. He looked at me with the brightest black eyes I have ever seen. We examined each other for a while and he smiled.

"Found the place after all these years. Good girl."

"Grandfather, what is this?" Samuel asked with irritation in his voice.

"Take your cap off, girl, and let Samuel have a look at you." I did as he asked, feeling unsteady. All eyes in the room were on me, and Samuel seemed amazed when he really looked at me.

"Little Sparrow?" The long forgotten name brought tears to my eyes and all I could do was nod at Samuel who was as shocked as I was.

"Ah," said the old man. "You forgot who you were for a time, eh? That's fine, you are here now and we can help you remember. I know you also. Lydia's grandson," he said to Jackson. "Welcome."

45

"Your great-grandmother was my mother's sister, Dances with Feathers, and your grandmother, Augusta, was Sparrowhawk, Bibiigiwizens. But we called her Iron Woman because she was strong. Iron Woman knew all this when she was very young, but Dances with Feathers died when Augusta was three years of age. Her second mother made her forget it and she became Augusta. An immigrant from Russia, the new mother knew nothing of our ways and she chose not to learn. Iron Woman was lost to us then. Times were very hard here in those days and there was no one to care for the child. She was Waabizhesi Clan, born of an Ojibwe mother and a white father. So, the clan gave her to your great-grandfather, Augusta's father, and his new wife to raise. That would not happen now, but those were different times." He smiled happily and continued. "Your great grandfather gave us back our land also. And now you are back home. But why has it taken you so long? One day you just disappeared and we never saw you again."

"My mother died the year I turned ten and no one brought me back here. When Augusta died, she left the property to me. She told me nothing, except that there were a lot of secrets to unravel here."

"Ah, I see…" The old man stared into the past while we all waited for him to continue.

"Your mother never knew us as family, but she did know us as friends and she brought you here often. You and Samuel were great friends, always in trouble!" He laughed. I took Samuel's hand. He gripped mine tightly, still staring at me in astonishment.

"I remember," I said, and I did. The fishing, the hunting with bows and arrows, painting flowers on deer hide, cooking over open fires, sewing our moccasins, and the stories by the campfires, the imagination game. Everything. Samuel had been as close as a brother. But I had forgotten all about him and this wonderful old man, living in another world from that of my young childhood.

"I went to see your grandmother before she died to remind her who she was. At first Iron Woman said we were not her family, but even then I think she really did know. Sometimes we forget things, you understand. She told me she would bring you back." The old man shook his head. "But she never acknowledged our bonds with words."

"Uncle," I began.

"You always called me grandfather." He interrupted me with a grin.

"Yes, I did. Grandfather, this is very confusing."

"Let me ask you this, child, do you still have the carving I made for you?" I nodded.

"That is what helped me to remember."

"That was its purpose. It is a picture of your family and your name and your totem. You are of the Hawk Clan and the Eagle Clan. They are very strong family ties and that is why you remember. You are as strong as your great-grandmother and Iron Woman were."

Samuel made us hot tea and venison stew and we listened to Grandfather's stories, until late in the day. He told us how he was injured in the Second World War, so he was able to teach us and spend time with all the children. It sounded to me as though he was the person who held the clan together and kept the stories alive. I smiled at the creation story, which was like all Native American creation stories. We, he said, were the original people, the first people, and we should never forget that. When we stood to leave, Grandfather grasped our hands and pressed something into mine. It was a blood red agate the size of a large frog, which was what it resembled.

"I found this," I said.

"Yes, and I kept it for you. I always knew you would come back, you see."

"I will come to visit you again very soon." I hugged him and Samuel also, and Jackson shook their hands.

The drive home was quiet. I wasn't sure what to say to Jackson. I didn't know how he would feel about this new family tie. He remained quiet also. When we got to the cottage, he kept the truck idling as I got out.

"I need to go and see Lydia," he said so quietly I was hardly able to hear the words. "I'll see you later? Can I take the picture of Bertel and Dances with Feathers with me?"

"Okay," was all I could answer as I handed over the picture. I didn't know what reaction I would get from Jackson, just that this wasn't it. I was extremely disappointed. I had been so sure Jackson was the one person I could count on to be there for me. When I thought about it though, we had only known each other since September. This relationship sure had advanced quickly! Maybe too quickly? Perhaps my first reaction to Jackson had been the correct one? I made supper, but couldn't eat it. The dogs were whining at the door and I knew they were looking for Jackson. I felt sick and upset and my heart was breaking. All I had needed was a word from him letting me know he loved me and was excited for me. Maybe even that this information just made me all the more interesting. I didn't know what to do about his silence. Could I have been so completely wrong?

"Damn this shit!" I yelled as I grabbed my car keys. My temper, that of Marie's, took over. I would not let this silence continue! I would go to Lydia's too, and confront Jackson and make him talk to me. However, my trusty old Saab would not start. I sat there, much too sad and frightened to even cry. I went to bed, but not to sleep. Sully snuggled close and even Lily lay up against me. By morning I was thinking of going to the Twin Cities by myself for a time out. But then what about the dogs? The birds? Did Jackson truly live here with me or was he more like a guest with privileges? I kept telling myself I was being extremely ridiculous and stupid, but I was hurt. Jackson hadn't come home.

46

I took the dogs for a long walk and we ended up at
Augusta's. There was a box of tiny multicolored lights still
to put up. With nothing else more pressing, I took them
out, plugged them in, and straightened out the tangled
strands. They looked so beautiful lying in their pools of
color. I unplugged them and just left them where they lay.
I went up to the attic to look for picture frames. I wanted to
hang the small photo of Bertel and Dances with Feathers on
the wall with all the other ancestors. It was a small photo,
but it was all I had. Dances with Feathers, Sparrow Hawk,
and Little Sparrow. I wondered if my mother had an Indian
name. I didn't think so.

Robert! He popped into my mind out of the blue.
Did he or his family know about this? I had just about had
enough of Augusta's secrets and lies! My life used to be so
ordinary and maybe I missed that a little. Although I was
getting to know who my mother's family had been and
therefore, who I was. That was exactly what I wanted.
Wasn't it?

269

I found a carton of empty picture frames and picked out a few that I liked. Now I just needed the picture. The light was fading, the dogs were sleeping at my side, and I heard the front door slam.

"Emily?" Jackson was here. I didn't answer and I hushed the dogs. I wasn't ready to see him. "Emily? Are you up there?" He was at the bottom of the stairs now and still I didn't answer. "Where the heck are you, woman?" He was mumbling as he went back downstairs and out the door. I went to watch him out the window as he crossed the yard. Twice he stopped and glanced back at the house. Sully and Lily raced down the stairs as soon as I stood. As he walked away I realized how much I cared for him. Tall and strong and trustworthy, remember? If I didn't fix this soon, we would end up like Robert and Marie. Hadn't I already vowed that wouldn't be my fate? For all I knew, there wasn't even a problem. Besides, I reasoned with myself, Jackson often went to talk to Lydia when something was on his mind. I think she had become his sounding board over the years. Feeling stupid, but better, I started home. Besides, I had been slowly realizing something new about myself. I wanted Jackson in my life, sure, but I didn't need him to be there. My joy and happiness was mine. I could share it, but it was mine.

I followed the cavorting dogs over the packed snow to the cabin. The windows were dark, but I thought I could see the flicker of the fireplace. Letting the dogs inside, I hung my jacket on its peg and went to stand by the fire.

"Where were you?" Jackson's voice came from the shadowy darkness.

"Just out with the dogs." I lied. "Where were you?"

270

"I told you, at Lydia's. I wanted to ask her about the picture of Bertel and Dances with Feathers. Something about it seemed familiar to me. It got late, so I stayed over. You don't have a phone, remember?"

"I guess I'll have to get one." I decided to act as normal as I could, in spite of my foolishness. I went to him and kissed him. Several times.

"I missed you," was all I said.

"Funny how used to each other we are already. I couldn't sleep either." He pulled me into his lap. "I'm sorry. I should have come home."

"I was afraid this new family might have been too much for you." Damn! I never meant to admit that!

"It wouldn't matter to me if you were half Eskimo or Chinese or Turkish. I thought you knew that."

"I did. I do."

"Okay then. Aren't you curious to find out what Lydia said?"

"Oh yes! I forgot why you were there."

Jackson led me to the kitchen and turned on the light. The photograph was on the table.

"Tell me what you see."

"Just a newly married couple all dressed up," I answered.

"Look closer."

"She looks more like me than he does. More than my own mother, actually, and I thought we looked alike." I kept looking. "What does she have around her neck? Is that part of her dress?"

Jackson went back into the other room and came back with a flat box about the size of a dinner plate. He set it on the table and took off the lid.

"This is what she has around her neck." It was a necklace. More like a collar really. About six inches wide and made of stones, shells, silver, ivory, bone beads, and turquoise. There were several blood red agates like the frog I had, too. It was stunning and should have been in a museum.

"It looks like a museum piece, doesn't it?" Jackson spoke my words out loud. "Lydia had it, but it belonged to Augusta. Until Augusta died, Lydia didn't know its significance, though.

The old Ojibwe man had come to visit Augusta and asked to see the necklace. All her years, Augusta had kept it in this box in the table next to her bed. It was an heirloom of sorts. Passed from mother to daughter for generations. It represents all the Ojibwe trading routes and different branches of the family. Lydia tried to give it back to the old man, so he told her the story. He also told her to give it to you."

"So why didn't she?"

"I think she would have. Lydia thought you had too much to deal with right now and just wanted to wait a little. She wanted you to be comfortable with all of us and know all the history before adding something new and possibly upsetting."

"Well, she was certainly right about that! Does anyone else know about my Ojibwe family?"

"No."

"Let's go tell them." I was ready.

272

"Right now?"

"Yes. No more secrets, okay?"

"Right." So we left for Petersons store.

47

When we pulled into the parking lot, the lights in front of the door blinked out.

"Perfect timing." Jackson took my hand and we entered the store. Myron, Selma, and Robert were all there. It felt late, but was only 6:30. I thought I should be nervous, but I wasn't. We all had had so many shocks already, what was one more?

"Just in time for some supper." Selma smiled. "Come in, come in."

Robert took our jackets and hugged me. "You look like you have a secret."

"I do. A very big one." We all settled ourselves around the table and I began. First I laid the photograph on the table.

Selma picked it up. "This is Bertel!" She said with no small amount of surprise.

"But who is the woman?" Myron was looking back and forth between me and the photograph. Lydia saw this and looked also.

"Why, it's Emily. But no, of course not!" She blushed. "It can't be, but it surely could! I mean..." Her voice trailed off into nothing and she began to pace the room.

Robert said to us all "Let's allow Emily to tell her story." He led his mother back to the table but he was the one to begin.

"Marie and I were friends of Samuel Grey Sand's father, Jem. We spent a lot of childhood time at the grandfather's, whose name I remember as Lost on the Lake. We called him Grandfather Grey Sand. And I think Marie took you there too?" Robert looked to me.

"Yes. Jackson and I were just there and we learned some things." Suddenly I was hesitant to speak. I took a deep breath and smiled at Jackson when he took my hand.

"The woman is Dances with Feathers and she was my great-grandmother, Augusta's mother, and Bertel's first wife." Selma gasped and started to question me, but Myron stayed her words with a silent hand.

"She died when Augusta was a baby and Bertel married Irena and they raised her. Grandfather Grey Sand didn't think Augusta remembered this so he reminded her just before she died."

"By god!" Myron burst out. "What I wouldn't have given to have been there for that discussion! The old bird never said a word."

"He told us that she pretty much didn't admit to remembering, but Grandfather Grey Sand thought she did. He told us he saw it in her eyes. Anyway, I guess I am part Ojibwe Indian."

"How do you feel about that?" Robert asked me.

275

"I think it's a lot more interesting than being just Swedish. I've gone from having no family left, to having two."

"Three." Jackson reminded me with a kiss.

"Ah, just when you think that you have life all figured out, it shows you another side." Selma laughed. I'm going to have a talk with Lydia, though. Shame on her for keeping such a secret from me."

"I think we all need to pool our information. Who knows what we can figure out?" Robert had a good idea going. "Is there anything either of you need to tell me and Ray? Like do we have lost relatives somewhere?" He winked at his folks.

"There can't be much more, can there?" I moaned. "I know who my parents are and I know who I love..." I stopped when everyone looked at me. "Well, that certainly can't be a surprise now!"

Sitting there, gathered around the table, we began passing plates of food and ate Selma's excellent supper. As we were finishing up, there was a knock at the back door. Myron opened it to Samuel. He stood there nervously twisting his hat in his hands.

"I don't want to butt in" he began. "I need to talk to Emily."

Myron took him by the arm and pulled him in far enough to get the door closed against the cold. Samuel saw me, and came closer.

"I'm taking Grandfather up north to my folks. They work at the casino in Walker, where my mother's band is from originally." He looked worried. "His health isn't good and I don't want him alone all winter with no help.

We will both be back in the spring, but Grandfather sent me here to tell you." He handed me a slip of paper and said his goodbye. In a way, I was relieved because I had been thinking about that also. Grandfather Grey Sand lived a tad too far away for me to be much help and neither of us had a telephone.

"What's on the paper?"

I opened it to a note written in a very shaky hand. "Go to my house and take what you find on the table."

"That's it." I told them. "I wonder why Samuel didn't just bring it, whatever it is."

"I'm wondering what it is." Selma mused. We speculated for a bit, and then went home.

48

I awoke before Jackson, dressed, and left the cabin with both dogs. My car started on the first try and I was glad it was parked at Augusta's house so it wouldn't wake Jackson. I refused to look in the rearview mirror as I exited the lane in case he was awake and following me. Some things I still like to do alone.

It was a perfect morning. A crisp, cold, sunny morning. A good day for a drive. The recent snowfalls were piled high on both sides of the narrow road, so it was like driving through a white tunnel. Not much was visible except tops of trees and snow. Every once in a while I drove by a driveway entrance. It appeared that the plow had been there not to long ago and no one else had ventured out yet. Just me and my dogs in my little green car in all that snow. I liked that feeling. A few mailboxes were barely sticking their heads out of the banks and some had been completely covered. Probably until spring. Most of the driveways hadn't been plowed, but they were the summer cabins.

When I got to the main highway the road was cleared and the white tunnel effect was gone. I stopped first at the Native American Museum and Gift Shop at Mille Lacs Lake. It was directly on the Highway, and I had been there many times as a child. This time I wanted something more than to be entertained. They weren't open yet, so I got a cup of coffee across the highway, and drank it in the car. It was warm sitting there in the sun and out of any wind. The dogs were asleep from sheer boredom. I watched a pretty older woman as she came down the street and unlocked the door to the museum. Leaving the dogs in the car, I followed her.

"Good morning." She greeted me with a bright smile. "The museum isn't quite open yet. Soon, though."

"Can anyone have access to the Tribal archives?" I asked politely, afraid of her answer. I was positive she would say no.

She looked at me with open curiosity. I'm sure she wondered about my reasons.

"I want to trace some family lines," I offered her as an explanation. Obviously it wasn't enough, as she began to shake her head.

"My great-grandmother was Ojibwe and I would like to know more about her family. She was named Dances with Feathers and she married a man from Sweden."

"Really? I thought I knew everyone in that family." I was used to the skeptical glance. "My husband's cousin is Jem Grey Sand, another tree branch of that family, but they live farther north now."

"And Samuel is Jem's son and there is still Grandfather Grey Sand." I was wishing I knew more names, but she seemed impressed enough.

"You look Indian except for that curly hair!" She laughed.

"My great-grandfather and grandfather were both Swedes. Bertel Lundguist and Rudolf Svensson."

Jem's cousin's wife looked pensive and a little sad. "Oh. That part of the family," she said. "I can let you look at the records, but you seem to know it already."

"I guess I just want to confirm it all for myself."

Does it upset you, to find out who you are?" She was a little cool now.

I couldn't help but laugh out loud. "No. Not at all. I was thrilled to find I had family. I pretty much spent half my life without any." I shrugged my shoulders and smiled warmly at her. "Now, I am finding all kinds of relatives, and I love it all."

I could see her visibly relax and she held out her hand.

"Hello. I'm Rachel and I am pleased to meet you."

"And I'm Emily, and very pleased to meet you."

Rachel dug out the clan's records and we examined them together. Great-grandfather's name was Lost on Water Grey Sand, married to White as Snow, with three children. Jem was the only one remaining. There were far too many cousins to take in at once. Rachel kept laughing at my confusion, but she understood it too.

"You'll get it all straight soon." She comforted me. "We have several family gatherings when the weather is fine and you can meet them all. We are a pretty good bunch." She laughed.

Bertel had indeed married Dances with Feathers, deeded land to the Ojibwe's, and was Augusta's father. Sparrow Hawk, rather. The name suited what I knew of her. She was not well remembered by Rachel, either, who said Augusta was a stranger to her family.

"No one could understand that. Family is family, after all. Of course we have no idea of what her Russian mother told her over the years," was how Rachel told it. I was liking Rachel already. She had gone to high school with Robert and Marie but didn't remember much about them. She had married very young, before she would have graduated from high school, and had several children of her own which had kept her too busy for anything outside of family. Now, her children grown, her life was her fisherman and artist husband, Thomas Grey Sand, and this museum. She took me through the rooms and pointed out several items that had been the Grey Sand ancestors and passed down through many generations. She was especially proud of the leather dresses with beaded local wildflowers on them. Even the shelters had beads woven or stitched into the hides. Everything, down to a common bowl, was decorated and beautiful to see. I was curious about the painted colors, but remembered the dogs and felt guilty for leaving them so long in the car. Rachel walked me out, met the dogs, and welcomed me again to the family. We agreed to meet for lunch soon, so I could learn more. I felt truly blessed as I drove to Grandfather Grey Sand's home.

With the car gone and no smoke coming from the chimney, the place looked abandoned and forlorn. Snow had already filled in the pathways. The door was unlocked and I left it open for some light. In the center of his table, Grandfather had left a rolled up deer hide. He, or someone, had hand drawn a family tree for me with little designs and sketches on the sides. He must have been working on it for years. Some of the sketches looked like people I knew and some were strangers, but the longer I looked at them, the more familiar they became. Everyone was there, starting with Dances with Feather's parents and trailing down to me. It was a lovely thing and meant so much to me; I couldn't stop the flow of tears. He had even drawn in Jackson, Lily and Sullivan. Suddenly I was shocked. How had Grandfather known about my dogs? Then I remembered the birch-bark canoe and the single man sitting in it, the brief odd experience I had had soon after arriving at the cabin. So, it had been Grandfather Grey Sand then, either real or in my mind, and the dogs had been with me.

There was an eagle flying above me with my mother's face, and a beaver, that look3d surprisingly like Robert, building a home. Myron and Selma were watching us through a window and smiling. Augusta was holding hands with Rudolf. This old man was a genius. I rolled up the deerskin and left for home securing the door firmly behind me.

Although it was afternoon when I arrived home, Jackson had breakfast all ready to cook. Eggs, bacon, sausage, and French toast. Yum! I was starving. I hugged him and pulled away so he could cook.

282

"Hold on there, Miss!" He pulled me back for a long kiss.

"How was your journey and what did you find?" he asked as he fussed at the stove. I shook out the deerskin and laid it on the table. Jackson smoothed it out and studied it.

"Wow," he stated with awe in his tone. "This is incredibly beautiful."

"Isn't it? I am so pleased." I also told him about the records and Rachel and the museum while we ate. The dogs were exhausted after their long afternoon nap, and decided more napping was in order. They settled again, in front of the cookstove, leaving us alone.

"I need to quit working them so darn hard," I pointed to them.

Jackson laughed at both the dogs and my lame joke.

That afternoon we decided to pick up Robert's puppy. Mrs. Anderson was glad to see me.

"Robert Peterson called to ask if there were any puppies left." She told us with a smile. "That's who the puppy is for, isn't that right? Anyway, I told him the pups were gone, but there would be more in a year or two. He seemed disappointed, though, so this will be a terrific surprise for him." The pup launched herself at Jackson, who knelt down to her level to play. She was all tongue and legs as she tumbled about.

"She's perfect." Jackson loved her already and it was mutual.

"She seems to prefer men, although she is friendly to everyone." Mrs. Anderson picked her up for a hug. "Matt is outside somewhere with the other dogs, but he knew you'd come soon for this one, so he's ready to let her go." She handed the puppy over to me. "I hope Mr. Peterson likes her," she said as we left.

The ride home was a lively one. Jackson drove and I attempted to keep the pup out of his lap, away from the steering wheel, and out from under the brake. She was all over the place and hard to contain. Jackson was laughing at both of us.

"Are you sure you've raised dogs before?"

I was laughing too. "I have, but not this one." When we arrived at the cabin, it was a wild scene. Sullivan's fur stood straight up along his spine and he walked around the pup with his tail up in the air and only the tip wagging. His gait was stiff and there was a low growl in his throat. The pup rolled over onto her back and whined a bit and it was all over. As soon as she realized Sully was the boss, he loved her. They dashed around the yard and out on the frozen lake until they dropped. Lily was somewhat more aloof, until the pup was tired. Then she checked her out thoroughly.

"Okay, we're all friends now," I said as we went inside. Lily and Sully led the way to the water bowl and then to the fireplace rug where they lay in a pile and napped.

"I hope housebreaking will be this easy." Jackson was still laughing. "They look so cute. Maybe we need another puppy, too." I shook my head.

"I don't think so." But as I watched them sleeping so happily, I wasn't so sure. I went to my easel and started a new canvas. The three dogs in front of the fire were too hard to resist. Jackson took out his museum work camera and snapped several photographs while I worked. We knew the pups wouldn't remain this still for long and I'd need something to work from. I did several quick charcoal sketches of the pile and even began the painting before anyone moved. I had never attempted animals before. Especially animals that actually looked like themselves. Maybe there was some R. G. Peterson in me after all.

49

Jackson was the one to be gone as I slept in the next morning. Turn-about is fair play, isn't that the quote? I could smell coffee as I dressed and it made me smile. Jackson must have known me in another life to understand me so well in this one. It was snowing lightly as I poured the beverage, but it rapidly worsened as I sipped. With only a few days until Christmas, I was becoming excited and full of the anticipation that the holiday used to bring out in me, but hadn't for so many years. I filled a plastic garbage bag with gaily wrapped gifts and decided to take them to the house. Ray's snowplow truck was parked in front, facing the lane and I wondered what he knew about the coming weather that I didn't. I slipped my boots off just inside the door and was unloading the presents when I heard the door open.

"Hello? Anyone here?" It was Maryalice and her two girls, Katie and Bettyanne. Phillip, the youngest son was lugging in a suitcase when I met them at the door.

"Oh, hello Emily, have you heard? The weather is going to be terrible." Maryalice said with glee. "Lots of snow over Christmas and we will probably be snowed in here. Isn't that great?"

"It's great if everyone can get here." I answered.

"Oh they'll be here. Ray will see to that. He is up at the store now to pick up his folks. They've had a sign on the door for a few days now to tell everyone they wouldn't be open for a week. They have never done that before so this will be so good for them. We all think they work too hard, but they don't agree. Robert and Greg will get here together this evening and Jackson is getting Lydia now. This is going to be so much fun!" Her daughters were gazing fondly at their excited mother, and her enthusiasm was contagious. They each had several bags and packages. Some for the kitchen and some for under the tree. Maryalice and I went upstairs to double check the bedrooms to make sure they all had enough blankets and that it was warm enough up there. To me, it all was as perfect as it could be.

"Where do you want to put everyone?" Maryalice asked me. I shrugged my shoulders.

"I don't care, I guess, just where you all will be the most comfortable. I think I'll take my mother's room." I gestured at the doorway.

"Great, if there is room enough for two?" She laughed her wonderful musical laugh. "Can Ray and I have the master bedroom then? So much space! Our room at home is like a closet. It will almost be like our first night together at that fancy hotel in Duluth." She took her bag into Augusta's room and her daughters were already settled in the adjoining parlor. They had their sleeping bags spread out on the sofas and they pushed us out of the room so they could wrap more presents in private. Soon we heard the beat of rock music coming from the other side of their door. Phillip was settling in one of the bunk bed rooms where he would sleep with his brother.

"I got the top bunk first," he announced with pride. "Greg has it at home. Fair is fair."

Maryalice thought Myron and Selma should have Lydia's old quarters, as she thought that room might make Lydia too sad. I didn't agree, but went along with her plans. So, Lydia would be in Grace's room and Robert in the other bunk bedroom. Wonderful. When we returned downstairs, Ray was helping his folks inside and the snow was getting so thick it was hard to see beyond the open door.

"I'm going out to do some plowing," Ray told us as he kissed his wife. "See you all in a bit." And he was gone.

It was only mid-day, but dark enough that we needed to turn on the lights. The girls had brought their portable CD player downstairs and kept us all in the mood with holiday music. Everyone who was there worked in the kitchen, happily making sandwiches and soup. I took a few minutes for myself and went up to Augusta's room to take down a picture of my mother and move it to her room with me. It showed Mom the way I remembered her best: in her early twenties, sitting on the end of the dock, smiling and reaching her hand out to whoever was behind the camera. I was thinking about her so intensely, I almost felt her with me again. After all these years, why wasn't the longing any less? There was so much fullness to my life now, I shouldn't need more. But I did. The pain of her loss was as sharp as it had been the day she left me. That was how I thought of it, I realized. The day she left me, not the day she died. I had never seen her and Dad hadn't held a funeral. There had just been a brief memorial service at a church I had never attended, so I felt like I never had a chance to say goodbye. Grandma Bengta shook her head sadly at her son and said she thought it was strange, but it was the way Howard wanted it, so there it was.

"Emily? Are you up there?" Jackson was calling up the staircase. I waited before answering, knowing he would find me. His beautiful face peeked around the open door and grinned when he saw me.

"Hey you! Where should I put Lydia?"

"Right next to us." I pointed to Grace's room.

"Terrific idea." I helped him unpack his grandmother, and hand-in-hand, we trooped downstairs for lunch.

50

Jackson and I left the family to get settled in and went back to the cottage to play with the dogs in the snow. We wanted them to burn off their excess energy in the deepening drifts. Sully and the puppy were wild things! Chasing tails and snowflakes out over the lake. Lily joined in and it was simply a frenzy of play. I slipped on the ice and a worried Lily sat down directly on my chest. The fall had knocked the breath temporarily out of my lungs, and I was laughing so hard, Jackson tried to rescue me. Lily, however, wouldn't let him near enough. I rolled over to dislodge her bulk and she ran off with the others. We threw snowballs for the puppy to chase and she'd willingly pick them up and trot back to us with her rapidly disappearing treasures. The look on her face when the ball had melted was priceless! She would return over and over to the spot to look, sure her treasure must be there somewhere. The puppy was the best behaved of all three and even came when called. We needed to come up with a name for her soon, or Puppy would probably stick.

We could hear Pearl squawking through the window. "Whatcha doin' out there?" and "Come here right this minute. Hello? Right this minute!" So, in we went to play with the birds for awhile. The dogs were almost too tired to eat, and they settled down immediately afterwards for a nap. We'd have to come back later to let them out again, but for now things were peaceful. Tomorrow Puppy wouldn't have to be a secret any longer.

The walk back to the house was thick with snow, both on the ground and in the air. I had never seen anything like it. It was so silent, our breathing sounded like brief gusts of wind and our steps were utterly quiet, muffled by the snow. The flakes were heavy and large enough to see the patterns. They were like the paper ones everyone made in grade school. With flakes stuck to eye brows and lashes we looked like figures from mythology.

While still not used to the winter silence of this place, I found it soothing, comforting, and entirely welcome. It was a live thing, a spirit form of what actually was the world outside my realm. I used to find quiet disturbing. At times, I left the radio or television on just for the noisy company it gave me. It kept me from thinking about my life too much. Now, I found that I wasn't able to think at all without the solitude of the quiet. Funny thing, life. This silence, on this particular day, made me smile broadly.

"What's up with you? Jackson inquired.

"Huh?"

"You are smiling. No, grinning," he smiled back.

"Just happy, I guess." I took his hand as we entered Augusta's house.

The rest of the family were gathered in the parlor and they all had safe trips to the house, but no one was willing to go out again, so, Myron said, we damn well better have everything we needed. The ladies had assembled supper while we were playing and we ate in a candlelit dining room. I loved the way the glass reflected the flame back into the room. It was enchanting. Fires were also lit in the fireplaces and it was cozy, making the house seem more homey and smaller. I was feeling more and more at home in this house all the time.

Sometimes I daydreamed about raising a family here with Jackson. I could imagine several children chasing each other about, playing with the pets, studying in the playroom upstairs, and reading together in the living room. We'd celebrate every birthday and holiday as a family, and no one would ever be lonely here. Not in my house. Oh boy, don't get so far ahead of yourself, woman!

The kids had set up board games from the playroom and after dinner we sat around the parlor and played Scrabble and Parcheesi, Monopoly and Clue. There certainly weren't any "modern" games in this house. We finished off several bottles from Augusta's wine cellar as well, and I fell asleep in the middle of my turn at Scrabble. I couldn't wrap my brain around my remaining letters to spell anything other than the word tea, so that ended the game. There were no more spaces where a word could be placed without breaking the rules.

"I'll go let the dogs out." Jackson was already pulling on his jacket.

"I'll go with you." Robert stood and I looked up in a panic.

"No, Uncle Rob, I need to get my gear out of the truck, so I'll go." Greg remembered the secret just in time. For a minute I thought we'd have to tell him, but Robert just shrugged and wandered out to the kitchen with the empty wineglasses. Soon the fires were burning low and people went off to their rooms. Jackson came back with Sully, who was thrilled to see me.

"I didn't have the heart to leave him behind. We could hear him crying before we even got to the cabin." Jackson handed him over. "He missed you, I think."

"Why didn't you bring Lily too?" Robert asked.

"She's soaking wet and smelly. I'll clean her up tomorrow and bring her over then." Jackson looked at me and I could see that even this small lie went against the grain. Robert gazed at us both with an odd expression, said good night, and went upstairs.

"This is getting too hard! Lily was very unhappy."

"Okay, we'll do it in the morning. Then they can all be underfoot, which is exactly where they want to be." Actually, I didn't want to wait any longer either. I wanted to see how Robert reacted to his puppy hoping he'd be as thrilled as I thought he'd be.

We all woke early, even the teenagers. It's hard to sleep when such heavenly smells are invading your senses. Of course, Selma and Lydia were up at dawn and busy in the kitchen. I was sure that cooking for their families was their greatest pleasure in life. They don't make women like that anymore. Everything needed to be made from scratch, no short cuts or boxed meals for these two. It was always the slow, traditional methods. No matter how hard I tried, I would always be a short cut cook. Jackson and I had made our plan before coming down stairs. He slipped out and I made an announcement.

"Okay, family, everyone in the parlor for the first Christmas surprise!" I herded them and their coffee cups along the hall. I glanced out the window in passing and saw Jackson coming so I collected the cups.

"No worries, I'll give them right back." Greg was laughing at everyone because they didn't want to give up the cups.

"Trust her," he said.

Jackson called out "Ready?"

"Ready."

First came Lily who promptly jumped up on the couch, forcing those seated there to make room for her, licking the snow from her feet. The puppy flew into the room and went straight for Robert! It couldn't have been better if we'd planned out her behavior. She gazed up into his face with pure delight and settled down in his lap with most of her gangly legs hanging over his knees. Jackson had tied a huge red bow around her neck and she actually left it there, bedraggled as it was, by the time they came in.

"Who is this?" Robert looked at me.

"This is your Christmas present. Do you like her?"

"For me? Have I been that transparent?" He seemed genuinely startled. Puppy was firmly planted in his lap.

"Yes, Robert, for you. And yes, we have noticed you watching these dogs for awhile now. I doubt we could get her away from you at this point. She seems to know who she belongs to already." The pup sat up straighter and planted a wet paw on Robert's flannel shirt and a sloppy tongue on his cheek.

Robert smiled down at her and rubbed her ears softly. "Hello Lucy." He said. He might have had a single tear in his eyes, I couldn't be sure.

51

This Christmas Eve was everything I had dreamed about and longed for in my lonely life. My new family was snug and cozy with me in every part of this decorated heaven. The older women kicked us youngsters out of the kitchen and tantalized us with smells never to be forgotten. The dining room was filling with finished delights and we all sat at the table to eat, drink, and laugh. Myron opened one of his bottles of homemade rhubarb wine and we all had to try and guess what the rhubarb was blended with. Not one of us was able and he refused to say. Together. We were truly together in every sense of the word.

The dogs were extremely tired by this time and collapsed at our feet. I noticed Lucy slept with her head on Robert's foot. Lily lay between Jackson and me and Sully went from one person to the next. The meal was a mixture of traditional Swedish food like barley and potato sausage and rice pudding. We also had more American fare like roast turkey and sweet potatoes and cornbread. We were nearly too stuffed to open gifts. Many of these were crafted by hand, like a heavy knit shawl from Lydia, mittens and socks from the girls, braided leather dog leashes from Ray, and so forth. It was a Christmas that would make my mother proud. Sully and Lucy had to be stopped from ripping off the wrapping paper before the gifts were opened. I think they watched us and figured out that this was the new game. We gave them the paper from the presents already opened and they shredded that happily, leaving trails of shreds in all the rooms.

Maryalice, Katie, Bettyanne, and I decided we needed some exercise so we started on the dishes while Jackson, Ray, and Robert cleared the table. Myron put away the leftovers and we made the cooks relax with their after-dinner coffee, with just a dab of Bailey's Cream added to each cup. I watched everyone with a full heart, wishing life could always be this way for everyone. Warm, sated, and loved. All that was missing from complete happiness was my mother. Robert, I was certain, was also thinking about her.

In the morning, we set up a buffet table in the dining room that would be ready when people arrived. There were empty spots for them to place their offerings. Piles of plates, silverware, sparkling glasses, and napkins were lined up at the end of the table; all was ready. The neighbors wandered in throughout the day. Matt Anderson was one of the first. He was happy to see Lucy, but she lost interest in him after only a couple of minutes and went to find Robert.

I hugged Matt tightly. "It's okay, honey. This is the way it's supposed to be. Aren't you happy that she likes her new home?" He thought about that and smiled when Sully launched himself at his face. They tumbled together and I figured all was fine. The rocketdog saved the moment once again. He had a real knack for distracting people from their tasks.

The day went quickly with comings and goings and music and food. Lots and lots of food. The men cleared the floor in the two larger rooms, rolled up the rugs and anyone who could play a musical instrument tuned up. The older guests showed the younger ones how to do Swedish folk dances. Amid much stumbling about, we finally caught on and had a great deal of exercise. People were dancing from room to room with infants held in their arms or young children standing on their father's feet. Wives gazed into husband's eyes and I saw several kisses exchanged. Someone, I never guessed his identity, came downstairs in a bright red Santa suit to distribute small gifts to the children. Everyone got a hand-sewn stuffed animal of some kind. Matt Anderson was thrilled with his stuffed Retriever puppy. Selma told me that her circle of friends had been working on these for months. I wondered if she'd guessed we'd celebrate this way long before I did.

Toward evening I dressed for outside, and took the dogs for a walk to the cottage and out on the ice. Like my mother, I thought I will never tire of looking out over this bay. My fingers were getting icy when I turned to go back to the party. Jackson was approaching. He hugged me and we both looked out over the ice. The pines appeared to be almost black against the blue-grey sky. Here and there small trails of smoke from fires or furnaces slipped upward through the trees. The moon was full and bright enough to cut a path straight across the bay directly at our feet.

"I love the desk," he said. He slipped off my new mitten and kissed my hand. When he let go, there was a spot of perfect glistening on my finger. I sucked in my breath audibly. It was a lovely ring of blue star sapphires and diamonds. The ring looked like the night sky with its inky-indigo blue and spark of stars. We spent a good deal of time there, out on the rickety old dock, just holding each other tightly.

We rejoined the family and I caught Lydia smiling at me. That woman must have second sight. I swear she knows everything. All the guests had gone home, following Ray as he plowed the way. We settled in for our last night all together in this house. I think the house enjoyed the excitement also. I could almost hear its sigh of contentment as lights were turned off. Jackson and I made love, but we kept giggling and it was very hard to keep quiet.

The world always seems a much diminished place when the holiday is over. Memories of family meals full of flavor and laughter, music everywhere. When the decorations are taken down and packed away, empty spots need to be filled up with something else. People go back to work, and life returns to normal. I've come to believe that I don't like normal. In my world, it would always be Christmas with snow and colored lights and candlelight and wonderful smells coming from kitchens, presents unopened under beautifully decorated trees. The people I love would always live under the same roof or, at the very least, within walking distance and in daily contact. I had spent entirely too much of my life being lonely and now realized I could not tolerate it at all. Being alone is okay as long as you know people are downstairs and just a yell away. There is nothing more human than sharing a bed with a lover. When you wake up to someone else next to you, all is right with your world. This was the first time I had experienced that and now Jackson was gone again. Only to Minneapolis this time, but gone is gone.

The months of January through March are the longest months of the year for me. There is little reason to move about as there is little to do. It was a really good thing I had the dogs to get me out of bed in the mornings.

I was babysitting Lucy this week because Robert had another show in Chicago. He also took two of my paintings, "just for fun," he said. He was teaching a brief oil painting class to college seniors. Lucy loved it at my cabin, but she looked for Robert everywhere. I had never seen a dog and a man bond so completely in such a short time. They were inseparable. Robert laughed when he said he couldn't even shower without her lying next to the tub. Like Sully, Lucy didn't like sleeping in her own bed, but in Robert's. It made me very happy knowing he wasn't alone all the time. I reached over to rub her ears and she moved her head to my lap. All three dogs were napping next to me on the couch, Sully on Lily's back with his head tucked under her ear. As the sun was going down, the remaining light caught my diamond ring and I missed Jackson all over again. He had completely taken me by surprise on Christmas Eve when he slipped it on my finger. We had never discussed marriage, only that we were in love.

"It can just be a present," he said, a little worry in his eyes. "It doesn't have to mean anything else. Okay?"

"Does that mean you don't want to marry me?" I asked him, laughing and kissing him.

"No, of course not! I just don't want to rush you into it."

"Jackson, I would love to marry you." Of course, I still needed to get divorced from Marcus first. I hadn't heard anything from him lately. Anderson/Erickson lawyers said I probably would have to settle some amount of money with Marcus in order to get the divorce, but they would take care of it. How lucky I had become. Augusta's wealth had certainly changed my life. I was willing to give Marcus almost anything in order to be rid of him. Just not this property.

I decided to go to the house to pick up some leftovers for my supper. I left the pile of sleeping dogs and trekked over. It was a warmer night, and had been that way for several days now, and the snow was beginning to rapidly melt. The moon was full and although it was better weather, large snowflakes wafted down lightly. Where they came from, I didn't know, because the sky was clear enough to view stars hanging low over the lake.

Walking over, I wished I had brought the dogs. It would be very dark soon, even with the stars. Why I didn't go back for them, I will never know. I needed a book to read so I went to the library first.

Grandfather's library held a vast collection of subjects. Many of the books were leather bound and many of them were classic novels. Books on geography, sciences of all kinds, history, archaeology, paleontology, some medical texts. It seemed both my grandfather, and my great-grandfather were men of many interests. There were more modern books here and there that told me this library was used long after Rudolf's death. I found personal letters and notes, too. It seemed Augusta had been wrong about Rudolf's motives in marrying her. It was obvious to me that he loved her. It was also apparent Bertel simply knew he was dying and wanted his estate cared for. It was actually left to both of them equally. I wondered if Grandmother ever figured that out. I hoped so. She hadn't been betrayed at all. Maybe she could have lost her hatred of men or at the very least, led a more comfortable life. She wouldn't have so completely lost her family.

I read letters from Sweden to Rudolf. They were from his parents and I needed help from a large Swedish/English dictionary. I got enough out of them to believe they were letters from loving parents who were worried about a son so far away. Letters from James and Myrtle to Bertel, Irena, and Augusta were stuck in a desk drawer. I had forgotten there were other relatives. Maybe I had some distant cousins somewhere in Sweden.

Most of the paperwork in the desk consisted of bills of sale for property around the lake. It seemed Bertel and then Rudolf, had made a fortune buying and selling land in central Minnesota, the lake district, as they called it. It appeared there was also a lumber yard and construction company that Augusta had sold several years after Rudolf's death. This family just kept getting more interesting all the time. Sometime during my reading, I had turned on the desk lamp, without thinking about it. It was now very dark and I was furious with myself for loosing track of the time so completely. I left the papers on the desk and rose to leave when I heard breaking glass in the kitchen. I froze and listened. More breaking glass and a door being kicked open. I switched off the lamp and held my breath.

"Emily!" It was Marcus. "We know you're here! We saw the lights. I just want to talk to you." His voice was excited, higher, and thin sounding, and that, I had learned, was always trouble. Marcus was mean and focused when he was excited about something.

I stepped into the hall and unlocked the front door to run away, but was too late. Rough hands grabbed me and slammed the door closed. It was slammed so hard that it popped back open a crack, but no one noticed. The man who had hold of me was huge. He smelled bad, too, of stale cigarettes, unbrushed teeth, and beery sweat.

"No, you don't!" He shouted in my face, his spittle spraying me. "We've waited long enough for you." he shoved me harshly into the wall. I looked at Marcus with disgust. He shrugged his shoulders. His face was shiny with greed, and he was drunk.

"I need money, Emily. Lots of it. I found out about you and this property and I stopped the divorce." He slurred the words some, but that was what I heard.

"Marcus, I took nothing from you."

"Yeah, well, nothing's what I've got and I need money! I've been telling you that for months! But you, with all this, paid me no attention. Plus you had that body guard hanging around all the time." He gestured roughly around him at the house with the expensive furnishings.

I looked at his companions. The woman I suspected was Connie, the flower thief. She had on a tight, short skirt and spike heels, tight tank top that showed a chubby belly, thin white bare legs with knobby knees. Did she not realize she was in Minnesota in winter? She looked cold as she snapped her gum. She also looked very young. Shaggy hair died several shades of blond had dark roots about three inches long. Too much makeup was smeared from constantly wiping at her eyes. The girl did not look well. In fact, neither did Marcus. Both had runny eyes and scratched sores on their faces, bruised and vacant looks, and were slightly unsteady. She was drunk too and swaying on those heels. Or was it something else? Something in addition to the alcohol?

The bully was a man I knew from Marcus's office. I think he was a bill collector, a wanna-be lawman. I remembered him as a loudmouth who never really said anything. He always smelled of gin, which he did now. His greasy black hair hung over his eyes. The muscles of his arms stood out even through his jacket. He was the brawn, and most likely the brains of this operation. He looked healthy enough. Unfortunately.

"Come on!" he yelled at Marcus, who flinched. "Where are the papers? I want the pen! Get me the money now!" Wait a minute, who wanted money, Marcus or this guy?

"What is going on, Marcus?"

"I made a bad business deal, and I owe Paul Cantine, here, four hundred and eighty-five thousand." Marcus looked a little sheepish but determined.

"A 'bad business deal!' You stole the cocaine you were supposed to sell, you idiot! I warned you..."

"A half a million dollars? Marcus! There is no money here," I told them.

"Maybe not, but this property on the lake is worth a fortune. We have someone who will pay top dollar and no questions. They will level all this woods, or whatever, and put up a fine resort." Connie, the slut, joined the conversation.

"Shut up! Don't tell her anything! She doesn't need to know our business, you stupid bitch!" Paul pushed her away. Connie huffed, stuck out her tongue and moved behind Marcus. Evidently this happened often. If she expected Marcus would defend her, she had much to learn. Wow, she was young. Paul turned back to me with a growl.

"All you have to do is sign these papers!" He pulled them out of Marcus' hand and shoved them into my face. "Sign! Now!"

"Do you think I'm crazy? I'm not signing any papers. Even if I did, they wouldn't be legal. I can get money, but not until the banks are open."

"They'd be legal enough if you were dead." He was snarling now, almost foaming at the mouth like a rabid dog in a movie, and I was terrified. I was also getting the bigger picture.

"You! Bitch!" Paul grabbed me quicker than I thought a man his size could move. He shook me and threw me back against the wall. I had braced myself for just this kind of move, so it did little damage.

"Hey!" Marcus yelped. "Don't hurt her! You said no violence! I don't want her hurt!"

"She's not going to be hurt; she's going to be dead. How else did you think we'd get away with this plan? Stay out of this Marcus! I'm taking care of business now, so get out of my way. It's my money on the line, and it's you and your little bimbo here, who created the problem for me to clean up!"

Paul swung around to Marcus with his fist clenched and raised. Marcus's face held total shock at Paul's words and his attitude. Obviously he'd had no idea of what Paul's real plan had been, that I was to be murdered right now, right there.

"It isn't about you anymore! You're a weasel, a weak junky, and a means to an end. I want my money! So I suggest, if you have no stomach for this, you and your little baby-doll just leave the room!" And as he let fly with his fists, I ran out the door. It was the best plan I had been able to come up with.

"She's getting away!" Connie was shrieking. "Stop her! Stop her!"

I stumbled out the door and soon was over the ice. The woods would have been better, but I wasn't thinking clearly. I knew I'd never make it to any of the ice fishing huts out in the bay. Besides, most of them were gone as it was warming up and the ice was thinning. He could see every move I made with the moon shinning over the lake, so I just ran. Half way out into the bay and toward the sandbars I stopped. The current under the ice here was swift and I could feel a difference in the ice below my feet. I heard the crack before I felt it. Looking up, I saw the big shadow of the man advancing rapidly. I held up both my arms and screamed at him.

"You have to stop moving! Stop now! Look at the ice!" But he didn't stop. He wasn't even listening. He had a large knife he must have taken from Augusta's kitchen, and held it up and in front of him. I was sure he intended to use it. When he was four or five feet from me, the ice gave way. All the stars that were nearly touching the lake went down with us, just like in my long ago dream. I had time for a deep breath and went under. The water was impossibly frigid and felt like brick walls pushing in on me from all sides. I felt Paul's body smack into mine and push me over several feet. I remembered Grandpa Algot telling me, while we were ice fishing on Mille Lacs Lake that people drown because they get lost under the ice. I knew I had to go straight up, not to even turn around. I tried to do just that, but I felt Paul grab my foot. I kicked and my Sorel boot slipped right off as I shot to the surface. There were long, white shadowy arms reaching for me through the ice and guiding me to the open hole. I could hear Connie still screaming. Were those arms hers? I reached the ice sheet and found the hole. There was no one there. I was trying to pull myself up onto the ice when Paul flung his beefy arms around my neck and held on tight enough to choke what little breath I had left in my lungs right out of me. He was coughing on icy lake water and having trouble breathing. The big man was panicking and clawing at me. He had also lost the knife. I couldn't dislodge his grip and we were going under again. Out of nowhere a shadow flew over us. Marcus had a hold of Paul's jacket and greasy hair and was pounding Paul's skull with his fist.

"I told you not to hurt her! Get off! Let's get out of here!" Suddenly they both slipped under the ice, their heavy winter coats now soaked with frigid lake water and pulling at their bodies, and I was free. Still not able to hoist up on the ice, I was afraid. But I felt something holding me up at the surface. I could no longer feel my legs and my arms, too, were losing ground. I knew there was very little time. I called out to Connie, who couldn't hear my weak voice over her own panic. Her screeching could be heard all the way to Brainerd, I was sure. I thought all was lost and I would die here, in my beloved lake, when a rope fell over my shoulders and Robert was there!

"Push the rope down under your arms, Emily. I've got you." His calm voice reached my dim brain and I did what he said. Slowly, I was inched up onto the thicker ice and out of the water. As Robert eased me onto the ice sheet, I felt the arms from below me, let go. Twice, ice broke off under me, but Robert's slow pulling didn't stop. Soon, I was in his arms and wrapped in his parka. I stood with his help and walked over to Connie, who was still shrieking: "Marcus, oh no!" Connie turned to an astonished Robert and held out her arms in pleading. "She's killed him! She's killed him! She's..." I punched her square in the jaw and she dropped like a rock. The sudden quiet was as startling as the ice water had been. I turned to a grim and shocked Robert.

"I don't care what you do with her; just don't bring her to my house!" Then I looked at the deep black hole in the ice and back at Robert, who shook his head no. Suddenly his eyes grew wide and stricken.

"Emily! You're bleeding!" He rushed to me and pulled the parka away from my body. My sweater and jeans were sliced from my left shoulder blade down to past my hip. The cut was deep and wide open and yet I couldn't feel anything. Blood was thick and slow and there was way too much of it. Robert swept me off my feet and ran toward the store dock, screaming for his father all the way. People were on the shore when we arrived. I was feeling quite faint and weak and couldn't stop my teeth from chattering loudly.

"Ray's in the car already to go!" Myron told us. Without stopping Robert yelled, "Call the police and get the woman off the ice. Keep her locked up somewhere. She tried to kill Emily! Two men are under the ice!" And we were gone.

"It doesn't hurt Robert. Why doesn't it hurt?" I mumbled.

"It will honey, it will."

52

I guess I was unconscious by the time we reached the emergency room, as I remember nothing firsthand. But eventually I pieced together the entire tale of woe, either from what I actually did recall as well as from what I was told. When I opened my eyes, Robert was holding my hand, half asleep next to the bed. Ray was also there, asleep in a chair.

"Hello." I tried to talk, but even I could hear how incoherent I sounded, like no words I had ever heard. What I was thinking and what I was actually uttering weren't even remotely the same, but it was enough to alert Robert that I was awake.

"Oh my god, girl! You had us scared to death. I thought I was going to lose you all over again." There actually were tears on his cheeks. Ray came over to give me a smile and kiss.

"I'll go tell everyone she's back," he said hoarsely, as if his throat was sore, and left the room.

I looked questioningly at Robert.

"The whole family is here," he answered the unspoken question. "We haven't found Jackson yet, but we will."

I cleared my throat and tried words again. "Tell me." It was all I could get out. Robert nodded and began.

"I had just returned and was getting into my truck to go and collect Lucy from your place. I heard you screaming out on the lake so I went to look. I was in time to see you go through the ice with two men on top of you." He paused for a bit to wipe a few drops of sweat from his forehead. "I grabbed a rope and ran. You know the rest?"

I nodded. "After?"

"Dad called the state police and they got the same diving team that found Grace and Karl. Anyway, it took two days, but they found them. The woman's not talking, but she's in custody. The troopers are here, too, to get your story."

"Two days?" I croaked. "How long have I been here?"

"Four and a half days."

We heard a ruckus in the hallway and the door burst open, slamming against the wall.

"Where is she? Is she hurt! Where..."

Suddenly I was half lifted off the mattress and held so tightly I could hardly breathe. When I pushed Jackson away a little to catch my breath, his lips were all over my face and hair.

"Emily!" was all he could say for awhile.

I winced and slightly pulled away.

"What..." Jackson looked at Robert.

"She's got over seventy stitches down her side," Robert said by way of explanation. "She'll be a little sore for quite awhile."

"Stitches? My God, seventy stitches?" Jackson's face paled considerably.

"Wow, I didn't know that," I said in a whisper. Some of the experience must still be a little foggy.

"I'm fine," I finally was able to mutter. "Robert was there."

"Thank God. But it should have been me. I should have never have gone. I am so sorry. No damn job will ever keep me away from you again." And he hugged me hard to his chest again.

"Jackson, I don't think she can breathe when you clutch her like that." Robert was laughing at us.

"Oh. Yeah." His grip eased only slightly. "Was it Marcus? Burglars? Tell me!" He shook me in his frustration.

"We will tell you all the drama, but let's let her sit up and have a sip of coffee at least." Robert chided. "She has only now regained consciousness."

"What? Emily, you were unconscious? My God..."

By this time, the rest of the Petersons and Lydia were there, as well as a state trooper.

"Are you good enough to talk, Ms. Lind?" He asked politely.

"Yes, I'm okay now." And I told my story.

"I'll go back to where I think it began, even if I'm not sure." He nodded. "Shortly after I moved here, the phone in the main house would ring, and no one was there when I'd pick up. A couple of times, doors would be wide open and I was fairly sure I didn't leave them like that." Both Robert and Jackson raised eyebrows at me, but I didn't let them interrupt.

"Then one day I heard Marcus's voice on the phone, sort of in the background. Several weeks ago, in the middle of the night, there were voices, three different ones, behind the cottage. They were looking for me, but didn't realize I lived there. Myron said they had been at the store, too, asking about me." The trooper looked at Myron, who nodded emphatically.

"Last night, I stayed too late at the house and had lights on, so they probably could see me through the windows. It was really stupid of me to lose track of time like that. They broke in."

"They?" asked the trooper.

"Marcus, Connie, and someone Marc called Paul Cantine. He seemed to be in control of the other two. At least he gave the orders. It was all about money Marcus owed Paul." I left out the part about the suspected drug use. For now, anyway. Marcus was dead, so what did it matter? "Paul had some papers I was to sign that would give him my property. I think Marcus must have told him I was pretty tame and would sign anything just to be rid of them. But Marcus was wrong, as usual. Anyway, things got rough and I ran out on the lake."

"Rough?"

"Paul threw me against the wall and I hit my head. Marcus seemed to object to this, so Paul turned on him. That's how I managed to get out on the lake."

"Not very wise, after this milder weather," the trooper said. I just looked at him and said nothing. Sometimes "wise" has nothing to do with anything.

"That's where I came in," Robert added to the tale. "I had just returned home and heard loud voices out on the narrows. It sounded like Emily needed me, so I got there as they fell under the ice. I got her out, but the other two never came to the surface."

"I wouldn't have either, but Marcus got Paul off of me." And then I remembered the arms under the water.

"Who else was there?" I asked Robert.

"Else?" He looked confused.

"Who held me up until you got the rope to me?"

"Emily, there was no one else out there except that woman, Connie, and she was worthless."

I didn't know what to say, so I said nothing. Maybe I was delirious from the cold, but I didn't think so. Maybe it had been Marcus helping me stay alive even if it meant his death?

"Next?" Asked the trooper.

"That's it. Marcus jumped on Paul when he was trying to pull me back under. Neither of them surfaced again. Paul must have cut me with the butcher knife before he dropped it in the lake. I'm not sure. I couldn't feel anything."

"And the woman?"

"She took a nasty fall, but she's okay now. One of your guys has her, I think." Robert grinned at me, then immediately dropped the smile.

"Anything else you want to tell me?" The trooper stood. I shook my head.

"Okay, then. About this woman, Connie…"

"She's Marcus' girlfriend. She didn't actually touch me, but she was definitely part of the plan."

"Okay then. I think that's all I need right now. Rest well, Miss Lind." He smiled as he went through the door. Jackson never took his arms from around me.

After the trooper left, everyone spoke at once. Selma finally shushed them all and we sat there in silence. I could hardly keep my eyes open. Eventually, I quit trying, and slept in Jackson's arms.

53

I woke from nightmares twice during the night, but both times Jackson was there next to me and I knew that I was safe and secure, so was able to go back to sleep. When I did wake, the sun was high in the sky and a nurse was checking my temperature and blood pressure. No one else was there. It was very hard to move around and I needed a nurse to help me to the bathroom. She wanted me to use a bedpan, but I declined until she just gave up. I was hungry and needed coffee.

Another nurse came in with a newspaper.

"You and your dad are quite the local celebrities," she smiled. "There hasn't been this much excitement for the newspaper in years."

My dad. That still came as a shock. On the front page was a photograph. On the ice was a flat bottomed boat with several men in state trooper uniforms or black slick diving gear. They had some long grapple hooks, ropes and other gear. I could see one body bag on the platform and it appeared they were in the process of hauling up the other. Most of the ice in that part of the bay was broken up and was beginning to refreeze in odd looking piles. They were some distance down from where I thought I had fallen through. One trooper was holding a huge butcher knife and my lost Sorel boot. Ah, evidence. I giggled with some hysteria. At least my humor was intact.

The door to my room opened, and Jackson, Robert, and the same policeman entered.

"Can you think of anything else?" he asked after inquiring about my health.

"No. I told you everything." I replied.

"Do you want to press charges against Miss Hall?"

I was confused again. "Who?"

"She's the woman who was with them. Miss Connie Hall." I thought about it for a moment and shook my head.

"You might want to reconsider, Miss. She is claiming you killed the two men. You led them out on the ice, because you knew it was dangerous, and they could fall through. She says you did nothing to save them, and prevented her from doing so as well."

I looked at him in shock. "That is ridiculous!" I looked to Robert for help.

"I was there also, officer. Did Miss Hall forget about that?"

"She says you came later. After she had already pulled Miss Lind from the lake."

I couldn't help myself, I laughed. I laughed so hard, I found it hard to stop. I'd better be careful or that hysteria that was so close to the surface might just make an appearance.

"Sorry! I'm sorry." I sputtered between gasps for breath. "Did you get a look at her?" I asked the trooper.

317

"She was nowhere near the break in the ice. I'm positive she wasn't wet, and that skinny twit could no more pull me out of the water than she could run in those shoes of hers!" The officer patted my hand and said "I just wanted to check. We have your statement, and Robert's, and we have this evidence…" He gestured at the photograph. "I wouldn't worry about any of this. I think it is clear what happened here."

Another policeman entered and nodded at the first.

"Miss Lind, if it isn't too much, we need you to formally ID Miss Hall for our records. I could hear a commotion out in the hall and very loud sniffling. There was a struggle happening out there beyond the door.

"Oh my poor, poor Marc! She killed you!" She wailed at the ceiling. "I told you she would." Connie was led into the room in the same clothes I'd remembered. Even the spike shoes. Connie swung around to face me and pointed an accusatory finger.

"You are responsible for this! I intend to sue for damages!" She threw herself down on the floor, pulled her hair, and put on a show for us. When no one responded and she couldn't think of what else to do, she stopped.

"This isn't over!" she spat the words at me.

"Okay, I've had enough. I will press charges, if only to shut her up."

"Good enough." The state officer slapped his notebook shut, took Connie by the arm, cuffed her, and hauled the sad creature away. As she was removed from the room, she was still yelling; "I am the victim, here! Me! I'll prove it! I will! Just because it's her in that bed doesn't mean anything! I'm the victim…"

She and Marcus must have been quite a soap opera. Oh Marcus, what happened to us? No matter what he had done, and I knew he hadn't been the only one to blame, he did come through at the end. It had cost him his life.

I insisted Jackson go back to Minneapolis to finish the museum job he had left to come to me. He didn't want to leave me, but I didn't want him to stay. Of course, I couldn't say it quite that way, but I needed to be alone. I think I needed to mourn Marcus for awhile. Jackson promised to get back when it was time to bring me home.

With the death of Marcus, I was no longer a married woman, nor did I need to worry about settling a divorce. It was over. That was a relief in a lot of ways, but I would have happily given Marcus some money. I had never loved the man, though. I knew that now. Loving Jackson had taught me real love and I was sure I hadn't felt that kind of love before now. In fact, I knew that Jackson had actually taught me *how* to feel. I'd spent my life not knowing. Except for my mother, I had never really known anyone and recently, I'd realized I hadn't known her well either. But I was beginning to.

54

The hospital kept me for two weeks. They were
afraid the long wound would become infected, and the loss
of blood had weakened me more than I cared to admit. It
was fine, though; I slept most of the time. Robert was
staying at the cottage and enjoying himself quite a lot, he
said. He loved the frolicking dogs and was teaching the
birds new words. The entire family came to the hospital
almost every day with flowers and tasty treats. Sure I was
going to be many sizes larger by the time I was released,
not to mention spoiled from all the attention and unwilling
to fend for myself. Jackson was home again and he
brought pictures of the dogs. They were trying to figure
out the melting ice at the edge of the lake. In one shot,
Sully's small body was floating on a sliver of ice not much
bigger than him and he had a comical expression, half
terror, half joy, as he slid farther from the dock. Jackson
said he had to rescue the little guy.

The day the doctor let me go, my left side was still
sore, but the stitches had been removed and it felt much

better. Just itchy. I was anxious to be at home and moving around more. I needed to take long walks.

"Just take it easy for awhile yet," Doctor Jacobs warned.

"Oh, she will. I'll see to it." This firm answer came from Jackson.

The drive home seemed to take a decade. I couldn't sit with any comfort in the truck. Everything hurt with each movement on the road. Jackson had the dogs confined until I was seated. When he let Lily and Sully out of the bedroom, they flung their bodies into me. It hurt like the devil, but I didn't care. It was so good to see them. Sully kept looking for a blanket to snuggle under, but finally settled for my sweater. Pearl was dancing up and down on his perch squawking nonsense words and Tinkerbell sat quietly taking it all in. My warm and wonderful home.

Myron and Selma brought supper. I'm afraid I couldn't do the excellent meal justice, though. My eyes kept wandering to the lake. I finally excused myself and walked out on the dock. Jackson got up to join me, but I shook my head no. I stood there for a long time. Remembering Marcus, remembering Mom and Grace, and thinking of the night I could have died in this ideal and beloved lake. I thought that I might feel differently about this place after all that. But I didn't. This was home and always would be. I felt Jackson's arms slide around my waist and he whispered into my neck.

"You are a free person now," he spoke gently.

"Not really." I answered as I turned into his arms. "And neither are you."

321

I realized I could hear the gentle lapping water on rocks again. That was the hardest part of winter, no sounds of water. Soon the time to plant flowers and vegetables and hang the hammock would arrive. I could hardly wait.

We got back inside in time to say goodbye to the Petersons.

"Get well soon, sweetheart." Selma gave me a hug. As they walked to the door, I noticed something new on my wall. It was a red telephone.

"Robert said he didn't care if you two wanted it or not." Myron grinned when he saw what we were looking at. "He had it installed when you were still unconscious."

"We can always turn off the ringer." I just laughed. Part of me was actually very relieved to have more access to people and now I could talk to Jackson when he was away from me. The real and modern world was edging its way more and more into my beloved cottage. It was necessary, I suppose, and most of it was my own doing.

Selma had dropped off the mail and a couple of seed catalogs. There was a letter from Marcus and another from his lawyer. I put Marc's unopened letter in a drawer unread for now, but read the lawyer's. All it said was there obviously was no need for a divorce and Marcus no longer owned the house or anything else of value. No surprise there. They had the nerve to send me a bill for services rendered in the amount of five thousand dollars. I promptly ripped it to shreds and stuffed it into the return envelope and sent it postage due. The next bill from them would get the same treatment and eventually they'd get the message.

There was a postcard from Georgia. No message at all, just the beautiful card. What was the deal here? Maybe

Jackson knew. It was addressed to the Augusta Svensson House on Bay Lake, Deerwood, Minnesota. I'm surprised it even got here. Maybe it was for some other Svensson on the lake. Still, Augusta....

"Hey Jackson, know anyone in Georgia?" I called out.

"No. I don't even work for a museum there," he answered me as he gazed at the card. "Pretty place, though. Too bad they forgot the message and signature."

The bi-monthly statements from Anderson/Erickson were there. A thin manila envelope of expenses paid and a running account balance. I still wasn't used to all the zeros. Thank you Augusta for this, anyway. I would have to think of something to do with some of it. Maybe summer art classes for the kids around the lake. Perhaps Grandfather Grey Sand and Sam would like to help. I had always loved children's art. Once, at the Minneapolis Art Institute, there was an exhibit of art students. The kids were eight to twelve and they all painted the same still-life. Each painting was unique and I would have hung any of them on my wall proudly. Or perhaps a reading program and books at the Native American Museum at Mille Lacs Lake. Or a nature summer camp for the locals....Funny, all my ideas seemed to do with children. Suddenly I heard a sound I hadn't heard since moving here last fall.

"Jackson! Listen." The loons had returned to the lake.

55

The ice had completely disappeared from the lake. Once the melting began, it happened swiftly. Myron said it would be an early spring since the winter had been so severe. I suppose we should have known that when the ice got so thin before it normally did, according to the ice fishermen who grumbled about having to dismantle their fishing shacks so early. The smell of cold and icy ground had faded to memory like it does each and every spring. The water was still extremely cold but the air was almost balmy. Jackets were no longer necessary. This day was heavy with dark grey clouds that hung low over the water. I sat on the end of my rickety old dock with my feet nearly touching the water as huge snowflakes were swallowed by lake water. It was the oddest event, not cold, but snowing. The water was darker than the sky, and these bright, white, large delicate snowflakes were drowning in the lake. I wanted to get Jackson, but I didn't want to miss this. Several good sized fish swam just beneath the surface, and they would occasionally stick their heads out of the water to grab the flakes. I laughed; maybe they thought it was bread crumbs like I fed them when I was a child. All too soon, the magical moment was over and the clouds moved away. That was a weather miracle; I was sure it had never happened before. My own personal weather moment.

Spring was always my mother's favorite season. I think she just liked the newness of it all. She and I would count the number of different green colors we could identify, and give names to the others. Names like parrot green or seaweed green, kiwi-green or lemon-green.

That original lake smell had returned and I breathed deeply. It was getting easier to move around and I did a lot of it. Walking with the dogs and Jackson was my favorite activity. We covered every square inch of the property at least once a week. We tried to teach Sully the parameters so he could possibly be off his restraining leash, but to no avail. The warmer ground turned our footsteps to mud, and I was constantly washing and vacuuming the floors. Cold water or not, I had been bathing dog feet often in the lake before they were allowed inside. The leaves were popping out daily and the dappled ground was back, but still a little sparse. We hung the hammock and I napped there warm afternoons, with Sully in the gently swaying motion. Sully, of course, fit his body in between my legs as it was the warmest spot without a blanket for him to utilize. Lily was too intelligent to try, after tipping herself out of it on one occasion. She growled at it when she brushed by.

Augusta's gardens needed weeding, but there were hundreds of blooms and buds and I could see I would have to come up with new names for the color green. We opened windows for balmy breezes to flow through our rooms and freshen up winter spaces. The lengthening days were too glorious for words and I think I was learning what true spring felt like. This kind of spring couldn't be experienced away from water. This was the way I had pictured my life. Here, in my cottage with my pets, my family, and someone to love who loved me back. I was delirious with life.

Jackson was in the main house turning the playroom-schoolroom into a work space for himself. I went to join him. He had moved the roll-top desk there, with help from Robert, as well as a large table with a drawing board. Most of the ancient school books had been boxed and placed in the attic to be replaced with museum pamphlets and architectural design manuals, work orders and a huge wall calendar with large square days for writing in dates and work schedules for Jackson's projects at the various museums. We had also moved my studio to this space, so we could work together. It felt that I was slowly moving out of the cottage to this house and I wasn't sure I liked it. The dogs did, though, as they ran from room to room, snuffling and sniffing every corner and closet. They managed to return with odd bits and pieces of things I hadn't seen yet. Like an old toy Jack-in-the-Box, very small in size; and after I rotated the handle until the clown popped out, I doubted Lily would bring anything else to me. This scared her for the remainder of the day. She will not enter the playroom if that toy is anywhere in sight. Just now, I could hear their nails scrabbling on the attic floor above me.

"What do you suppose they're searching for?" Jackson cocked his head to listen. At that moment, he reminded me of every dog I ever had. Curious and trying so hard to listen and determine what he was hearing.

"Invisible mice." was my guess. We heard something heavy fall over.

"Really big ones." Jackson laughed.

"Sounds like they found one." I went to check on them. By the time I got up there, both dogs were innocently feigning sleep on the bed. Two heavy iron floor lamps were knocked over but not broken, as there were no shades or bulbs.

Jackson was hard at work on a new project for one museum or another and didn't want to be interrupted, so I took Lily, left Sully gnawing on an old shoe at Jackson's feet, and wandered back outside. I headed home to cook something, an "easy" recipe from Maryalice. As I rounded a corner of the cabin, I noticed a woman standing at the end of the dock just gazing out over the lake. She was tall and thin and dressed in a long dark wool coat, scarf, and hat with a rather large brim, looking both old-fashioned and otherworldly. Lily took off at a trot to greet her.

"Hello there!" I called out to her. "Are you looking for someone? Can I help you?"

She jumped as if startled by my voice and whipped around to face me. Lily had reached her side and I was afraid she would knock the woman into the lake, but Lily minded her manners and simply nuzzled her fingers. She nervously stroked Lily's head and looked like she could just slip over the edge. She seemed fragile and nervous.

"No, I didn't…I mean I wasn't expecting…I thought no one would be here…" She started moving off toward the lane. "I am so sorry to intrude!" She apologized as she rapidly moved away.

How strange, I thought. Was she lost? I went to ask, but I heard a car engine kick in and she was gone. Maybe she was looking for that other Svensson family. Or the McKennas. I knew they had relations elsewhere. Oh well. Time to make supper.

The Swiss steak with potatoes and carrots was simmering on the cookstove when Jackson came in with Sully on his heels. Funny, I noted, Sully didn't need a leash when he was with Jackson. Maybe the dog had been paying attention. Jackson went immediately to the row of windows and cranked a couple open wider.

"Man! It's warm in here. Maybe for the spring and summer we should move the outside." He lifted the lid on the soup pot and sniffed. "Smells terrific. You're getting so domestic." He wrapped his familiar arms around me and kissed my neck.

"How soon before we can eat?" he asked, but with his mind obviously elsewhere.

"Now."

"Darn…"

I told him about the woman while we ate.

"Yeah, I think I saw her earlier from the upstairs windows at the house. Who was she?"

"I never got the chance to ask. She was too nervous to stay and talk."

"Well, either she will come back or she won't."

"No kidding! Sometimes you are so irritatingly logical." I lightly punched him in the shoulder as he pulled me into his lap. "Yeah, but you love me anyway, right?" His kisses soundly sealed off my retort.

Later, we packed the dogs into the car and headed to Petersons General Store. My tulip bulbs and peony bushes had been delivered there. Jackson had a shopping list as well.

"Hello?" We called out when we entered to an open but unoccupied space. Myron popped up from beneath the counter with a pile of mail in his gnarled fingers.

"Hello to you too, Selma!" he yelled to the back of the store. "The kids are here."

I mentioned the strange woman to the Petersons, but they had no idea who she might be, nor had they seen her.

"Maybe she was looking for a summer place, not realizing you lived there year round?" Selma ventured a guess. "There are always people stopping by to find a place to rent for a summer."

"That makes sense; she was surprised to see me." I answered and promptly forgot about the incident. We shared tea and freshly baked chocolate cake before we went back home. Lily had gone off in search of Lucy, so it took a little while to locate and separate them. They both smelled of long dead fish and had to be bathed right then and there. Robert, Myron, and Jackson thought it was hilarious, so I made them do the bathing. God! It would take three days for Lily to dry out completely. Grandpa Algot used to say that a smelly dog was a happy dog. However, this dead smell was a little too much happiness for my nose.

"I am not putting her in my car!" I announced when I saw the dripping creature.

"Okay then, I'll keep her until tomorrow or bring her in my truck?" Robert raised his smiling eyes to mine. "Which is it?"

"Truck." I answered.

When we drove up my lane followed by Robert, our way was blocked by a small car. I had a premonition, and jumped from the still moving car and ran to the lake. Sure enough, there she stood, again looking out on the lake. She stood there gazing and I was immediately put in mind of both me and Mom in exactly that same pose. The premonition deepened to the point of taking me over.

"Who are you?" I called to her. I stood directly in her escape route at the land end of the dock. She would have to jump over me or push me into the water to get past.

56

The woman in the long black coat turned slowly to face me. The wide-brimmed hat was tilted back from her face and I saw that she wasn't tall at all, but was about my height. Her eyes took in all of me, until I was feeling somewhat uncomfortable. I'm sure it was just a minute, but it felt much longer.

"Emily?" she asked in a tiny voice. "Are you Emily?"

The next several minutes moved both in slow motion and warp speed simultaneously. Robert and Jackson had rounded the corner of the cottage with the dogs racing ahead of them. The woman swayed and began to fall to the ground as Robert's color drained from his face. He reached her before her head hit the dock and cradled her in his arms. I just stood still, not even breathing. Afraid, shocked. Finally, time returned to its usual speed, and I backed up until I ran into Jackson and he steadied me.

I thought I heard the woman whisper "Robbie," but it was so faint, I couldn't be sure.

Robert was smoothing the woman's hair back from her face and murmuring softly as he kissed her over and over again, her eyes, her forehead, and her lips. When she stirred, he pulled her closer. "Oh, my darling," we could hear him whisper to the woman.

My darling? My darling? I looked at Jackson, but he was staring at the couple on the ground with his mouth open and eyes wide. Robert's gaze shifted to me and he had tears running down his face. It couldn't be true! But who else would Robert refer to as "my darling?"

The woman stood, still somewhat shakily, and walked to me. I tried to back up even more, but Jackson prevented it. In fact, he pushed me slightly toward her.

"Emily." She held out her arms to me. "My baby." I couldn't move, so she came to me.

"I have dreamed of this for five years," this woman, my mother, told me as she wrapped her arms around my stiff body. That sentence got to me and I looked into her face.

"Five years?" I screamed at her, this moment taking away all my self-control. "Five years? What about twenty years! What about that?" I didn't even try to control the myriad of emotion that was all over the place. I loved her! I hated her! I was betrayed and abandoned by her! No one had ever hurt me like she had. I had never trusted anyone enough after her to ever let that happen until Jackson. And here she was, back in my life, alive and uninvited. I wanted her, I didn't. I had wished so hard for her, prayed for her to not have died and left me. I was nearly screaming in pain. She was Augusta, she was Grace, and she was me. All the confusion I had tucked safely away resurfaced once more to slap me across the face.

"Why are you here? Why did you come back? And..." I continued to yell at her.

"Emily. Please don't." Robert's voice, soft and gentle, stayed my flow of anger.

My mother wisely just held me, until my storm dissipated and I quit struggling against her.

"There is so much to say," she began. Robert came to us and put his arms around both of us. His warmth and love, I think, reached me. Finally, I was able to take it all in. My mother was not dead. She leaned her head against Robert's chest and sighed.

"I wasn't sure I'd have the courage to face you both. But when I saw you earlier, I knew I had to try."

Jackson led us all into the cottage, which was still warm. The dogs lay down on the fireplace rug, unsure of what was happening. Pearl was uncharacteristically quiet. My mother looked around happily and smiled through her tears.

"This is so perfect." She took my hands. "Just like I remember." She sat in the chair closest to the fire.

"Do you remember sitting here in my lap while I read to you? Even when you were too big. Neither of us wanted to change it." I did remember.

"You must be tired, Marie. Why don't we wait with this?" Jackson said.

"No! I want to hear the story now!" I couldn't ever sleep again, until I knew why she left me willingly and so suddenly. Marie took a deep breath as if to prepare for an ordeal she didn't want to begin. Robert pulled a chair next to her and held her hands. He gazed at her with complete love and trust, like she had never been gone from his life, never married another. I marveled at how he could do that.

"When we were here that last summer, Emily was when I realized I had lost Robert completely. It was a total shock. I knew I did not want to go on living without him." She hesitated. "I know how selfish that sounds now, but I was so lost in my grief. When we were back in the Twin Cities and I was facing a future with Howard, I was broken and couldn't mend myself. We argued constantly. Well, Howard tried to argue, but I didn't care anymore. One morning after you left for school, I called a taxi and left. I left Howard a letter saying I was leaving him, and to take you to Robert. Howard knew all along he wasn't your father. At that time, I was positive that Robert would be able to better raise you than I, damaged and unreachable as I had become. I simply hoped Robert would accept you and care for you, and I see that he did." She smiled through her tears at all of us.

"But Howard didn't do that, Marie," Robert told her gently. "Emily and I just found each other last fall. And it was because of Augusta, not Howard."

"I don't understand." Marie looked so vulnerable, so lost and confused; even I was thawing several more degrees toward her. I told her the story of Augusta's will and the provision that I must live on the property.

"But, she told me nothing about you and Robert, or me," I added.

"She didn't know about Robert and me," Marie stated. "No one did."

"Oh yes she did! Robert never got any of the letters you wrote to him, nor did you get his! Augusta saw to that herself."

"This is true, Marie. We only know because of Emily's tenacity. She figured this out herself and she found the letters. We pieced the long story together."

Marie sat in silence for a long time before she spoke. "You never read the letters I wrote to you year after year." It was a statement, not a question.

"Not until last fall. Then I read them all."

"So you never knew how I truly felt...or that Emily was..."

"I should have. My heart knew." My parents just looked at each other and those looks spoke volumes. The two were so completely lost in each other it was almost too intimate to witness.

I waited as long as I could before I interrupted.

"Where have you been all this time?" Marie's eyes came back to me.

"Okay. Here it is as best as I can remember and as much as I now know."

"What does that..." I started, but Jackson stopped me.

"Let her tell this, Em." I stifled my questions and nodded. Just when you think life has returned to normal and you have everything figured out, something else slaps you in the face! Who had told me that?

335

57

"When I left the Twin Cities and Howard, I was headed for the airport, but went to a car dealership instead. I bought the first car I looked at and just drove. I ate when I was hungry; I got a hotel room when I was too tired to drive. I got all the way to the east coast of Georgia. I sat on the beach for a week then decided I had to go back for you." She looked at me with huge sad eyes.

"I couldn't go on without you, do you understand?" When I nodded she continued with her story. "But I was emotionally exhausted and from what I've been told, so much so, that I caused a terrible accident. No one was killed and I am grateful for that, but there were many with injuries, including myself with a serious head injury." She lifted her hair from the right side of her face and a thin, long scar was faintly visible along her hairline. It traveled from her forehead all the way down into her neck. Robert caught his breath and moved even closer to her.

"I was hospitalized for several months, and when I couldn't tell the doctor who I was, he took me to his private convalescence home where I helped out as a sort of nurse.

It turns out I have a natural talent for that." She got up and paced the room, stood at the windows for a moment, and returned to her chair. Jackson got her a bottle of water and a glass which she accepted.

"Doctor Findley and his wife, Caroline, treated me like a daughter. They were elderly and had no children of their own, so, in a way, we helped each other. For years I was happy and even fulfilled. But I knew much of my past was gone and I did wonder about it, who I was, did I have a family somewhere, where was I supposed to be? That sort of question was constantly on my mind. The Findleys had run ads in area newspapers, radio, and television, but there had been no response.

One day, Caroline came home to Savannah with a painting. She had been to Chicago to visit her sister and they went to a gallery and met an artist. They loved his work, and she purchased the painting." Marie turned to Robert. "It was your painting, Robbie. I didn't recognize your name, but I knew the place in the painting. This place. There was a young woman sitting on the dock and somehow I knew she was me. Even the Findleys thought so." Marie paced again and then went out to her car. I saw that Robert held his breath and his eyes were glued to the door until she returned. She brought the painting with her.

"I remember this sale!" Robert said. "The woman who bought it told me she knew the girl in the picture, but I, well I knew she couldn't, because that girl was dead. So I just sold it and forgot it. I never even questioned her."

"I did not remember anything yet. Mr. Findley did some checking, though, but didn't say anything until he was sure. He started to tell me a story that sounded a little like a book I had read once, or a movie I had seen a long time ago. Gradually, I knew it was my life he was telling me." Tears were running freely down her cheeks now, but she let then come.

"I didn't know what to do. Doctor Findley died last fall, and he encouraged me to look for you. He left me enough money to do just that, so here I am."

I abruptly left the cottage and walked. I walked until it was too dark to see where I was going and then I simply sat down on the ground. This past year had been too much for me. Too much had happened. Most of it glorious, yes, but too much, none the less. I needed time to absorb all this information, to make some kind of sense out of it. But then I thought about Marie and all she had been through, and my confusion was nothing compared to hers. I felt small and selfish and I wished Jackson was beside me. And then, unexpectedly, he was. His warm body wrapped around my chilled one, he held me while I cried.

"Okay now?" he asked gently when I had stopped sniffling.

"Very okay. I've got to be the luckiest woman in Minnesota. Now, take us home, because I think I'm lost!"

We really were not that far from the cottage, it was just dark and I hadn't been paying any attention while I simply walked in circles. When we entered, only Robert was there. I must have looked panicky, because he said, "Its fine, Emily, I just put her to bed in your spare room. She is so worn out." He neglected to ask if that had been alright with me, assuming it would be.

"That's fine. This is her place too, and that was always her room." I went to her door and listened. I

338

needed to be sure, I think, so I went in and sat on the edge of the bed.

"Emily, I am so happy to be here with you and Robbie!" She took my hand. "I can recall more and more of my life every day. But I am sorrier than I can say that it took me so long. I'm sure that I never intended to leave you alone. I don't think I could have done that. You and Robbie were all that I had of importance. Even without him, I would have come back for you. We would have gone on together somewhere else. Some place that didn't constantly remind me of what I'd lost."

"No Mom, this isn't anyone's fault. Things just happened to us. This has to be some kind of miracle, though. And you did come back. Please stay."

"I will, baby. Of course I will." And she fell asleep, her hand still resting in my own.

58

Jackson had alerted the remaining family of this unexpected arrival and many tears were shed. I even caught Myron crying when they had stopped by to see Mom for themselves. Lydia, especially, seemed emotional to have Marie back. The next days were full of introducing Marie's story to the family. She was remembering things and stories about most everyone, especially Lydia, who hadn't left her side. We visited the grave of Augusta briefly, but there was no forgiveness there. She lingered over the graves of Rudolf and Grace, though.

"I think I knew something terrible had happened to my sister when she never returned for me. I believed her when she said she and Karl would come back. I begged Mother to ask for help from the police to find them, but she said that her oldest daughter was as dead to her as Rudolf." She drew a deep steadying breath. "I never could forgive her for that. And now, to learn what else she was capable of..." She looked at me helplessly. "I guess I haven't been much better as a mother to you, have I?" I shook my head, but said nothing. All the loneliness of my last twenty years was still so fresh and the pain of it was right there in front of me. I wanted to just tell her to hold me tight and tell me she loved me even though I already knew that. I simply held her hand more tightly.

I looked up to see Jackson coming toward us with both dogs frolicking along his side.

"I like your Jackson very much." Marie squeezed my hand.

"So do I. We are going to be married eventually." We all walked together, following the creek to the lake. Jackson and I left my mother there, lost in her own thoughts. She didn't seem aware when we left her. I could not imagine what all these memories, betrayals, and loss were doing to her heart.

Back at the cottage, Robert was pacing. Edgy and nervous, like I had never seen him.

"Where is she? Is she still here? Is she okay?"

"She is by the lake behind the house," I started to say, but Robert was gone before I finished the sentence.

"Wow, he is a man in a hurry." Jackson laughed. "He still loves her, I think."

"He does indeed. He told me that months ago. He said he had never loved anyone else, either. Guess he refuses to waste any more time. Amazing, huh?"

Jackson hugged me to his chest. "Not so amazing maybe," he said into my hair. He pulled me toward Augusta's house and upstairs into her bedroom.

"This is our room now, Emily. Our house. Our life together. We should give the cottage to your mother. She loves it as much as you do, and she needs it far more. Like you did, when you first arrived."

I nodded, kissed his mouth and pulled him down on the bed. Several entertaining hours later, we woke to grumbling stomachs and Robert calling us.

"Hey, Emily? Jax? Are you two here?"

"Be right there, Robert!" Jackson answered pulling on his jeans and tossing me my sweater.

We spent a quiet but joyful evening, just the four of us, cooking, eating, and laughing easily. Marie and Robert seemed delighted with each other, almost like high school sweethearts, just the way I imagined they always had been, and I bet on a wedding soon. It seemed like the last twenty-two years that had separated them were nothing, nothing at all. It blew my mind.

"Mom, Jackson and I want you to make this cottage your home. Unless you'd rather have the house?" I realized I had no idea, really, what she'd want and, after all, she had more rights to this property than me.

"Are you sure you can give it up?" Marie looked both pleased and surprised. "It seems like you have enjoyed this place and you have done such a great job modernizing it. It really looks like you in each and every corner."

"Mom, it looks like you. When I did this, Jackson and I, you were with us. And if you live in it, I'm not really giving anything up, am I?" I still had years of exploring to do in Augusta's house. There was the second silver key to find a lock for and the attic had a lot more to check out. Besides, I had yet to even open the basement door.

"Oh, Emily! Thank you. Robbie and I always planned to live here." She sat in Robert's lap and kissed him soundly.

Robert smiled shyly at us. "Marie and I have decided not to waste any more of our lives apart from each other. We will be married as soon as it can be arranged." Marie laughed at my expression and I remembered the charm of that laugh. My mother was indeed back home. The mother I remembered with all my heart.

With Myron, Selma, Lydia, and the rest of the family, a wedding was put together at record speed. For two days, wonderful smells came from each of our houses and, since my cooking still left a little to be desired, Jackson and I once again decorated the big house. The gardens were blooming with the earliest of the flowers, and we bought some to fill in. It would be a perfect country wedding. Selma had hung a handwritten invitation up at the store and we were ready.

The minister from the church camp across the lake came to do the ceremony. It was not a traditional wedding, there was no one to give away the bride, and we all were witnesses. I swear I had never seen two happier or more beautiful people than my parents on that day. All they had to do was see each other and the world was brighter. It made me even surer of my feelings for Jackson. As my parents stood in front of the pastor, holding hands and glowing, unable to take their eyes off the other for even a moment, I marveled at what fullness was possible. Even after all the lost time, hurt feelings, and misunderstandings between them, my parents had weathered it all. Without hesitation, they vowed to spend the remainder of their days loving and caring for each other. I realize how corny that sounds, even to my own ears, but it was absolutely real in spite of that. They were so beautiful: Mom in her pastel dress covered in bluebell buds, borrowed from Maryalice, Robert, in an ivory linen suit with bluebells pinned to his lapel, I could see the teenagers they had been. They stood shoulder to shoulder, hip to hip, arms wound around each other. Their love still as fresh as it had once been. I must have sighed in my happiness, because Jackson suddenly took my hands in his and pulled me closer.

The house was full of well-wishers. Everyone in this neck of the woods had heard the miraculous story by now, and wanted to see Marie for themselves. I had decided to let go of my sadness and sense of loss and just revel in the here and now, which was as good as it could be. I was relaxing in Augusta's rocking chair with my tired feet up on a hassock. There was a more recent photograph of Augusta and Lydia framed and on the table. I held it and actually smiled at Augusta's bitter frowning face.

"We've come full circle, Grandmother. We have undone nearly all of your deceit and treachery. The wedding you worked so hard at preventing has happened. This family is whole and happy and you are still dead. You told me that I would never be happy, but you were so wrong. About all of us. We are high on life and in your house, too. How about that, Grandmother?"

I thought of her now with pity. Her life had not been an easy one and perhaps that explained some of her deeds. I couldn't forget what she'd done to us, but maybe, just maybe, I could forgive her. I think Marie and Robert had already done so. I slipped the photo into a drawer.

Then I noticed a new painting over the mantel. It was Robert's painting of the cottage, complete with the old white beacon of the boathouse door. Robert came looking for me and found me in the middle of a daydream, again. There were children racing around the grounds with a litter of retriever puppies. Happy adults setting the picnic table up for lunch and then maybe a boat trip out on the lake to show the kids the boathouse door as the way home. I was complete sure this future would happen.

"Do you like it there? The painting, I mean." He inquired, pulling me to my feet.

"Oh yes. Very much. Dad." I reached up and kissed his cheek.

He got this huge silly grin on his face. "I wondered if you'd ever call me that. Come on, your mother is waiting. Our Marie."

"How would you feel about being a grandfather?" I asked him, still lost in my daydream.

"Emily! Are you and Jackson…?"

"Pregnant? Not yet…" With our arms around each other, we rejoined the party.

THE END
IN SEARCH OF EMILY